THE
MERVYN
STONE
MYSTERIES

THE MERVYN STONE MYSTERIES

1

GEEK TRAGEDY

NEV FOUNTAIN

First published in November 2010
by Big Finish Productions Ltd
PO Box 1127, Maidenhead, SL6 3LW

www.bigfinish.com

Project Editor: Xanna Eve Chown
Managing Editor: Jason Haigh-Ellery
With thanks to: Matthew Griffiths and Lisa Miles

Geek Tragedy
978-1-84435-530-3 (numbered edition) 1-84435-530-6
978-1-84435-513-6 (hardback) 1-84435-513-6
978-1-84435-531-0 (paperback) 1-84435-531-4

DVD Extras Include: Murder
978-1-84435-532-7 (numbered edition) 1-84435-532-2
978-1-84435-514-3 (hardback) 1-84435-514-4
978-1-84435-533-4 (paperback) 1-84435-533-0

Cursed Among Sequels
978-1-84435-534-1 (numbered edition) 1-84435-534-9
978-1-84435-515-0 (hardback) 1-84435-515-2
978-1-84435-535-8 (paperback) 1-84435-535-7

A CIP catalogue record for this book is available from the British Library.

Cover design and photographs by Alex Mallinson.

Printed and bound in Great Britain by Biddles Ltd, King's Lynn, Norfolk.
www.biddles.co.uk

Secret passcode: 2M

To Iona, who loved mysteries

Thanks to...

Nicola Bryant. If I had to list all the things she has done and said to help this book, then I'd sound like the Spanish Inquisition sketch. She has been an amazing source of information. She has also been wonderful, and invaluable, and very wise.

Big Finish Towers. Thanks to Jason Haigh-Ellery, for seeing the potential, David Richardson, Nick Briggs, Alex Mallinson, Xanna Eve Chown, Paul Wilson and Toby Robinson, for being so positive and working so hard on this and the 'Whatever Happened to Babel-J?' podcast.

Terrance Dicks, for writing words that made me interested in reading, Iona Fountain for buying them, and Barbara Corby for encouraging me to write my own.

Jonathan Morris and James Goss, for their help, their comments and their unrelenting positivityness.

John Banks for his support, his performance, his time and his talent.

Dolya Gavanski for her great work on the 'Babel-J' podcast.

Tom Jamieson, Rob Shearman, Ann Kelly, Peter Ware, Steve Berry, Debbie Hill, Ally Ross, David Tennant, Jill Foster, Dominic Lord and Paul Magrs for their help, advice and suggestions.

Andrew Beech and Shaun Lyon for inviting me to science-fiction conventions.

Tony Fountain, for almost getting me to a science-fiction convention in 1983. Nice try, Dad. Much appreciated.

Paul Cornell for asking me for a short story and starting the whole prose thing.

Dan Freedman and Gary Russell, for dragging me into the fold.

Simon Brett for his inspiration.

To everyone who thinks they're in this book. Even if they're wrong.

Foreword by David Quantick

Jesus Jones wrote a song about it, you know. It wasn't very good – '*Vixens from the Void* / We want to avoid!' I think it went.

There was a game for the ZX called *Styrax Race*. It should have been called *Styrax Load for 54 Minutes and Then Race. A bit.* It was an awful game.

Simon Pegg has over 117 *VFTV* action figures, most of them in the original blister packs (but he hasn't got the Babel-J 'Desire' respray figure, and I have).

It's hard to think of a show that sums up the era so well. I mean, it's not *that* hard, but if I said, 'It's easy to think of a show that sums up the era so well,' it would sound arrogant. *Vixens from the Void*, notwithstanding, is as much of its era as MTV, Norman Tebbit, Classix Nouveaux and legwarmers.

I think when that annoying man off *Springwatch* picked it as his specialist subject on *Celebrity Mastermind* was the moment we realised *Vixens* had finally left the cosy confines of cultdom and become a part of the mass nostalgia bank (ironic now that a show so forward-looking should become yet another plank in the walkway stretching back to all our yesterdays). Certainly that nostalgia bank has served me well – shows like *I Love The 80s, Top 100 Sci-Fi Telly Of All Time, Whatever Happened To The Vixens?* and their like have made me both a popular and wealthy man. Often lorry drivers will lean out of their vehicles and shout, 'Oi, mate! I also liked that show!'

And when, in 2007, I was asked to pitch a storyline for an audiobook version of the series (for which quite a few of the original cast were able to appear in) nobody was happier than me when that storyline was accepted. The CD of the episode – 'Death In A Starwell' – didn't sell well, true, which I put down to the original Vizor, Roger Barker, being unavailable for the money asked, and replaced, bafflingly, by Sir Anthony Hopkins, but it is still out there and I have copies myself for sale at my website. But I digress. There's a whole universe out there. Explore! Enjoy! Exterminate!

(Sorry, wrong show.)

David Quantick. Exmouth, June 2010

Extract from the *Vixens from the Void Programme Guide*, originally printed in the fanzine *Into the Void #26*.

DAY OF THE STYRAX (Serial 2M)

Transmitted:	3 December 1987
Recorded:	Studio: BBC Television Centre, 11-12 June 1987 Location: Betchworth Quarry, Reigate, 25-28 May 1987

Medula:	**Tara Miles**
Arkadia:	**Vanity Mycroft**
Tania:	**Suzy Lu**
Elysia:	**Samantha Carbury**
Excelsior:	**Maggie Styles**
Velhellan:	**Jennifer McLaird**
Major Karn:	**Roderick Burgess**
Doriel:	**Jane Ferrier**
Miklos:	**Mike Edwards**
Force-field Tech:	**Katherine Warner**
Styrax Sentinel:	**William Smurfett**
Sryrax Voice:	**Arthur Stokes**
Groolians:	**Joseph McAndrew, Tim Warne, Rick Amory**
Production Design/ Special Effects:	**Bernard Viner**
Script Ed/Writer:	**Mervyn Stone**
Director:	**Trevor Gosling/Nicholas Everett**
Producer:	**Nicholas Everett**

Synopsis:

MEDULA'S murder of the Groolian ambassador is discovered by MAJOR KARN. He demands she give him The Device (episode 2C: 'Demons of the Outer Darkness') but she refuses and flees. KARN pursues her, but he is killed by a Styrax. Convinced the Styrax are the new power in the galaxy, she betrays the location of PANDORUS, the asteroid containing the empire's planetary defence system (episode 1B: 'The Pandorus Paradigm') and unleashes war on the empire, on the very same day that ARKADIA is inaugurated as the Prime Mistress of Vixos.

Notes:

- Yet more production problems beset this, the climax of series two. Once again, Nicholas Everett took over the directing chores. Assigned director Trevor Gosling withdrew because of 'personal difficulties' - the third time since the series began that a director had what appeared to be a nervous breakdown on set.

- Everett's problems were compounded during filming, when many of the production team were re-assigned to the BBC's coverage of the 1987 general election. Indeed, in the years after leaving the BBC, Everett has pulled no punches when talking about the suspicious absence of actors and technicians on the last day of filming, which coincided with the day after the election. Everett has often mentioned spurious 'sicknotes' from people who he suspected didn't feel like coming into work after 'pulling an all-nighter'.

- Everett was candid about the problems during a documentary about the making of the TV series also broadcast in 1987, saying that (quote) 'first the miners, then the dockers, then the nurses, then the teachers, then me. I was last in a very long line of people to get fucked up the arse by Margaret Thatcher.' The comment was discussed in parliament, and Everett later apologised at the behest of the BBC.

- Everett ascribed the comment as the reason he had been given nothing to produce by the BBC since 'Vixens' finished. During the 'ConVix 5' convention in 1997, Everett joked that clause 28 was brought in as a direct reaction to his comment, saying: 'the policy was designed to prevent the promotion of gay literature, gay teaching and gay producers.'

- Once again, script editor Mervyn Stone had to pen a story at short notice. Veteran writer Cedric Lime (creator of children's TV series 'Pixie Patrol') had sent his script in very late, and what he'd written was completely unsuitable. His episode featured a vindictive magic robot regressing the Vixens back until they were the age of children, and hurling them into a surreal dimension containing flying teddy bears and giant talking cushions. Given that the script was so out of character for the style of the series thus far, one might uncharitably assume that Cedric had dusted down an old 'Pixie Patrol' script and changed the names of the main characters.

- After some months, the production office rang up Lime, and was informed by Lime's wife that Cedric was 'too dead' to complete the necessary rewrites in time.

- So once again, Stone stepped into the breach. The result was rushed, sketchy and somewhat illogical, but it was still a compelling episode, charting Medula's season-long character arc. Her tragic journey began in episode six 'Quest to Danger' with the growing resentment of her older sister Arkadia, leading the character further into darkness, culminating in the death of Major Karn and her ultimate betrayal in the final thrilling minutes, plunging the Vixen empire into war. Nothing was ever going to be the same again.

- This was to be Vanity Mycroft's last appearance as Arkadia for the time being. She declined to appear in series three, but re-emerged in series four. The explanation given for her sudden disappearance was that she'd been held on a Styrax prison planet for the past eighteen months.

- Interestingly, during Mycroft's absence, no director of the series underwent any personal difficulties. Though five more did undergo 'difficulties' once she'd returned to the show.

- The show wrapped on the 12th June amid general optimism about the future, which was well founded. The ratings for series two would be the highest of the show, peaking at 13 million viewers.

- The celebration was marred by one sad note. At the wrap party that night, it was announced to the cast that former Styrax operator Sheldon Ellis had died in a house-fire at his home earlier that evening. Even though Sheldon had parted company with 'Vixens' some three months before on less-than-amicable terms, he was still good friends with a lot of the cast, so his death came as a great shock.

- An investigation concluded that the fire was caused by faulty wiring. The verdict was in no doubt that his death was nothing more than a tragic accident.

CHAPTER ONE

Murder. No doubt about it.

'Mervyn!'

That taxi ride from the station. Murder. A complete nightmare. As he checked in at the reception desk of the Happy Traveller hotel and business centre, Mervyn's hands were trembling so much he could barely sign for his little plastic key.

'Coo-ee! Mervyn!'

His driver had had a nodding Buddha in the rear window, a dream-catcher hanging from his mirror and a luminous plastic statuette of Jesus on the dashboard. He believed in everything but traffic lights.

'Mr Stone!'

All Mervyn wanted to do was go up to his room and calm his jangled nerves.

'Mervyn! Mr Stone!'

Getting his name bellowed in the busy foyer was the last thing he needed.

'Over here sir!'

Pity, that.

Mervyn surrendered and turned round to acknowledge the voice. A young man with an explosion of curly orange hair and big-framed glasses appeared, as if by magic, from the crowd. Mervyn's hand was grabbed and pumped vigorously. His face froze, and his mind groped around in a blind panic for the man's name.

'Hello, sir! So, the prodigal returns. Such an honour. So glad you could be here, sir. When Morris told me he asked you and you agreed, I just didn't believe him. "Morris," I said, "the Great Mervyn Stone hasn't done a convention in seven years, what could possibly tempt him out of retirement?"'

'Well, I thought it was time to revisit things, you know, take a fresh look at the past...'

'I hope the fee he mentioned was sufficient,' said the man with a grin, as if he knew *exactly* why Mervyn had agreed to do the convention. 'So how the devil are you, sir? I do hope your journey wasn't irksome.'

'Well it was a bit of a nightm–'

'It's just been calamity after calamity this morning,' sighed the man. 'The big screens aren't up yet, the office they've given us is completely inadequate – the photocopier keeps jamming – and the staff are proving very obstructive. The hotel's been taking down our signs telling people where the events are being held.'

'Oh dear.'

Mervyn's eyes strained to read the name badge on the man's lapel. It was unhelpfully written in a blocky squared-off font that had been universally embraced in the 70s as 'futuristic'.

'They're saying we didn't tell them about the sellotape, and they say that's wear and tear on their infrastructure, fixtures and fittings. We've put Blu-Tack on the table but they're just not biting. We may have to work out a compromise, some kind of combination of smear-free adhesive applied on windows and other shiny surfaces as well as free-standing pin boards clear from fire exits.'

'Right...' What did his bloody badge say? Steven? Stefan? Sidney?

'Do you know, I'd only been here 20 minutes and the hotel tried to stop us putting any of the original props in the main hall? "Fire regulations," they say. I told them beforehand about the props, and so I said to them, "Look," I said, "look, those props are part of the programme's history, they see them every year, if they're not there then people will feel short-changed. So they've got to be there, end of story."'

Samuel? Scott? Sean?

'"They're our customers, and so they're your customers," I said to them. "If ever I've learnt anything from my training in management consultancy, it's that the customers set the parameters of your business, and your business is meeting those parameters. You agreed to put this convention on," I said, "and this convention includes those props."'

Sandy? Spiro? Spandex? Anything was possible in this place.

The man pointed into the main hall. 'Just look. We haven't even got them in yet. It's a complete madhouse in there.'

Mervyn looked. The room was filled with convention staff quietly and smoothly unfolding chairs, testing microphones and putting up speakers. It looked very sane to him. Not what he would consider a madhouse at all.

Which was ironic; because the foyer they were standing in looked *exactly* like a madhouse.

It was filled with people dressed in weird and wonderful home-made costumes. Some were flapping around with claws fastened to their extremities, others had coloured their faces bright purple and wore bathing caps on their heads. Some had covered themselves from top to toe in silver boxes and stood motionless in corners, allowing themselves the odd robotic twitch. It was the darkest, most gibbering sweat-stained nightmare of any children's television presenter. These were *Vixens from the Void* fans, and they were truly in their element. Teased by Trekkies and Time Lords, and jeered at by Jedi, *Vixens* fans were the oddest and dampest of them all: the science-fiction fans that put the 'sigh' into science and the 'ick' into fiction. It was an accepted fact that *Vixens* fans only existed so that *Xena Warrior Princess* fans had someone to pity.

Through a strict lifestyle of avoiding daylight, dedicated Doritos consumption and a rigorous regime of ill-health, most looked inhuman enough at the best of times – and this was a chance for them to go that extra mile, strap on a tentacle and look completely alien for a weekend.

The man prattled on: 'Anyway, they say they *might* agree to sell us a man with a bucket of sand, and I'm trying to persuade them to use one of our people with a bucket of sand, but they say the person holding the bucket has to be trained. How does one get trained to hold a bucket of sand?'

The hotel doors crashed open, and three people struggled into the foyer, their official mauve 'ConVix 15' sweatshirts clashing with their gasping red faces. They were grappling with one of the disputed props. To the uninitiated, the object looked like a huge moth-eaten piece of fibreglass and papier-mâché, a green shell-like structure about the size and shape of a golf buggy. To those in the know, of course, it was the casing of one of the galaxy's most fearsome creatures and implacable arch-enemy of the Vixens. They plonked it down in front of Mervyn and the man.

'Simon!' shouted one of them, a big man with a heavy ponytail and an exhausted scrappy beard that had tried to reach his face but had given up and died somewhere below his chin. 'What do you want us to do with this?'

Simon. Simon *Josh*. It all came flooding back. Simon Josh, convention organiser and über-fan. How could he have ever forgotten?

'Careful with that, Morris!' Simon snapped. 'That's an original Styrax Sentinel from series two. It's irreplaceable, and very delicate.'

'But *where,* Simon?' gasped Morris.

'Now you know where you're supposed to put that,' said Simon to Morris.

Morris stared breathlessly up at Simon, bent double with his hands on his knees. His eyebrows were raised helplessly, as if to say 'How the hell should I know?' Simon gave a long-suffering sigh.

'It goes on the middle stand of course. In amongst my most precious collection of knick-knacks.'

From the expression on Morris's face, Mervyn had an idea which particular precious collection of Simon's 'knick-knacks' he'd like to put it amongst, but all he managed were a few breathless nods.

Simon beamed, and rested his hand on the Sentinel's flaking carapace as if posing for a photo. 'Marvellous isn't it, sir? I bet it takes you back.

What does it feel like to once again be in the presence of the most evil creature in the universe?'

'Oh, I wouldn't put yourself down, Simon.'

Simon stopped talking for a few blessed seconds, then he realised what Mervyn meant. 'Oh very droll,' he said, flashing one of those smiles given by those who are congenitally humourless but have learned to detect the shape of a joke and move their faces accordingly. 'You writers!' he clucked. 'Your schedule's in this programme leaflet.' He handed Mervyn a programme 'leaflet', which was about the size of a telephone directory for a large village. With no small effort, Mervyn stuffed it in his pocket. 'Autographs at eleven, panel at one, and I know you're going to love this, you'll be judging the fancy dress in the evening.'

Mervyn looked around at the foyer, at the creatures clad in cardboard, tissue paper and bubble wrap. Fancy dress? Surely everyone here had peaked far too soon? There was nowhere else for them to go in the 'acting like an evil alien' stakes, unless they went down the road and invaded Brent Cross shopping centre.

Simon was talking Mervyn through the schedule, running his finger along some insanely complicated boxes and offering a translation. 'You'll be signing autographs in "Arkadia's Boudoir" – that's what we call it. It's actually room 1013. And after that it's the panel in what we call "Vixos Central Nerve Centre", and that's the main hall here, and the fancy dress is also in "Vixos Central Nerve Centre". I'll get someone to show you up to your room.'

'And what's my room called?'

Simon grinned a humourless grin, and Mervyn caught a flash of something nasty beneath. He realised he'd made one joke too many.

'Room 2224,' Simon said, a little too loudly.

Out of the corner of his eye, Mervyn noticed a hairy herd of bespectacled creatures in rock T-shirts and jeans. They were shuffling in their direction. He was sure some of them had overheard where his room was.

'Don't worry,' said Mervyn, 'I'll find my own way.'

He started to walk away.

Very, very fast.

CONVIX 15.
EARTH ORBIT ONE:

9.00am start

EVENT	*LOCATION*
REGISTRATION AND IDENTITY TAG COLLECTION	Prison Planet Docking Bay (hotel foyer)
'THE BURNING TIME' **EPISODE SCREENING**	The Catacombs of Herath (video lounge room 1024)
WHY VIXENS FROM THE VOID IS BETTER THAN STAR TREK **FAN PANEL** with Graham Goldingay, Fay Lawless, Craig Jones, Darren Cardew	The Seventh Moon of Groolia (room 1002)

Tomorrow People and Blake's 7 schedules are found inside free copies of Into the Void available from Checkpoint Doomworld (reception desk).

CHAPTER TWO

The Happy Traveller hotel was tucked behind a slip road somewhere around the M25. It was a modern hotel, a square ugly building in orange and yellow brick. The only difference between it and an open prison was that the hotel had a bigger sign, smaller rooms and palm trees in the car park.

The reason *why* hotels wedged in such sweaty rectums of the country decorated themselves with palm trees always eluded Mervyn; presumably to entice the kind of person who gets impressed by pineapple *and* ham on pizza.

The carpet that Mervyn jogged along was from the same identikit book of bland hotels. It was covered in a pattern of vomit-coloured splat shapes arranged about 10 inches apart, designed that, should anything vomit-coloured and splat-shaped descend upon it, the mess would be cunningly disguised. Unfortunately, as no one has ever yet learned to vomit precisely 10 inches apart (even engineering undergraduates), the nastiness usually showed up anyway.

Why was he running? Because he was special.

Not special in many respects, of course. He was in his late 40s, hovering on the wrong side of stout, with soft, perplexed features and a large nose. Middle age had mercifully left him his hair, which was grey and thick, and grew in every conceivable direction but down. Mervyn looked like a hedge that had been dragged through a man backwards.

His dress wasn't particularly exceptional either. He wore the standard uniform of television writers everywhere; black jeans, black shirt and black corduroy jacket. There were certain writers' panels he'd been on in years past that looked more like a convention of retired and rather portly Milk Tray men – the ones who'd skipped the speedboat, given up on the sexy lady and kept the chocolates for themselves.

No, he wasn't special. Not in any respect. Except one.

Mervyn had *Vixens from the Void* on his CV, and that made him very special indeed.

The Happy Traveller had played host to a lot of strange and wonderful gatherings in its history, but this particular event took the complimentary plastic-wrapped biscuit.

The convention – known as 'ConVix' – had been in existence for 15 years now. It was a convention devoted to many forms of cult television. For this event, there were a smattering of *Tomorrow People* cast members, a few luckless red-shirted extras from *Star Trek* and one rather dog-eared space rebel from *Blake's 7* – but mostly ConVix was concerned with celebrating the exploits of the *Vixens from the Void*.

Mervyn had co-devised and script-edited a brazenly cheap and exploitative piece of sci-fi kitsch that cast a day-glo spell over the BBC1 schedules in the late 80s to early 90s.

In the mid-80s, TV sci-fi was unfashionable at the BBC. *Doctor Who* had been prescribed a rest, *Blake's 7* had been tragically cancelled, and *The Tripods* had been even more tragically made. It would have been suicide to propose another space series in this climate, but BBC drama, with that appetite for suicide shared by most publicly funded organisations, decided to make one.

Mervyn came up with an epic that contained elements of classic BBC serials such as *I, Claudius* and *Fall of Eagles*, but on a much larger scale, recounting the decline and fall of a vast intergalactic empire through in-fighting, betrayal and war.

That wasn't how he pitched it to the BBC, of course. He wasn't completely mad.

He sold it shamelessly like a whore, dressing it in primary colours and daubing it with cheap lipstick, showing it off in a way that would make sense to the brain of the average BBC boss. He winced as he remembered the first line of his proposal document: 'Think of *Dallas* meets *Dynasty*... but in space!' Mervyn reasoned that, even if they didn't understand science-fiction, they might at least understand science-fiction containing nubile young women in corsets and skin-tight lycra a little better.

He wasn't alone in pitching an SF series – not by a long shot. There was also an 'I see this as *Howards' Way* – but in space!', an 'Imagine the kids from *Fame* – but in space!' and then an 'It's like *The Money Programme* – but in space!' Mervyn couldn't imagine how *that* one would have worked. He'd even heard of one old and rather baffled producer who went into a meeting with the words: 'Think *Star Trek* – but in space!'

Mervyn found his room. The moment he placed his suitcase on the bed, he noticed the revving of engines. He crossed over to the window and peered out, his spirits sinking. A Mondeo Moron and a BMW Bastard were having a 'Who's Got the Smallest Penis?' competition in the hotel car park. Mervyn was a light sleeper, and he just knew that he would have problems with sales reps from Crawley gunning their engines in the early hours. He needed his sleep; if he couldn't move rooms, he would have to resort to the little coloured pills in his suitcase.

It was Mervyn's deep-held conviction that, throughout his life, he was destined to be forever in the wrong place at the wrong time. He measured how badly located he was in life by degrees of wrongitude and crapitude. '20 degrees wrong... 30 degrees crap,' he muttered.

Today was particularly wrong *and* crap. He knew where he *should* be, of course. He should be lying in bed, contemplating a shower, and then a quick Tube ride to ITV's magic castle of opulence, where the lifts contained live jazz bands, and the automatic urinal cleaners in the men's toilets gushed forth vintage claret. He should be having a power lunch of milk and rusks with a bunch of fresh-faced media toddlers, and they would ask him how many shovelfuls of cash it would take for him to agree to adapt his best-selling novel into a stupidly successful TV series.

Yes, that was definitely where he *should* be.

The best-selling novel was, of course, unwritten as yet. It was nothing more than a few kilobytes lurking in his laptop, and the ITV toddlers weren't having any meetings with any writers, particularly not him. They were all probably sitting in a room working out if it was in poor taste to do a mini-series on the life of Pope John Paul II starring Ross Kemp. Still, until the non-existent novel magically wrote itself and leapfrogged over the Dan Browns in the bestseller lists, the Happy Traveller would have to do.

It felt like a grim penance for his indolence: to return to the convention circuit after all these years; to be *forced* to return to the endless rounds of anecdote-telling and autograph-scribbling due to an irritating lack of cash. Something had gone badly wrong somewhere.

He toyed with the idea of seeing if he could get a change of room, but decided against it. He'd had quite enough of Simon's benevolent tyranny for one morning. Perhaps later.

Mervyn unpacked, then had a shower, made himself a cup of tea with the tiny plastic kettle, ate the plastic-wrapped digestives, ordered a burger and chips from room service, examined the quality of the adult channels on the television, received and ate the burger and chips from room service, re-examined the adult channels, and, when he had finally exhausted the delights his room had to offer, went downstairs to brave the convention.

He opened the door, and was immediately faced with a *Vixens* fan standing across the way, emerging from an adjoining room.

The fan did a double take in his direction. A meaty grin slowly smeared its way across his face and he gave a wave.

'Hi, Mr Stone!'

Something deep inside Mervyn instinctively recoiled. He had a notion that he was going to be in for an awful time.

CHAPTER THREE

'Hello, my name is Mervyn Stone, and here I am at ConVix 15 having a *wonderful* time!'

Blast it.

'Um...'

His mind always went blank at times like these. In all of his friends' video cabinets, there were home movies containing parties, weddings, christenings, and a few seconds of Mervyn going 'Um...'

'Anyway... hope to see you soon!'

Morris looked up from the camera tripod, and held his thumb aloft. 'Perfect. Great. Thanks. I'll play it back in a minute.'

It didn't sound very great, judging from Morris's reaction, but then Morris always sounded bored. Morris was Simon Josh's lieutenant. He handled the audio-visual equipment and was the guy who really ran the convention while Simon Josh gibbered from one room to the next.

They were all in the convention's hospitality room, a room distastefully covered in avocado wallpaper. It was Friday morning and the guests were starting to assemble; people Mervyn hadn't seen in years, and some he hadn't much liked when he did.

Feeling self-conscious, Mervyn needed a friendly face to latch on to. Luckily he saw just the chap.

He helped himself to a filter coffee from the refreshment table and slumped down in an armchair next to Roddy Burgess, who, as usual had his nose deep in a glass of something liquid and amber-coloured.

'How go things at the front, Major?'

The actor beamed woozily at Mervyn. He was a man in his late 60s, the personification of ageing ham, complete with immaculate grey hair, moustache and silken cravat. His eyes twinkled above silver-framed half-moon glasses. 'Oh, tip top, old boy, tip top, enjoying myself terribly. The troops are awfully well drilled.' The 'troops' was Roddy's pet term for the hotel and convention staff. If they fed him, gave him drink and led him around the hotel so he didn't have to read a schedule or think for himself, they were 'well drilled'. If they allowed him to look after himself at any point they were 'a bit of a shower'.

'I say, don't think I've seen you in active service for a while, have I?'

'No Major. It's been seven years since I last did one of these.'

'Thought so... thought so... Seven years eh? Long time to go AWOL,' he rumbled.

'Oh I don't know,' Mervyn nodded at the over-familiar faces dribbling into the room. 'Things don't seem to have changed much.'

There was a meaningful cough from behind the video camera. 'Mr Burgess, would you mind taking a seat, please...?'

Roddy Burgess groaned. 'Do I have to, old boy? I'm not on duty until 1100 hours.'

'Just a little message will do. It's to put on the official website.'

'Ahm... Don't think so, old chap. Remaining incognito for this mission, I think. Maybe next time.'

Morris let loose a sigh. 'I think you were told in your letter that part of the requirement for guests was to contribute to publicity when requested –'

'Are you giving orders to a senior officer, corporal?' Roddy snapped.

'No, but...'

'Then until fresh orders come through, I'm staying posted right here.' Roddy pointed his nose back into his glass of scotch.

After years of being worshipped and lauded by obsessives, trawling around the country from hotel to hotel and forced to recount the same anecdotes, it wasn't surprising that a few stars of *Vixens from the Void* had gone ever so slightly doolally. It was even less of a surprise that they'd grown into complete barking head-cases. There was only one reason they hadn't been given a cell with double-quilted walls long ago; the convention circuit provided better secure accommodation than the state ever could. Constant supervision, regular meals and whole roomfuls of people willing to humour any delusion they had, no matter how deranged.

Roddy was a case in point. He'd played Major Karn, the head of the Vixen guard. He hadn't had a large role in the series, but he was fondly remembered for dying nobly in a favourite episode, and he was a good convention guest – when they were able to lever him out of the comfy chair where he'd managed to wedge himself.

He'd also been deferred to as 'Major' for so long he seemed to believe he was ex-army. He'd started to scatter military jargon erratically into his speech, and developed a gruff no-nonsense delivery. Truth was, the nearest he'd been to any kind of military rank was the Private Hospital he'd kept finding himself in after a variety of blurred drink-related accidents.

Morris scratched his beard wearily. 'I do really need you to say a few words. Simon'll be upset if you don't.'

Roddy pretended not to hear.

'I will have to tell him...'

'Hello all. Everything all right?'

Speak of the devil, Mervyn thought.

Simon Josh had glided back into the green room on one of his irrelevant missions to nowhere in particular. All of his errands had the same purpose; to make Simon Josh look busy and important. He was like a shark; he had to keep moving otherwise his existence had no meaning. He smiled like a shark, too.

Morris cleared his throat slowly and deliberately and nodded towards Roddy. 'Roddy doesn't want to say hello to our online customers,' he said darkly.

'Really?' said Simon brightly. 'I think I need to explain to Mr Burgess how important our official website is in our public relations arsenal.'

Here we go... Mervyn turned back, anticipating an explosion from the old warhorse bigger than anything the BBC special effects department ever produced.

But Roddy wasn't there.

To Mervyn's astonishment, the old man had sprung out of his chair and was sitting happily in front of the camera. 'Hello chaps,' he chirped, 'the Major here... Having a marvellous time at this convention... First-class billets, excellent tuck and well-drilled troops!' He signed off with a brisk salute, and sprinted out of the room, casting a wary eye back at Simon.

The old man looked almost terrified.

CHAPTER FOUR

As was now traditional at these conventions, Vanity Mycroft was holding court in the middle of the hospitality room, glass of champagne held carelessly in one hand, dwindling cigarette in the other. Slumped gracefully on a high-backed chair, she had a semi-circle of adoring faces listening to her impromptu lecture and chuckling dutifully at her outrageous statements. She looked utterly at home with her 'audience', as all true stars do.

'You see a lot of... lesser people... let's call them TV reviewers...'

'Smoky' didn't begin to describe her voice. 'Cured like a kipper' was a more apt description.

'No, no, let's call them by their proper name... You see, a lot of bastards...'

This elicited a polite chuckle from her followers.

'They looked down on us; they looked down on me... They looked at *Vixens* and they said "What a load of rubbish"...'

Cue sympathetic noises.

'And they were right of course... It is rubbish...'

As the sycophantic chorus were all fans of *Vixens*, this polite chuckle sounded a little more forced.

She meandered on. 'But the mistake they made was going: "It's rubbish, so it's all rubbish... So the acting's rubbish." But it's not. It's the most marvellous acting there is. It's better than the RSC, you know.'

'Oh I agree,' one was eager to chip in. 'It's just what I've been saying for years. It's what I said in the piece I wrote for *Into the Void* fanzine... "Both *Vixens* and Shakespeare have metaphor and meaning that strike to the very heart of the human condition."'

'That's right, Darren darling,' Vanity agreed drunkenly, nodding vigorously but not listening to a word. 'Absolutely... I mean, any old fart with a cravat and an Equity card can make Shakespeare sound good... But to make the crap we were forced to spew up week in, week out sound like it wasn't written by an illiterate hack...' She raised her voice so it could reach the other side of the room. 'No offence, Mervy dear...'

'None taken, dear,' yelled Mervyn affably, who knew Vanity of old.

'No, to make that old toss sound decent. That took *real* talent... Hmm? Hmm?' Her head swivelled around glassily looking for endorsement, but she found only terrified smiles.

'I've got a present for you. I got it at auction,' cooed Darren, seizing his chance to stem her tirade. Reaching behind a table, he pulled out a Sketchleys bag. Tearing the plastic covering off, he revealed an eye-watering tangerine outfit which was a shiny basque combined with lycra sleeves and tights, and bedecked with silvery epaulets and a shimmering cloak. He also produced some fearsome-looking knee-length boots, and a hat which he perched on the ensemble – something not unlike a Roman legionnaire's helmet, but with a very 80s-style mirrored visor fastened to the front.

'Now this, would you believe...' he said with a breathless pause '... is one of your actual costumes from the original series.'

Vanity wrinkled her nose and blew a drunken raspberry with her lips.

'It smells a bit, I'm afraid,' grovelled Darren. 'I think it's mothballs.'

'More like fag ash and KY jelly...' said a voice in an incredibly loud stage whisper.

The level of noise in the room dipped as every third conversation ended. Everyone knew that the ill-disguised whisper came from Katherine Warner.

Here we go, thought Mervyn, *again.*

Actresses don't have face-to-face cat-fights. Mervyn had never seen the screeching, face-slapping, cheek-scratching, hair-tugging or blouse-ripping found in 1970s British sex comedies. In his experience, actresses do their scrapping while pretending to do something else – like magicians; ostentatiously flourishing their cuffs and talking nineteen to the dozen to distract the audience's attention from what they're *really* doing.

By way of example, Vanity Mycroft's eyes didn't flicker. She didn't look over to Katherine Warner, or even acknowledge she'd heard anything. She simply carried on her conversation, patting Darren ostentatiously on the knee and raising her voice. 'Don't worry about the smell, Darren dear. It's a lovely gesture...' She held it admiringly. 'It's nice to have it. I don't expect they kept yours, Katherine darling. They probably sent it back to the hire shop with all the other *extras*' costumes...'

Over in the corner, Katherine continued talking to a man who'd been invited because he'd played one-third of a crab creature in 1988. She also acted as though she hadn't heard anything, but her smile intensified, her conversation grew more animated and her laughter tinkled in the air as if crab-man was the most fascinating person she'd ever met. It didn't escape Mervyn's attention that the red-slashes of her fingernails were massaging the flute of her glass as if they were contemplating smashing it on the table and shoving the jagged remains into someone's face.

'But surely,' one of the fans said to Vanity, with a touch of desperation, 'you must have some affection for the time you spent on the show...?'

She looked at him pityingly. 'Oh, I suppose so... One does sometimes get misty-eyed for the old days.'

The voice from the corner floated up again. 'That'll be the cataracts, dear.'

Vanity continued talking without missing a beat. 'But it's so difficult to be nostalgic about it...Unlike *some* actresses it wasn't my whole career, just a very small part of it...'

'Yes...You did have a very *long* career. What was it like, working with Muffin the Mule...?'

'No dear, I'm so forgetful about those days... faces... scenes... scripts... I can't remember any of my lines any more... What about you Katherine? Do you still remember your *line?*'

Thankfully, it was nearly ten o'clock, and a couple of stewards came in to take the actresses to the stage. They all set off to tell the attendees their chummy backstage anecdotes. For an hour, their bitchiness would be buried beneath a practised air of bonhomie. Mervyn smiled. Through their networks, fanzines and exhaustive research, the fans knew about every temper tantrum and spat the women ever had. Vanity and Katherine wouldn't be fooling anybody.

Simon glided past, and Mervyn grabbed his arm.

Simon recoiled like he'd been touched by a passing vagrant. *It was always the paradox of these conventions,* Mervyn thought. *The fans love us, and want us to be with them, but hate us for having nothing better to do BUT be with them.* 'Actually Simon, I wondered '

'Lumme, it's been an utter nightmare out there, I have to say. The dealers are at war over their tables. One's got a wobbly one and is worried about souvenir mug breakage...'

'Actually Simon; could I have a word about my room? You see, it's right over the car park, and I did ask if I could – '

'Ah, sorry Mervyn, hotel's completely chocka. I'd like to help, but they're being difficult as it is, and I don't want to give them more ammunition in the Blu-Tack war.' Simon pulled a tight little expression intended to show some kind of regret, which was as insincere as a spam e-mail informing you that she'd seen your profile on a website, was waiting for you at the end of a phone line and was as horny as hell.

'Is that all right?'

'No problem,' said Mervyn lamely, but his response was drowned by an eruption from the other side of the room. Morris had just told Vanity something she didn't like.

'What? I'm *where*?' she screeched. 'First floor? With the plebs?'

Simon hurried over and flashed his teeth. 'Vanity, the room you've been given is perfectly adequate.'

'Well that's easy for you to say. You rub shoulders with these "people" all the time. There's an aura I have to cultivate, a distance. They'll be pushing notes under my door and trying to pick my lock to get at my knickers.'

'Husband finally got you to wear that chastity belt, then...' muttered Simon, not quite under his breath.

If Vanity heard him, she chose not to mention it. 'God knows, I can see I've done far too many of these things. I'm old news, far too ubiquitous to be given decent treatment any more. I'm a convention whore. A fixture.'

She gestured around the room to the inoffensively offensive hotel décor and focused on Mervyn. 'I'm always here, Mervy. You can just nail me up on the wall with the fire-regulations and pictures of fruit. Oh no. He wouldn't do that.' She eyeballed Simon. 'Not allowed to use nails on the hotel walls are you? Perhaps you could stick me up using a combination of Blu-Tack and pin boards?'

Simon glared at her. 'We do have a rule, don't we Vanity, the one about hissy fits at conventions...?'

'Not this time, Simon!' She levelled a finger at him and jutted her jaw defiantly. 'Not now my autobiography is out! Not this time and not any more!'

She turned abruptly, the coat draped on her shoulder swirling around her like a cloak, and left.

CONVIX 15. EARTH ORBIT ONE:

10.00am

EVENT	*LOCATION*
VANITY MYCROFT, Katherine Warner **INTERVIEW**	Vixos Central Nerve Centre (main stage,ballroom)
'ASSASSINS OF DESTINY' PART ONE **EPISODE SCREENING**	The Catacombs of Herath (video lounge - room 1024)
PHOTOS PAUL CHESTER-ALLEN	Transpodule Chamber (room 1030)
AUTOGRAPH PANEL NICHOLAS EVERETT, WILLIAM SMURFETT, ANDREW JAMIESON	Arkadia's Boudoir (room 1013)
WHAT IS 'CANON' **VIXENS EXPERTS PANEL** with Graham Goldingay, Fay Lawless,Craig Jones, Darren Cardew	The Seventh Moon of Groolia (room 1002)

CHAPTER FIVE

The convention was getting under way.

Mervyn remembered the routine. All around the hotel, confused convention attendees who didn't know when anything was happening were talking to other confused attendees who didn't know where anything was happening, and seeking out stewards who didn't know when *or* where or *how* anything was happening, if indeed anything was going to happen at all.

There were one or two elusive people who did know when, where and how everything was going to happen, but they were hiding in the green rooms with the guests who didn't need to know what, when or how everything was going to happen as they were shepherded everywhere by attentive staff for the whole weekend.

Even further down the evolutionary scale from those getting their bearings in the foyer was the sad collection of people who had just got to the hotel, and were milling around reception, carrying coats, lugging holdalls and dragging suitcases on wheels.

Mervyn did know where he was going. He didn't trust anyone to show him anywhere, so for his journey to the autograph room, he'd marked it very clearly on his little map with felt pen. He didn't like nasty surprises. But he got one anyway.

The moment he left the hospitality room, someone leapt out and grabbed his arm. He screamed with sheer brain-addled terror.

'Roddy! You nearly gave me a heart attack!'

'Is he about?' Roddy blurted.

'Is who about?'

'You know very well, old chap. Him. The Quisling.'

He must have meant Simon. 'He's just left.'

Roddy stared at him with wide, poached-egg eyes. 'He keeps us here against our will you know... We can't leave.'

'Roddy. It's a hotel. You can leave whenever you want.'

'Nonono... He won't let us... Because his masters won't let him.' He nodded his head downstairs. 'The ones... down there. His robot masters.'

'What?'

'It's like the Japs all over again. The war's over, but they won't admit it... There's only one way out of here and that's in a wooden box.' A thought seemed to strike him. 'Unless... well, there is a way out, isn't there?'

'What's that?'

A sly look flickered in the old man's eyes. 'I'm not going to dig a tunnel, am I, old boy?'

Not for the first time, Mervyn wondered how much of Roddy's bewildered bluster was an act, and how much was a whisky-induced plunge into fantasy.

'Really, Roddy... That's very... Interesting.'

Mervyn retrieved his sleeve from Roddy – not without some difficulty – and stumbled to the lifts.

CONVIX 15.
EARTH ORBIT ONE:

11.00am

EVENT	*LOCATION*
THE DVD TEAM INTERVIEW: ROBERT MULBERRY TREVOR SIMPSON IVOR QUIGLEY	Vixos Central Nerve Centre (main stage,ballroom)
'PRISON PLANET' **EPISODE SCREENING**	The Catacombs of Herath (video lounge - room 1024)
AUTOGRAPH PANEL VANITY MYCROFT BERNARD VINER MERVYN STONE PAUL CHESTER-ALLEN	Arkadia's Boudoir (room 1013)
PHOTOS RODERICK BURGESS	Transpodule Chamber (room 1030)
WRITING VIXENS FAN FICTION **FAN PANEL** with Graham Goldingay, Fay Lawless, Craig Jones,Darren Cardew	The Seventh Moon of Groolia (room 1002)

CHAPTER SIX

Back in the mists of history, when he was introduced to his first ever autograph session, Mervyn thought it looked like a sweatshop.

Two hours and several hundred signatures later, after he'd lost the feeling in his wrist, he realised it *was* a sweatshop.

This one was like most others. There were the stars sitting behind tables against the far wall, and there was an incredibly long queue of fans stretching through the hotel lounge, clutching books, posters and bits of paper. Every so often the stewards would allow a half-dozen of them through, and they would rush eagerly to their chosen idol.

Posters were everywhere (attached to the wall with Post-it notes, which weren't proving very effective as some were already peeling off). On them, scrawled in fat, hostile capitals, were the words:

PLEASE NOTE!!!

1) ONLY <u>ONE</u> AUTOGRAPH PER PERSON!
2) ONLY <u>OFFICIAL</u> MERCHANDISE!
3) PUBLICITY PHOTOS WILL BE AVAILABLE FROM THE STARS <u>FOR A FEE</u> IF YOU HAVE NOTHING TO SIGN!

Simon Josh was there, a grin sliding around his face. Mervyn remembered Roddy's words, and it did strike him that Simon was strolling around in a way not unlike that of a Nazi commandant of a prison camp.

Tucked in at the end of a long line of tables, Mervyn could see a spindly man with greasy hair and shiny black eyes, sitting like a sinister teddy bear, magic marker at the ready.

He couldn't be here could he? Signing autographs? Not him? But yes, it was Bernard Viner.

Bernard was the special effects supervisor on *Vixens*, and a deeply angry person. He was a man who constructed grudges as slowly and methodically as he constructed little model spaceships, and he had a huge grudge against Mervyn. Mervyn had lost Bernard his job on *Vixens*, and even though it was pretty much Bernard's fault, he hadn't forgotten and hadn't forgiven. Mervyn made a mental note to avoid him as much as he possibly could.

Bernard hadn't lost his touch. Every so often he would snarl at a luckless fan: 'I told you – I do signatures only! I don't do personal messages. Are you deaf or something?' When he did sign a picture, it was done slowly and methodically and in complete silence.

Mervyn hoped this wasn't going to be too arduous. With any luck this convention was full of fans uninterested in the behind-the-scenes team and they would flock to the actors instead.

As if on cue, one of those actors made a fashionably late entrance into the hall. Vanity Mycroft sashayed in through the double doors like a catwalk model, surveying the room with a graceful sweep of her whole body before striding in. Assorted fans and hangers-on chugged along in her wake, like tiny boats tooting the homecoming of a mighty battle-scarred warship.

At first, Mervyn assumed she had dressed down – jeans, jacket and plain blouse – but as she got closer he realised that the ensemble was a riot of labels; Gucci this, LaCroix that, Paul Smith the other. Mervyn wasn't an expert on such things, but even he could recognise the studied casualness of designer clothing when he saw it.

Wait a minute... As she got *closer...?*

She was heading straight for him. Mervyn realised with a start that the seat next to him was empty, and the tiny printed card on the table by his right elbow read 'V. Mycroft'.

She threw herself into the seat, and addressed her entourage. 'Right. Mummy's on duty now. Off you fuck.' Her fans dribbled away, save for one thin-faced girl in a cardigan who produced a number of sparkly magic-marker pens, an ashtray and a packet of Benson and Hedges and arranged them in front of Vanity. The girl then pulled a number of photos from a folder and fanned them out on the table. Vanity pulled her sunglasses down her nose and turned her bottle-green eyes towards Mervyn.

'Mervyn darling, what a lovely surprise. How are you?' She grabbed his knee with surprising force.

Close up, Vanity was impressive. She had a striking, chiselled face, well preserved by alcohol and botox. A face which had only recently begun to curl at the edges. In ten years' time it would probably implode, the wrinkles would mesh together to form the gnarled look that was the trademark of oak trees and the long-term chain-smoker, but for the moment she was an impressively attractive woman.

Vanity didn't bother to introduce the girl, who had meekly taken a seat and was lurking somewhere to her right. Presumably she was a personal assistant and general dogsbody.

The actress pulled a cigarette out of the packet, slotted it in her mouth and ignited it with a huge gold lighter (*did anyone ever have the courage to tell her the hotel was non-smoking?* he wondered). Her face almost turned inside-out with pleasure as she took a grateful drag.

'Ready for another hour of legalised slave labour under the lash of Mr

Josh?' she drawled. 'Greasy little bastard wants a pound of my flesh. I should have sent him the off-cuts from my last surgery.'

'I noticed you weren't happy with him,' said Mervyn.

'You could say that, darling. All settled now. Tripled my fee and got a better room so I don't have to choke on the great unwashed's BO. I showed that pubic-headed prick who's boss, thanks to my book. If the pen's mightier than the sword, I've given him a good hard jab in the arse with my biro.'

Mervyn was curious. 'Good autobiography is it?'

'Of course it is, darling. It's all about me.'

'Am I in it?'

'Darling! How could you not be in it?' And she winked slyly.

He looked down. Nope, they were still there. He could have sworn her eyes had just scorched the buttons off his shirt.

'So how does your book tame Simon Josh?'

'Read it and find out, darling. It's very reasonably priced on Amazon. Apparently they've taken 40% off me – just like my second husband. Bastard. Anyway, time to open shop. The barbarians are massing at the gates.' She gestured towards the doorway. Through it, Mervyn could see that her entrance had been noted and the ordered queue was swelling into a sizeable crowd.

'Looks like you're going to have your work cut out getting through that lot,' he said.

She sighed. 'Yes. One does yearn for a shorter name, Sue Bloggs or something chavvy like that. Writing "Vanity Mycroft" a thousand times in a row does make the fingers ache somewhat.'

'Worth it though. It's a great name. Unusual too.'

'Thank you darling. And it's my real one, you know. Not a stage name. If you read my autobiography you'll find that out...'

'I'll make it a top priority.'

'... But I'll tell you anyway, darling. It's all down to a quaint family tradition we Mycrofts have, of naming our children where they were conceived.'

'I've never heard of a village called Vanity.'

'Not quite, dear. I was spawned during a desperate fumble in a Cardiff dressing room. My mother was playing Becky Sharp in an ill-advised tour of plays adapted from classic English novels. This one was *Vanity Fair* – hence my name. Vanity Mycroft.' She took another drag. 'Should count my lucky stars they weren't doing *Fanny Hill*.'

Mervyn looked again at the queue. All eyes were focused in her direction. 'I don't envy you, the amount of "Vanity Mycroft"s you're going to have to write today.'

'Oh don't worry about me, Mervy...' She gave him a smouldering look. '... As well you know, I happen to have *very* supple wrists...'

She swung round and took a photo from the simpering girl who had scurried in front of her, lucky enough to be at the head of the queue. 'Thank you, dear. Ooh! That's a good photo. I like that one.' The fan blushed with gratitude at the compliment. *Same old Vanity*, thought Mervyn. *Able to switch from pleasure to business and back again as quickly as the hotel rooms above them.*

'So what are you doing at the moment, dear?'

The fan muttered, 'Well, I'm thinking of doing a physics degree at Middle–'

'Not you dear, I was talking to Mervyn here. Anything interesting?'

'Well, ahm...'

'I just know you're writing a lovely big telly show, with a smashing part just for me.'

'Actually Vanity, I've been a bit out of the telly loop recently...'

'God,' she sighed, 'not you as well! Andy Jamieson has just left *The Bill*, Nicholas is touring the nether regions of the country... What's the point in cultivating all these contacts, having to pretend to be nice to you during the series, when you all give up being useful to me?'

'I was thinking of writing a book.'

'Who's it for?'

'It's not for any publisher yet, it's for myself really...'

'Not you, Merve dear.' Vanity was talking to the fan again. 'Who shall I put it to, darling?'

'What?'

'The name dear, who's it to?'

'Just the signature please.'

'Fine.'

Vanity signed her name with a casual flourish. The girl gave a nervous nod of gratitude, bypassed Mervyn with a simpering grin, and asked for the autograph from the man on Mervyn's left; the actor who played one-third of a crab creature in 1988. The left claw, apparently.

She jerked a thumb at the fan's retreating form. 'Another bloody gold-digger. That'll be on eBay come the morning.'

'Surely not.' To Mervyn, the fan looked like a sweet little thing. Shame she bypassed him. He remembered now that he always got overweight, intense men who wanted to discuss plot holes.

'She didn't ask for a dedication. Dead giveaway. Can't flog them if they've got, "To Mildred and her pet cat Nibbles, lots of love Vanity, kissy kiss kiss" on the bottom.'

'Oh', said Mervyn. 'She seemed nice.'

'Same old Mervyn. Always thinking with this,' she suddenly grabbed his crotch and gave a little tickle under his scrotum with a long pointed fingernail. 'Can't blame her though. More power to her elbow. We're all here to make money. Just look at these...' She indicated the photos. They were prints of *Vixens* publicity shots; Vanity laughing at the camera with the other characters carefully cropped off; shots of her pointing her gun aggressively at nothing in particular, shots of her in a tight T-shirt leaning casually on a shiny new Styrax.

'These are... um...'

'£15 for an eight-by-ten black and white, £20 for a ten-by-twelve black and white, add a fiver on both prices for colour.'

'Very nice...'

Vanity made a dismissive snort. 'Titty pics for the lonely mummy's boys and the fat lezzers.' Mervyn had to concede that an inordinate amount of the waiting fans were either pale scrawny men in black T-shirts, or extremely sturdy women who seemed to have left their necks at home. 'Ah! It's these that I want to sell, darling... come to mummy!'

She held her hands out, as a man rushed in with piles of books and deposited them on the table. The thin-faced girl instantly sprang to her feet and started to arrange them like battlements in front of Vanity. Mervyn picked one up. It was a chunky tome; the sort that appeared in huge displays by the tills in supermarkets and in airport bookshops. In gold embossed lettering (so italicised it was hardly legible) was the title:

Vixen to Fly

My autobiography
Vanity Mycroft

If the title wasn't very inspiring, the cover certainly was. It was an 'artistic' black and white photo. Vanity was draped across the Styrax Superior prop like a model in a motor show, completely naked. She was lying over the front of it with her feet in the air behind her, crossed playfully at the ankles. Her head was cradled on the backs of her hands, a pose beloved of 60s models (and very typically Vanity) with her arms resting on the bonnet, elbows conveniently covering the nipples.

Her face, complete with wicked grin and arched eyebrows, looked up at him. Apart from a few tell-tale liver spots on her hands and the neck starting to do a Bernard Matthews, she looked like the old Vanity he'd known and fondled.

'Put it down carefully darling. It's very explosive. It could go off in your hand.'

'I'll bet.' Mervyn put the book down.

'It's certainly ruffling a few feathers,' she drawled on in a bored voice. 'Apparently *some* people don't like to be reminded what naughty little boys they used to be...' Her eyes flicked momentarily to William 'Smurf' Smurfett, pushing his Styrax prop out of the room and down the corridor. He was very small, and the prop looked very big. Smurf didn't look very happy. Many fans offered to help, but he batted them away like moths.

'... And, alas, I had to take a few things out. The lawyers, God help their twisted little knickers, went on about this and that, blah blah, you can't say this about X, you can't reveal that about Y, and Z might get upset if you said blah... I say to them, X was a shit, Y was a poof and Z was a gullible idiot, and they say prove it, and I say Y shagged Z in Y's dressing room and X shopped them to the tabloids. But will they admit I've got a point? Will they buggery boll–'

Vanity stopped in mid-sentence, staring off to her left. Puzzled, Mervyn followed her gaze, and soon realised why. Near the head of the queue there was a handsome young man in his 20s, with clear brown eyes and spiky blonde hair. He was wearing white chinos and a black t-shirt, impressively filled by his tidy physique. He was carrying a big black satchel.

The effect on Vanity was instantaneous. Like Jekyll and Hyde in reverse, the crabby old chain-smoker disappeared and was replaced by the dazzling enchantress who smiled out of the covers of TV listings magazines in the 80s and 90s. But to the bewilderment of Vanity – and the utter astonishment of Mervyn – the young man *bypassed* her and stopped at Mervyn, his face a picture of hero-worship.

'Mr Stone, I wondered if you could sign this for me?' He put down a big glossy picture. It was a computer-generated montage of Mervyn surrounded by creatures from *Vixens from the Void* – a Styrax, a Maaganoid, a Gorg, and a Groolian.

'Goodness,' said Mervyn, as flustered as the breathless fan appeared to be. He tried to remember how he wrote his signature. 'You certainly took your time over this.'

'I had the most trouble finding a nice photo of you. Most of the ones I found on the internet had you looking a bit gormless, or your hair was too mad.'

The photo was indeed a good photo. It was a moody black and white one, with Mervyn leaning forward into the camera, his hand thoughtfully resting on his chin and hiding his jowls.

‘Well it’s a good photo of me. I had that done for my book sleeve.’

‘Yes, when is that coming out? I’ve been scouring Amazon for years.’

‘Just in the final stages of proofreading,’ Mervyn lied. He looked at the picture in frank disbelief. ‘I don’t think anyone’s made anything like this of me before.’

‘You changed my life,’ said the boy simply. ‘I’ve followed your career incredibly closely.’

‘Which is more than I ever did.’

‘I can name you all your career highlights.’

That won’t take long, thought Mervyn. ‘Oh really? What’s your favourite highlight?’

‘Oh, definitely the bit when you caught Bernard Viner for stealing from the set and got him sacked.’

‘Um... Oh.’

‘I loved your whodunnit episode in series three, “Hyperdeath”, when the murderer turns out to be the malfunctioning robot... But when I found out that you actually did some actual detective work in real life? That was amazing!’

‘Well, I don’t really like to talk about that,’ muttered Mervyn, casting a nervous glance over at Bernard’s corner.

‘But wasn’t it just amazing? Gosh! I’m definitely coming to your panel after this. Just imagine... you and Bernard actually on the same stage together...’

‘What?’ He should have looked at his schedule more carefully.

‘It should be, oh, just great!’

Oh, just great.

Mervyn picked up a pen. ‘What’s your name?’

‘Stuart. Oh, sorry. You mean for the autograph. Well actually, could you not put Stuart...’

On the very edge of his peripheral vision, he could see Vanity mouthing ‘eBay’.

‘Could you put, “To Stu, from a fellow sleuth, best wishes, Mervyn Stone.”’

The young man held the resulting signature close to his face with an awed fascination.

‘Gosh thanks. This is great.’ His eyes flicked around it, as if he was mentally absorbing every dash and squiggle. ‘This is *really* great. Thanks. Great. Thanks.’ He struggled with his satchel. ‘Do you think I can show you something to you. To both of you?’

Vanity leaned forward, bosoms skating the flyleaves of her books.

‘Oh darling, of *course* you can show me anything you like.’

'Well, okay...' said Mervyn doubtfully.

But the young man's laptop was already out, powered up, and pointing at Mervyn. The screen exploded into life, and he was greeted by an old episode of *Vixens from the Void*. An actress coated in 80s make-up was chewing her lip and wrestling with an Atari joystick, while sitting in an MFI swivel chair.

'Oh God it's me, isn't it?' said Vanity. 'I'm really not a fan of how I looked in the show. Do you know, most people say I look better now... What do you think?' she gave the fan her sauciest smile, but his eyes were completely on Mervyn.

'It's "Day of the Styrax" from series two,' mumbled the young man.

'I know,' said Mervyn, puzzled. 'I wrote it.'

'I know you know. But look! I've remade it.'

The shot of Vanity wiggling her joystick was suddenly interrupted by a terrifying burst of noise, and CGI spaceships burst across the screen, firing and spitting bolts of pink lightning at each other. Everybody in the room turned, looking at where the noise was coming from.

Then the screen went back to Vanity/Arkadia, pacing around a cheap corner of a set, tapping the keys of BBC Micro keyboards, before leaping into action again with more frenetic CGI space battles.

'You see, I've added my own state-of-the-art special effects. I know you and Nicholas didn't have a lot of time and money, and it looked a bit ropey at the time. No offence, of course. I know the pressure you were under. So I've made it exactly the way you would have wanted it, if you'd done it properly.' The young man prodded the screen. 'I spent ages keying in the Styrax warship behind Arkadia's shoulder using Adobe AfterEffects.' He mumbled to Vanity: 'I hope you don't mind. I had to colour-grade you and overlay you onto a matte.'

'Oh darling, don't apologise! You have no idea how many times I've been overlaid on a mat.'

The boy stared fondly at the screen and then barked: 'I've got more shots to show you, if you like.'

'Perhaps later,' said Mervyn. 'There are other people waiting for autographs. Probably. Don't want to keep them hanging around.'

'Absolutely.' The boy nodded vigorously. Mervyn was struck how the young man's behaviour was like his little computer clip. Quiet and scarcely audible one minute, a burst of noisy energy the next. Mervyn wasn't certain if it was the young man or his 'restored footage' that was giving him his headache.

'I'll tell you what,' said Mervyn. 'There's Bernard Viner over there. Why don't you show him how you've improved on what he did? He's always going on about how rubbish he thought his finished work was,

I'm sure he'll be very excited to see how much better you've made it by taking it all out.'

'Great idea. Thanks, Mr Stone.' He packed his computer away, and made a beeline for Bernard.

'Mervyn, you are still a very naughty man,' hissed Vanity.

'Yes, I am,' said Mervyn simply. 'I shouldn't have done it really. He was a nice boy.'

'Oh yes... *Very* nice.' A sardonic grin skipped across her face.

'What?'

She looked at him with a profound pity, her eyebrows cocked and ready. 'Oh come on, Merv. He was as bent as a paperclip. Anyone could see that.' The Fan Who Did Not Fancy Vanity was summarily dismissed. 'And my God, I really thought all that computer stuff of his was hideous, didn't you Mervyn?'

'I wasn't impressed, no.'

'All tarted up to look like something it was never meant to be like. Ugh. So vulgar. It's like some old woman wearing boob-tubes, short skirts and crotchless panties. Catch me 'improving' myself like that, Mervy, and you can put me up against a wall and shoot me.'

'I'd rather just put you up against a wall.'

Vanity's eyebrows arched into her hairline. 'Mervy! You are *still* a very naughty man!'

Soon the allotted time was up and Vanity's entourage descended on her once more. Her ciggies and pens were duly collected by the thin-faced girl.

The girl stared at Mervyn, unblinking. It unnerved him.

Vanity stood up and tousled Mervyn's already unkempt hair. 'Come into my room and we'll talk about projects you can write for me to star in. Perhaps if I'm in the mood, I'll even tell you what I've written about you in my autobiography.' As she made to leave, she flicked him a predatory look and lowered her voice to a growl. 'Perhaps we could even re-enact a few chapters...'

'Now Vanity,' he whispered. 'You're taking advantage of a randy old man. You're not being fair.'

'Fair? Fair?' she hooted at full volume. 'My dear Mervy. "Fair" is my middle name.' She grinned wolfishly. 'Literally...' She squeezed his wrist, and then was gone in a cloud of Chanel.

Mervyn was surprised by how flirty he'd been to Vanity. True, they'd used each other shamelessly for sex in the past, but that time was long gone. They'd both stayed out of each other's underwear for some years now, each preferring to use their convention days to prey on the young, firm and easily impressed.

Still, the offer was there... And even if he was well acquainted with what lay beneath her bedcovers, getting acquainted with what was beneath the covers of her autobiography sounded just as enticing.

He was just about to follow her when a large sweaty fan hove into view, blocking his escape. He had thick glasses and rigid black hair sculpted into a drastic parting. He wore a black T-shirt with an impossible looking woman on it – breasts the size of dustbin lids straining against a skimpy leather outfit that would have made it difficult for the poor girl to draw breath let alone fight crime in a dangerous galaxy. It proved, once again, Mervyn's pet theory on science fiction and fantasy attire. The more attractive and athletic the character depicted on the T-shirt, the less attractive and athletic the fan wearing it.

Mervyn was irritated; the autograph session was now over. This gormless bastard had just taken advantage of the fact he'd not yet risen from his seat. He looked around helplessly but no help was forthcoming.

'She's great isn't she? A wonderful lady.' Mervyn realised the fan was clutching a signed photograph of Vanity; the one with her nipples prodding through the T-shirt. 'She's really real. Genuine. She's always like that with me. We share something really special, Vanity and me,' the fan continued.

He was tempted to say 'Oh really? What do you share exactly – bra size?' But he managed to stop himself. Good Mervyn. Nice Mervyn. 'Oh really?' he eventually said.

'Oh yes. A real psychic bond.' He put his photos in a leather file, which he had in a satchel. Then he pulled out a large piece of cardboard from the satchel, which he unfolded and plonked unceremoniously under Mervyn's nose. The whole process took an inordinately long time, and Mervyn's patience withered like the plants he tried to keep alive in his house. 'You have to sign there,' said the fan, pointing.

Mervyn inspected it. The piece of cardboard was smothered with photos, video covers and magazine articles. The fan indicated the bottom left corner.

'Here?'

'Yes'

'Right, and to whom should I put it–?'

'Just put your name.'

'Just the name. Right.' Another one for eBay, then.

He dutifully signed his name over a photo of a smiling man in a sparkly uniform.

The fan peered at the autograph. 'What does that say?' he

demanded.

'Um... "With best wishes, Mervyn Stone."'

The fan peered again. 'You're not Major Karn played by Roderick Burgess,' he said, the flat voice not wavering by a semitone.

'No, no I'm not,' said Mervyn. 'I have to admit it, I'm not. You've caught me fair and square. Devilishly sneaky trick of yours to blow my cover, getting me to sign my name like that.'

Enough with the sarcasm, Mervyn, he told himself. *These people have paid a lot of money to be here, and they're paying your fee. Have some* patience, *for God's sake.*

The man blinked several times, as though he was trying to reboot his brain. 'That's Major Karn played by Roderick Burgess. I wanted Roderick Burgess's autograph on Roderick Burgess's photo.'

'I'm sorry. I think it's a magic marker. I don't think it'll rub off.'

He blinked again. 'You've signed your name on Roderick Burgess's photo.'

'Excuse me?' Someone had approached them. It was one of the stewards who patrolled these conventions. With bright mauve sweatshirt and identity pass round her neck, she looked like a prim-yet-sexy gym mistress. 'The autographs have now finished. We have to clear the hall.'

'He signed his name on Roderick Burgess's photo.'

'I see,' she said. She took the cardboard collage, inspecting the offending scribble with great solicitude. Then, like a nurse removing a chest bandage, she suddenly ripped out Roddy's photo and gave his collection back to him. 'There. You can put another photo in your little collection and get Mr Burgess to sign that one instead, can't you?'

The man walked away in a daze where he was joined by other fans. Mervyn could just hear a faint disbelieving monotone saying 'She tore out Roderick Burgess's photo.'

This steward was young, pretty and had just rescued him from a large annoying fan. He was definitely in love. What was the name on her tag? She wasn't standing near enough, and, like Simon's tag, it was printed in that unreadable squared-off futuristic font. Bugger.

'Thanks for that,' he said, staring at her tag like a cross-eyed buzzard. He made out the name 'Minnie Moncreif' or 'Montrose'. Or something like that.

'That's all right. It's my job to keep the scary ones at a safe distance.'

'Is it? Thank God. You couldn't escort me full-time, could you?'

'Do you want me to?'

She tilted her smooth innocent face at him, and then she grinned, the dirtiest grin he'd ever seen on any woman's face. Even Vanity's.

And then she was gone.

What the...?

He hurried out of the autograph room, head cocked like a spaniel, eyes darting from right to left, looking for her. Was she at the end of the corridor by the lifts? He broke into a determined lollop, eyes craning to see a splash of curly auburn hair. Unfortunately, someone else happened to be heading swiftly down an intersecting corridor, and as Mervyn wasn't looking where he was going, the collision was inevitable.

'My portfolio!' wailed Simon, as photos, papers and postcards scattered down the corridor, falling like large multi-coloured snowflakes.

'Oh dear. I'm really sorry...' He went to pick up a few, but Simon screamed as he pulled on white cotton gloves. 'Don't touch the deceased ones! A lot of these artistes have been unavailable for decades! They are priceless!' Simon's face folded into an unpleasant scowl, which suited him. It was as if, with no others around, he no longer had to waste energy on his artificial bonhomie.

Obligingly, Mervyn picked up an autograph slip which had become separated from the photo, but Simon snatched it off him. 'I *told* you...'

'I know this actor! This is Samuel Johns. He's not dead!' Mervyn protested.

Simon glared at him, smoothing it. 'He *happens* to be very, *very* ill,' he snarled. 'Who knows, when you snuff it, your signature might be worth something...' He huffed off, holding his piles of photos like a newborn baby. 'But I doubt it, Mervyn. I doubt it,' he called back.

Mervyn resumed his trot along the corridor, but with little enthusiasm. She was long gone. *Oh well*, he thought. *Might as well head back to my room.*

He pressed the button to open the lift, only to find her waiting inside for him. One hand on the 'hold' button, the other placed provocatively on her hip.

'Are you stalking me?' she asked.

'Ah... well. No...'

She smiled wickedly. 'Would you like to?'

Mervyn's hands were trembling so much he could barely insert his key-card into the door slot. Fortunately, that passed. He had no more problems with slots after that.

CHAPTER SEVEN

The steward scooped up her ferocious bosom in a sturdy bra and shrugged on her sweatshirt.

'You off?' said Mervyn, watching her from his bed. He was self-consciously hiding the more wobbly and careworn bits of his body under the duvet. So basically, it was tucked tight up under his chin.

He'd been much less self-conscious half an hour earlier. He'd been hopping round the hotel room, doing the dance known as the 'Man Desperate for a Shag Shuffle'. This involved trying to take shoes and socks off with jeans puddled around the ankles while hurling a shirt above the head, trying to shake it free from the wrists.

'Got to go. Soz. Got to get ready for your panel. The whole convention will turn out for it. If I'm not there with the other stewards to sort the queues out, Simon's gonna get killed in the stampede.'

'Now that's something I'd pay forty quid to see.'

She bounded off the bed. Her arms were surprisingly large, threaded with muscles. Her shoulders were bigger than Mervyn's. Mervyn was under no illusion that she led a very active lifestyle; the sides of his stomach ached from the workout.

She bent over the hotel mirror brushing her hair, her buttocks raised and pointed in his direction. 'You'd have to buy a ticket and wait in line.'

'Oh yes?' Mervyn tried to spin the conversation out. Anything to keep that impressive bottom hovering in his vicinity. It was like two pink helium balloons bobbing across his eyeline, so smooth and shiny he swore he could see the hotel windows reflected in them.

'Is he not popular then... Minnie?' He used the name tentatively. In the excitement of the last half-hour, he'd forgotten to check her tag properly.

But he'd obviously read it right, because she turned and grinned at him. 'Yeah, you might say that. All us stewards, we all muck in for a laugh, really. Have a boogie at the disco, meet the stars. He takes it far too seriously, like a business. He's always oiling after the big names, but he treats them like kids, really.' She paused, thinking. 'No. Not like kids. More like things. He talks about you lot like he does all those ray guns and robots and props he owns. "Get Jamieson out of the bar and put him where he's supposed to be!" he says, and "I want my prize collection on stage in five minutes," when he's talking about the Vixen *actresses*, would you believe.' Her face darkened. 'And then there's what else he's done. He's not done a nice... Well, let's just say he's not popular. Patronising tosser. We call him Slime-on Josh. We got loads of nicknames for the stars. They aren't all flattering so I'd better not tell.'

'I shudder to think. Are you lot thinking up a nickname for me?'

'What's to say you haven't got a nickname already?'

'No I haven't!' He threw a pillow at her.

'You have too!' It was chucked back with a giggle. Minnie leapt on the bed, lying on top of him, nose-to-nose, with only the duvet separating them. Mervyn felt like a teenager, larking around with his new girlfriend in her parents' bed, his head buzzing with excitement and danger.

'You're teasing me.'

'It's true. You've got a nickname.'

'How can I have? I haven't done a convention in seven years.'

She smiled her dirty smile. 'What can I say? You've got a reputation that don't die easily. Let's just say you've made a bit of a name for yourself among the girl stewards. They say you always used to go on patrol, case them all for fresh talent. They call you "the Stone Ranger".'

'The *what?*'

She kissed his nose. 'You heard!'

'What do you mean "case for talent"? I do not "case for talent".'

'Oh really? And you weren't staring at my boobs all the while I was dealing with that fat bloke and his autographs?'

'But I was only –' He was about to protest that he'd only been trying to read her name tag, but his survival instinct took over. Probably not the best time to bring that up. Besides, if he hadn't been trying to focus on her name, he'd most likely have been staring at her breasts. It was his good fortune he'd accidentally given her the right impression.

'Anyway. I'm profoundly grateful to you.'

'You should be, mate.'

'No, not about what we just did! Though of course, that was nice.'

'Nice?'

'Great!'

'I'll take great.'

'I meant I was profoundly grateful about you rescuing me from that mad fan.'

'No worries. All part of the job.'

'They can get a bit much, the ones with their anal addiction to crossing the stars off their little lists.'

'I can believe it.'

She leapt off the bed and dived for her jeans, slipping them on. Then she dashed to the door, turned and said, 'Oh, before I go, could you do something for me?'

'Again? I'm an old man.'

'Not that! Though I'll be back for more, don't you worry,' she chucked a small black leather book on the bed. 'Could you sign the postcard on page 23 and get the book back to me after the panel? I'd be really grateful.'

And she was gone.

Mervyn picked up the book. It was an autograph book, sheets of plastic envelopes filled with photos and postcards; most were signed, in very fulsome ways, 'To Minnie.'

All the postcards and photos were of *Vixens* celebrities. All men.

Mervyn's was about the only one left unsigned.

I'll be back for more. Don't you worry.

CONVIX 15.
EARTH ORBIT ONE:

1.00pm

EVENT	*LOCATION*
BEHIND-THE-SCENES PANEL NICHOLAS EVERETT MERVYN STONE BERNARD VINER	Vixos Central Nerve Centre (main stage, ballroom)
'ASSASSINS OF DESTINY' PART TWO **EPISODE SCREENING**	The Catacombs of Herath (video lounge - room 1024)
AUTOGRAPH PANEL JOSEPH McANDREW TIM WARNE BRYCE CAMPION RICK ARMORY	Arkadia's Boudoir (room 1013)
PHOTOS VANITY MYCROFT	Transpodule Chamber (room 1030)
WRITING VIXENS FICTION **PROFESSIONAL WRITERS' PANEL** with Graham Goldingay, Fay Lawless, Craig Jones, Darren Cardew	The Seventh Moon of Groolia (room 1002)

CHAPTER EIGHT

As Mervyn entered the ballroom for his behind-the-scenes panel, he was plunged into darkness.

He could dimly see about 200 people on chairs, their faces shining with the reflected light from a projection screen. Booming from the speakers was a distorted conversation. On the screen, her features blown up to monstrous proportions, was Vanity. Her hair was lacquered into a golden mane that crested a good half-foot above her head; cheeks and eyelids plastered with a shade of shocking pink that had died out nowadays – thankfully – along with pirate shirts, suede pixie boots and T-shirts instructing the world in general to 'RELAX'.

'How could you do this to us. How could you do this *me*?' she over-enunciated, moist lips quivering. The camera cut to the room she was in; a cross between a Russian palace (curtains and props courtesy of a BBC production of *War and Peace*) and an ultra-modern control centre (set borrowed from *Blake's 7*). There was a large screen, crudely pasted on the wall with BBC special effects.

'Forgive me sister. I have this weakness for wanting to be on the winning side.'

On the screen was the evil Medula. She was wearing a jet-black wig in a severe Cleopatra style. Her costume and make-up were all in blacks and purples. One might as well have CEEFAX subtitles flash up the word 'villainess'.

'But they'll destroy the whole Vixen empire!' wailed Vanity as, yet again, her face filled the wall of the ballroom.

Medula folded her arms in triumph. 'The Day of the Vixen is over. The Day of the Styrax is just beginning!'

The credits rolled. There was spontaneous applause and whooping from the murky figures in the chairs.

'Aren't you dead yet?' hissed a voice to Mervyn's left. 'I could have sworn I'd read your obituary in *The Independent* at least four times.'

'Now you're just being silly Nicholas. There's no way I'd be seen dead in *The Independent*. You know and I know if I go, it'll be nine inches in the *The Telegraph* or nothing.'

'Nine inches? You'd have to mow down a bus queue for that, petal.'

Squinting in the semi-darkness, Mervyn could see a tanned, well-fed face under a flamboyantly dyed bouffant.

'Dodgy old rubbish, isn't it old love?' The ex-Producer of *Vixens from the Void* pointed at the screen, grinned, and immaculately capped teeth glowed out of a well-trimmed beard. 'But not bad for a budget of fifty quid and a toffee apple per show.'

'Let me tell you, Nicholas, it's got its own primitive charm. I've just seen it with very loud state-of-the-art effects and it's not pretty.'

Mervyn liked Nicholas, and thoroughly enjoyed the time they'd worked together on *Vixens*. It was a rare thing for script editor and producer to get on so well, but Nicholas wasn't one of those TV types who thought that being ostentatiously gay gave him the automatic right to throw his toys out of his pram and sulk at the production teams. Nicholas's overt campery was the gloss on a deeply sensitive and shy man who listened very carefully to people who knew their jobs. Mervyn was deeply touched that Nicholas counted him among those few people.

'How's business in the touring game?' he asked.

'Oh positively booming, dear heart. This summer, I've shunted three arty exhibitions, two tribute bands and a rather spectacular pyrotechnic light show around the country. I've also had the dubious honour of being nursemaid to a particularly innovative – read dodgy – production of *Midsummer Night's Dream*. I'm pleased to have the opportunity to shake the crumbs off my favourite old double entendre and say that the whole south coast of England has seen my experimental Bottom.'

Mervyn's eyes adjusted to the gloom. He noticed Bernard Viner, the third member of their panel, sitting sullenly on a chair near the stage. He didn't look very happy.

Oh dear, thought Mervyn. *I really shouldn't have sent that fan to show him his CGI stuff.*

The behind-the-scenes panel was to follow the clips. While the screens showed more highlights from *Vixens from the Void*, four large comfortable chairs were placed in a semi-circle on stage. After five minutes, the screens went blank. On cue, the crowd stopped milling and found a place to sit.

Minnie was there by the sound desk, arms folded. She caught his eye and blew him a kiss. Mervyn gave her a grin. Then he noticed his new fan, Stuart, sitting in the front row. Mervyn only glanced across to the audience for a second, but Stuart was waiting to catch his eye. The fan assumed the grin was for him, grinned back and gave a fluttery little wave like an adoring girlfriend, much to Mervyn's embarrassment.

Simon Josh came on stage, clearly savouring his moment in the spotlight. 'Ladies and gentlemen, we are so privileged to have with us three people who were, literally, the life blood and soul of *Vixens from the Void*. Let me invite on to the stage, Script editor Mervyn Stone, Producer Nicholas Everett, and last, but by no means least...'

Waiting in the darkness, Mervyn could have sworn that someone gave a bitter chuckle. It sounded like Bernard.

'... Special effects wizard Bernard Viner!'

They mounted the stage to thunderous applause.

'So, Mervyn, what made you come up with the idea of the Styrax? What made you come up with a race of supercars who rebel and take over their planet?'

'What *made* me? Our audience figures made me.'

There was a well-rehearsed ripple of laughter as Mervyn gave his equally well-rehearsed opening line, of which the attached anecdote had become part of fan folklore since it started popping up on convention videos. Mervyn gave a 'but seriously though' cough and continued. 'Well... I had been scratching my head all day thinking about what we could possibly do to open series two with a bang, and Nicholas thought it would be a great idea to have an original and distinctive new monster to kick things off.'

'Oh yes,' said Nicholas, deadpan. 'Brilliant idea of mine... To have an original and distinctive monster...'

'... And of course he left *me* with the task of coming up with said original and distinctive monster...'

Nicholas gave a theatrical sigh and pulled an expression of world-weariness.

'Well it was my idea, Merv... You can't expect me to do *everything...*'

More titters from the darkness.

'Well I was stumped, wasn't I, Nicholas?'

Nicholas dipped in with practised ease.

'Oh yes, he was indeed. He was pacing up and down in the production office just above TC8 with a face like thunder, shouting "I must have a monster! I must have a monster!" I popped my head round the door, and said "Merve, love, if you'll just let me finish this scene, I'll come out there and shout with you."'

Another familiar burst of laughter and applause. Nicholas had done nothing of the sort, of course. It was a spontaneous ad-lib from a panel some years ago which went down very well, so it had stayed in. It helped to 'oil the wheels' in the telling of a tale that had already been told too many times before, and wasn't really true in the first place.

Mervyn continued the anecdote. 'When I finished that evening – still scratching my head over the lack of a monster – I found I couldn't leave. My car had been boxed in by a rather stylish Austin 11. I was stuck there for two hours – security was ringing round like mad trying to find the owner, and while I was sitting there on the wall with darkness falling like snow around me – not to mention the *snow* falling like snow around me – I realised that I was in thrall to this damn machine. Of course, this was the mid 80s, and the fact the country had been held to ransom by weekly fuel crises was still in living memory... I was, in effect, a slave to my car at that moment, so what would it be like if they really took over? So the idea came there and then.'

Nicholas was smirking now.

'So I rushed up to the production office to tell Nicholas, only to find he'd disappeared... He'd been called out by security to move his new car...'

'... My newly bought Austin 11...' supplied Nicholas.

'... Which was thoughtlessly blocking in the script editor of *Vixens from The Void*,' completed Mervyn.

There was a warm round of applause, as if they had just completed a particularly good card trick.

Simon Josh intervened. 'Now, Mervyn, you left the show at that point. To quote a certain programme starring Patrick McGoohan: "Why did you resign?"'

'Well, you know what old Samuel Johns used to say... "It's when your memories are at their happiest, that it's time to say goodbye..."'

An appreciative murmur of recognition spread around the room as the fans recognised a notoriously meaningless quote from an old actor from series one of *Vixen*s, who was too bored and drunk to do series two.

'Seriously?'

'No.'

Laughter.

'It was creative differences,' said Mervyn solemnly. 'I could no longer work under this ogre beside me.'

Nicholas put on a ferocious 'Grrr!' face to the audience, which elicited a shriek of delight.

'But then you suddenly came back a month later. Why was that?'

'I'd changed my aftershave,' quipped Nicholas.

Bernard had been lounging sullenly in the end chair since the panel started. Suddenly, however, he spoke in a bored voice. 'It wouldn't have anything to do with fact that, if you had invented the Styrax while you were script editor, they would technically be BBC property and you wouldn't keep the rights?'

Mervyn was annoyed. Bernard was technically half-right, but the part he chose to get wrong made Mervyn look like a money-grubbing bastard.

'Well Bernard hasn't got it *quite* right...' He stole a glance to his left, where Bernard had returned to his sullen state, idly staring at the Happy Traveller's light fittings.

'We'd had a bit of a crisis with our scripts. As usual. A couple of new chaps we were trying out for the series hadn't come up with the goods... Andrew Jamieson had let us down...' He saved a frisson of comic world-weariness for his last word: '... Again.'

On hearing his name being taken in vain, fellow *Vixens* writer Andrew Jamieson waved cheerfully from the back of the hall where he was leaning on a loudspeaker (on which also perched a large glass of wine). No one on the stage could see him in the darkness, but there was a delightedly ragged cheer from fans at the back, who suddenly realised a celebrity was in their midst.

'As a lot of you here know well, the BBC used to frown on script editors commissioning themselves. They saw it as a sort of self-nepotism. I'd already asked permission to write a substantial amount of the previous series when things started to get a bit fraught...'

Bernard tittered to himself, and Mervyn could have sworn he heard him say 'Well, naturally' under his breath.

'... So in case they said "no" this time, I removed myself from the in-house job, and that way I was able to write the story.'

Bernard swivelled his eyes towards Mervyn, '... And that way, as an ordinary freelance writer, you were able to keep sole rights and cash in on the merchandise. Funny that...'

Mervyn had had enough. 'All this interest in why I resigned! It's all very flattering, but this conversation does seem to be getting very "me, me, me". Let's talk about why someone else resigned. How about you, Bernard? Why did you resign?' Mervyn slapped his forehead in mock realisation. 'Oh, I'm sorry! I forgot. You didn't resign, did you? You got sacked. That's right. You got fired. For nicking props off the set. Oh yes. How could I have forgotten?'

Bernard's eyes became slits.

He stood up, and started to leave the stage in a huff. Then turned round abruptly and lunged, punching Mervyn full on the jaw.

'You smarmy little shit!' he yelled.

The room erupted. Two stewards in mauve sweatshirts raced to the stage, helping a dazed Mervyn to his feet. A third steward attempted to restrain Bernard, only for Bernard to swerve around him and knock Mervyn off his feet again.

Nicholas lunged out of his own chair and, in a surprising move that was distinctly at odds with his camp persona, grabbed Bernard's legs in a neat little rugby tackle, which sent Bernard staggering backwards into Mervyn, who was struggling to get up for the third time.

Mervyn staggered...

Fell off the edge of the stage...

And...

Right on top of the Styrax prop.

The fibreglass and papier-mâché disintegrated, and Mervyn was enveloped in a huge mushroom cloud of paper, glue and paint flecks.

The fans were stunned into silence. The young man who showed Mervyn the 'restored footage' on his laptop was the nearest. He was frozen in shock, looking at the remains of the Styrax and the body lying in the middle of it. His hands were clapped to his mouth at the horror before him. There was no restoring this old effect, no matter how many hours spent on Adobe AfterEffects.

A St John's Ambulance man rushed into the hall, carrying a first aid box. 'Where is he?' he panted.

'Down here,' a man pointed. 'He went down quite hard. I think his nose is broken.'

The crowd parted to give access.

'Are you all right?' the St John's Ambulance man asked. 'Can you hear me?'

Simon Josh's eyes fluttered open. 'I think so,' he said drowsily, trying to sit up from where he'd suddenly collapsed, eight seconds after Mervyn fell off the stage. 'I'm sorry, I think I must have fainted. I...' he levered himself up on an elbow, '... I thought for a moment that someone had crushed my Styrax Sentinel.'

At precisely the wrong time, a steward came up to Simon with an armful of papier-mâché. 'What should I do with this?'

Simon took one look at the sad, crushed fragments in the steward's hands, and fainted again, his head hitting the stage with a satisfying 'thunk'.

CONVIX 15. EARTH ORBIT ONE:

2.00pm

EVENT	*LOCATION*
MY LIFE AS A GROOLIAN JOSEPH McANDREW TIM WARNE BRYCE CAMPION RICK AMORY	Vixos Central Nerve Centre (main stage, ballroom)
'THE DOOMSDAY SEQUENCE' **EPISODE SCREENING**	The Catacombs of Herath (video lounge - room 1024)
PHOTOS WILLIAM SMURFETT	Transpodule Chamber (room 1030)
AUTOGRAPH PANEL RODERICK BURGESS Katherine Warner	Arkadia's Boudoir (room 1013)
VIXENS FROM THE VOID: WHAT THE FUTURE HOLDS **FAN PANEL** with Graham Goldingay, Fay Lawless, Craig Jones, Darren Cardew	The Seventh Moon of Groolia(room 1002)

CHAPTER NINE

Mervyn headed into the lift, nursing his swollen jaw and picking chunks of Styrax out of his hair. Nicholas rode up with him. The doors pinged open.

Of all the bloody luck. Bernard was in the room next to his.

'You talentless hack!' he screeched. 'I'm going to see you in court and sue your arse off!'

'Oh really,' said Mervyn drily. 'I'm not an expert, but as I understand English law, slander only works when you say stuff which *isn't* true.'

Bernard looked like he was going to say something else, but decided against it. He gave another furious look and slammed his door.

Nicholas turned to Mervyn. 'Are you all right?'

'I'm fine. Really.'

'Well I'm not. I'm shaking like a leaf. I don't know about you, my sweet, but I'm gasping for a ciggie. I could eat a packet and spit out the filters.'

'I don't smoke any more'.

'You could watch me. You'll get a moral buzz, if nothing else.'

'I'll meet you outside in 15 minutes.'

Mervyn examined the damage in his mirror. There was an angry red mark tattooed across his chin. Fortunately his hair hadn't been affected – it always looked as if he'd collided with something large and dusty.

There were white marks streaked across his jacket. He attacked them ineffectually with his hairbrush. Fortunately, he had an identical jacket waiting in the wardrobe. If your choice of outfit was any colour so long as it's black, it was as well to have a spare to hand.

Order had been restored to the room with spectacular efficiency. Morris had taken advantage of Simon Josh's comatose state to improve things. Four actors who had played Groolian ambassadors had been rushed on early and were desperately trying to find something new and interesting to say about a job they'd done for six weeks, 20 years ago (there were only so many times you could point out how itchy the bald caps were and how the purple body paint never washed off, no matter how many baths you had).

As Mervyn walked towards the foyer, he found himself in a narrow corridor, having to inch his way past a long queue waiting for something or other. They all stared fish-eyed at him. Dust and fragments of Styrax flaked off Mervyn's hair. The attendees grabbed at the bits as they floated down as if Mervyn was covered in gold.

Some of then started to nudge Mervyn, unbalance him, trying to make more bits fall off. He started to feel like he was Jesus, surrounded by a crowd of particularly assertive and demanding lepers.

There was an open door at the head of the queue. He dived inside. Morris was in there, taking photos of *Vixens* fans as they posed alongside another Styrax prop – similar to the one Mervyn had scattered to the four corners of the hotel with his descending backside.

'Don't lean on the Styrax, please,' said Morris casually, staring through his camera at a fan who had unwisely rested his elbow on the prop. 'It's only papier-mâché and fibreglass on a wooden base. They're old and rather fragile. They get damaged easily.' He caught sight of Mervyn. 'Speak of the devil.' He indicated the Styrax. 'Watch yourself around that. There's not many left now.'

'Thanks. I'll try to resist smashing it to pieces.'

The photo was taken, money changed hands and the fan left the room. Morris took the opportunity to shut the door on the queue, prompting muffled and indignant cries.

'Are you okay?' Morris asked, in a sepulchral tone.

'I'm fine. Just a little shaken.'

'It was quite a punch he threw.'

'Yes. Yes it was.'

'I hope you don't blame us for this.'

'No no... It's just a personal matter between me and Bernard.'

'That's great'. Morris patted the case of his video camera. 'Because it's going to look great on the website and the souvenir DVD.' Morris looked him up and down, as if sizing him up for a coffin. 'Are you're sure you're all right? You know, you really should get your head looked at...'

I've been thinking that ever since I got here, Mervyn thought.

'A knock on the head, well, it can be more serious, you know.' Morris waggled a fleshy finger against his head to reinforce his point. 'I'm going to the bar. Do you want anything?'

'No thanks.'

'I'll be right back.'

Mervyn was left alone with the Styrax Sentinel. He sauntered up to it. 'I don't know what they've been telling you. But I didn't really mean to crush your colleague. So don't worry, I'm not going to hurt you,' he said jokily.

'I'd like to see you try, chummo,' said the Styrax.

Mervyn staggered, took several backward steps, and fell over on his bruised behind.

'Can we take a break? I'm dyin' in here, man,' it said.

'Who's that?'

'Hey, who's *that*?'

'Smurf?'

'Merv?'

Mervyn edged towards the Styrax. 'Smurf? Is that you?'

'Get me out of this bastard thing, will you?'

Mervyn unbolted the back of the Styrax and two sets of stubby fingers grabbed the rim of the shell. A sweaty dwarf eased himself out, grabbed a towel from a chair, rubbed his face vigorously, and left it flapping on his head like a boxer.

'I'd give it ten minutes if I were you,' the dwarf said, jerking a finger at the open lid of the Styrax. A ripe smell, Essence of Dwarf Sweat, was starting to fill the room. 'Those things don't half stink. Going in there... it's like getting stuffed inside your own armpit.' He looked around, scowling. 'Don't tell me the bastard's gone for another tea break and left me. I'll bite his bloody kneecaps off.'

'He went to the bar.'

'Huh. Didn't ask if I wanted anything. As usual. When you're in there you might as well be on another planet for all the notice gets taken of you.'

'Smurf... what were you doing in there?'

'I'm getting my photo taken.'

'In there?'

'The fans like it like that. We sell loads.'

Mervyn looked at the pile of photos on the table, all featuring grinning fans standing by the Styrax. 'Wouldn't they prefer it, if you know, they could see you?'

'How would I do that, then?'

'You could stand *outside* of it...'

'I can't do that. It's my costume. Why would they want me out of costume?'

Something had definitely got shaken loose in his head when he hit the floor. He tried to digest the logic of it, but his brain spat it out.

'But... if you're in there, in the Styrax. Well, they can't, you know, *see* you in the photos. What's the point?'

'What do you mean, "What's the point"?' You think a photo taken with one of the stars of the show in his costume is pointless?' Smurf was getting indignant.

'No. Yes. I mean no. Of course it's not. I mean, look. How can they even prove to anyone looking at the photo that you were actually inside it?'

'Oh, they can.'

'They can?'

'Oh yes. They get their photos stamped.' Smurf picked a rubber stamp up off a trestle table, slammed it down on one of the spare photos, and handed the shot to Mervyn. It read: *This photograph depicts me with a Styrax Sentinel from* Vixens from the Void. *The Styrax is being manned by original operator William 'Smurf' Smurfett.* 'It's a nice little convention sideline, this is.' Smurf started dusting himself down with a clothes brush.

'I suppose you heard about what happened on stage this morning?'

Smurf gave a throaty chuckle that sounded as though it belonged in a much larger person. 'Oh yes, I heard about it. I would have given real money to see Simon's face. Andrew Jamieson said it was the best panel he's ever seen at a con.'

'Did he really.'

'I think there'll be quite a few people queuing up to buy you a drink at the bar tonight. The little snit makes me want to vomit, always preening and showing off his stuff. Couldn't have happened to a nicer guy.'

'Well, at least he's got one left,' said Mervyn, indicating the Styrax Smurf had just climbed out of.

'Oh, no he hasn't. This one's mine. And if he comes sniffing around it he's going to be sorry. I don't care how much he offers – he can whistle for it.'

He patted it proudly. 'Picked it up in a car boot sale in '98. Even if it's seen better days and it's a bit flaky round the edges, I still don't mind climbing inside it for a few hours.'

Mervyn smiled. 'A lot of people would say that about Vanity Mycroft...'

Smurf's face froze. 'What?'

'Joke. Seen better days? Flaky around the edges? Sorry, bit naughty that –'

'I don't appreciate cracks like that – from you of all people!'

'Sorry?'

'I had nothing do with her. All right? Nothing! And I'll thank you to keep your witty bloody comments to yourself!'

'I'm sorry. I don't understand...'

'Just don't mention that woman's name all right? Just don't mention it! She's a lying cow and don't let her convince you any different!'

Mervyn looked at him, dumbstruck.

CHAPTER TEN

'Sorry Mervyn. I thought you'd heard about it. Everyone else has.'

Smurf and Mervyn emerged from the hotel into the car park, where the smokers skulked. It was much brighter than the gloom of the hotel and they blinked like startled librarians. Nicholas was already there, dragging greedily on his cigarette.

'So what does she say about you?' Mervyn asked.

'I'd rather not repeat the old witch's libel, if you don't mind. I'm putting everything in the hands of my lawyers.'

Nicholas's mouth twitched. 'I expect you can go through the small claims court.'

'It ain't funny, Nicholas!' Smurf fumed. 'I'm not having her chuck lies about me left, right and centre. I'm going to take this all the way, you know. I'll take a DNA test if I have to.'

'Quite right, quite right,' said Nicholas, looking concerned. He hastily changed the subject. 'Anyway. How are you feeling, Mervy? Recovered from your battle with the Styrax?'

'I think so. Thank God we didn't have the money to make the things in aluminium.'

'Good was it?' said Smurf eagerly to Nicholas. 'Didn't see it meself.'

'He fell beautifully, dear heart. Such grace. What a stuntman he was. Duggie "Don't lean against that window" Fletcher would have been proud.'

It was Smurf's turn to giggle along with Nicholas, and Mervyn's to scowl.

'Just what is Bernard's problem?'

'Don't be too hard on him, Merv. I don't know if you know this, but Bernard's had a rough time of it these last few years. He couldn't get another job in telly after the incident. After you –'

'After *we* –'

'Alright, after *we* caught him leaving the BBC with half of studio 6 up his jumper. And after *I* had to fire him.'

'So what's he been doing?'

Smurf had wedged a large cigar in his mouth and lit it with what looked like a small flamethrower. 'He set up a special effects company in the late 80s, didn't he? Lasted all of ten minutes before it went tits-up.'

'I hardly see why he should fail. He made great model spaceships.'

'He did it just before computer graphics became the in thing.'

'Oh dear.' Mervyn felt guilty now. *I definitely shouldn't have sent that young fan to show Bernard his 'improved' footage. Perhaps I should apologise to Bernard.*

Their chat was interrupted by an unhealthy revving. They turned to see a huge wedge-shaped object growl into the hotel car park. It was a much larger and vibrantly coloured version of the Styrax Sentinel. Built around a car (a clapped-out Mini Metro, to be precise), it was a formidable-looking beast. A bunch of fans were clustered around it, giving off appreciative noises. Bernard stood to one side, eyeing them suspiciously. Occasionally, one would get near enough to touch it, and he flapped them away as if scaring crows from a field.

Mervyn whistled appreciatively. 'Crikey, that's the Styrax Superior, isn't it? I'd forgotten how damned impressive it was.'

'God yeah,' said Smurf, admiring the fibreglass monolith. 'A bit more bloody comfortable than the little ones, I can tell you that for nothing. Me and Sheldon used to fight over who got to operate it. Sheldon always won. Always. Let him do it just to shut him up. Prickly little bugger he was. Always giving it that.' He flapped his hands like a glove puppet. 'Yap, yap, yap... Used to call me "small fry" he did! *Half an inch* between us, and *he* called *me* small fry! And as for his politics... To tell you the truth, I'm glad the little fascist got turfed out during series two.'

Mervyn glared at Smurf reprovingly. Smurf realised what he'd been saying. 'Course, I wasn't glad about the other thing that happened. Not his burning to death. No,' he gabbled hastily, 'not that.'

'It's the best thing Bernard ever made,' said Nicholas, looking at the Styrax Superior with genuine awe. 'He really is a very good designer.'

'So how did he get hold of it, then?' said Mervyn. 'I doubt he was able to shove that thing down his trousers during a quiet moment.'

'No, he didn't.' Smurf piped up. 'He bought up a lot of props quite legit after the series ended. He exhibits that thing around the country, doing fêtes and conventions. He does charity events too.'

'Ah! Enlightenment dawns!' Mervyn snapped his fingers under Nicholas's nose. 'I now understand this "Don't be too hard on him" stuff. Don't tell me. Let me guess. You and he are putting a little something together, aren't you?'

'Me?' Nicholas said innocently, 'Merely a little touring exhibition of props from the show, dear heart. Money in the bank.'

Smurf looked curiously at the machine. 'If Bernard's out here... Who's driving the thing?'

Andrew Jamieson sauntered lazily up to them, a cigarette dangling from his lips. 'I'd watch that habit of yours,' he said to Smurf, pointing at the cigar clenched between the dwarf's teeth. 'It'll stunt your growth.'

'If I'd had a penny for every time you've said that,' growled Smurf, only half-jokingly, 'I'd have enough to stand on and punch you right on the nose.'

With an impressive 'phtttsh' noise the Styrax door opened (a recorded sound effect – the doors were like any normal Mini Metro) and Simon Josh poked his head out with a beaming smile and a regal wave.

'What's he doing in there?' muttered Smurf. 'It's not like Bernard to let anyone near that, let alone that little tit.'

Andrew grinned. 'He can't do much about it since it's not his any more. Bernard sold it to him about five minutes ago.'

'*What?*' erupted Smurf, 'I've been trying to get him to sell that to me for years! And he sells it to Simon arsing Josh without so much as a squeak? What the hell does he think he's playing at?'

Andrew shrugged. 'Might have been Simon's price for not booting him out of the convention.'

'Hell of a way to say sorry,' muttered Mervyn, 'I'd have just bought him chocolates.'

Nicholas said nothing.

There were 'oohs' and 'aahs' from the onlookers, as if someone had let off a firework. It wasn't too far from the truth. Simon had thrown a switch inside the machine, and the Styrax Superior lit up. Red lights designed to give the impression of robotic eyes glowed from the front, and strip lighting pulsed around the weaponry. The whole effect was like a lovingly preserved mobile disco.

There was a cheer, and respectful applause. Simon bowed.

The crowd barely noticed Bernard slinking back into the hotel like a wounded animal.

Smurf did, however. 'I'm going to see about this. Sell that thing to Josh? What the hell's he thinking?' The dwarf marched hotly into the hotel after Bernard, the glass door revolving angrily behind him.

'Lunch?' Mervyn said to Nicholas, but there was no reply forthcoming from the ex-Producer. Nicholas was also looking in the direction of the hotel entrance. He seemed lost in his own thoughts, his normally placid features knotting in concern.

It's amazing, Mervyn mused, *all this fuss over that old thing. When all's said and done... it's just a used car.*

CHAPTER ELEVEN

Mervyn went back to his room. No sooner had he stretched out on the bed and closed his eyes than there was a dull thud on the door – not quite a knock, but too deliberate to be an accident either. He got back up and opened the door. On the floor was a large jiffy bag, sealed and unaddressed. He picked it up.

He suddenly tensed, realising what he was doing. One learned to be wary of anonymous packages when one lived in London. Perhaps it was a piece of hate mail left by an angry fan? Or worse – some kind of explosive device courtesy of the paramilitary wing of the *Vixens from the Void* Appreciation Society? Bloody vengeance for the dead Styrax?

Oh what the hell...

He tore it open. Incredibly, it contained Vanity's book. Had Vanity dropped it off? Probably. Like a lot of larger-than-life female stars she was always firing off presents, more out of a need to be reassured that someone somewhere was thinking of her, than any feeling of generosity.

One of the pages had been folded over. It was the first page of Chapter 13. He read quickly, his eyes tumbling from left to right.

Chapter 13: From Little Acorns do GREAT BIG Oak Trees Grow!

Let me let you into a little secret. I've always wanted to shag a midget.

Don't get me wrong, I'm not some midget fetishist. I don't get my kicks while watching *Charlie and the Chocolate Factory* or anything, but ever since I'd played the Wicked Queen in a production of *Snow White and the Seven Dwarves* in Bromwich, I'd always been curious about what it would be like, about whether they're 'to scale' downstairs, if you catch my meaning!

I don't know if you're aware of this, but midgets (or dwarves, or whatever they like to call themselves – in these days of political correctness, they probably demand to be called vertically impaired persons. VIPs. Geddit?) are hell to get hold of at Christmas time. Everybody wants them for their pantomimes. This particular pantomime had so much trouble getting hold of the darlings, in fact, that the only way we could make the quota of seven was if Dopey, Happy and Doc were all played by girls!!!

I'd just finished my fourth curtain call and was heading offstage when I heard noises from a dressing room. The door was ajar, and I peeked in. Well, my stars! It was like that old joke about the dwarves in bed all feeling happy, and happy got out and they all felt grumpy!! They were all at it; their tiny wee bodies humping away, still with make-up on their little cheeks. It looked like a porn film in Lego. And my young co-star was there too! Well, if she was Snow White at the beginning of the run, she certainly wasn't by the end of it!

I suppose I shouldn't have been surprised. I had heard all the stories from the filming of the *The Wizard of Oz*, about how those munchkins were at each other like jackhammers. Like midget jackhammers, I guess. Or like those little hammers doctors hit your knees with.

Naturally, from that point on I was keen to try one on for size, so to speak. I'd become well acquainted with the old showbiz adage 'the bigger the star the smaller the twinkle,' if you catch my drift! Many's the time a leading man has dropped his pants in front of me and I half expected the police to enter, put a cordon round him and say 'Move along Vanity! Nothing to see here!'

Talking of police, I've already mentioned I'd stepped out with a certain actor – Mr X – from *Juliet Bravo,* who I can exclusively reveal had a truncheon that was FAR from arresting!

Anyway, this is about *Vixens*, isn't it? As you know, I had already tried out a few of the full-size actors, and the old saying was pretty true. Poor Roddy. When he sat down his great sweaty belly almost covered everything save for his tip and balls, bulging out from underneath. It was like he was squashing a surprised ostrich to death.

Mervyn flicked hastily through the rest of the chapter. It was with some relief that he didn't see himself name-checked – not in relation to having a disappointing 'twinkle' anyway. He flicked back and resumed reading.

Sorry, I'm being vulgar. That's the thing when you're not saying these things out loud. No one shushes you or takes you away to have some black coffee.

I was desperate to try one of our fun-sized cast members, so I aimed to make certain before the end of the series. By the time we started filming series two back in 1987 (God, is it over 20 years?) we had two, Sheldon Ellis and Billy 'Smurf' Smurfett. Smurf and Sheldon were the guys who operated those Styrax robot monsters.

I bet you thought they were moved by remote control, didn't you? Everybody does.

It always got Smurf annoyed when anyone thought that, but then everything got dear Smurf's dander up! He was an 'angry young man'. Well... they say it's always the short ones, don't they? He was always rowing with the other dwarf, Sheldon, about this and that – mainly politics. Thing was, Smurf was a leftie – up the workers and all that. Sheldon fancied himself as a bit of a posh boy. He wore a monocle and everything! He even invented himself an extra name so he could hyphenate himself. He got quite irritated that Forbes-Ellis never caught on! Oh yes, he really wanted to be a yuppie. Young, upwardly-mobile blah blah. Well, as upwardly mobile as a dwarf can get!

He appeared with Mike Batt and Tim Rice on one of those Conservative election rallies as a 'celebrity', would you believe! They introduced him as 'the man inside the monster'. That wasn't very clever! If you remember, there were loads of cartoons in the papers the next day, showing him sitting in Maggie Thatcher's head, pulling levers.

Anyway, darlings, let's say Smurf and Sheldon didn't get on... particularly when Sheldon called Smurf 'small fry' because Smurf was a whole half an inch shorter! I presume he meant height! Otherwise that would have decided it for me there and then!

Well, which one was I to have? Sheldon had a certain class. He had manners after all, and I could have sensible intellectual conversations with him. I agreed wholeheartedly with him about world affairs. I mean, what was all that fuss about Nelson Mandela? He had a lovely smile and everything, but so do most criminals. Look at Buster Edwards.

So Sheldon was civilised, but Smurf was cute. Nice bum, cheeky little grin... Most importantly from the way those dinky little jeans hung on his crotch, it looked like he had one as big as a baby's arm! Not bad for four-foot nothing!

Well... who to pick? Funnily enough, as it turned out, the decision was made for me. Sheldon got tossed off! The show I mean!

Suddenly, Sheldon was let go. I don't know what happened, but my guess is that Smurf had something to do with it, because on Sheldon's last day he went up to Smurf and punched him right on the nose! They had an almighty fight in the car park and a lot of the lighting crew came out and took odds on who would win. I suppose most of those bent-nosed, cut-throat socialists missed their dog and cockfights.

Mervyn remembered that was the last he'd seen of Sheldon: lashing at Smurf, struggling and wriggling, trying to escape the grasp of a stage manager who had him by the scruff of his neck, yelling expletives at them all as he was carried from TV Centre like an angry ventriloquist's doll.

The next time Sheldon's name had been mentioned, it was three months later, at the season two wrap party, when a tearful Nicholas was informing the production team about Sheldon's death at a fire at his house.

It was a sad end to a friendship. Well not a *friendship* exactly, but Mervyn had nothing against the little man, despite his pugnacious 'sod the poor' attitude, and his gloating about the Tory Party's iron grip over the country.

He remembered how shocked they were at the wrap party, when his death was announced. How unbelievable it all was. Vanity cried loudly, honking into a silk handkerchief. Smurf went deathly pale, face agape in disbelief, like a tiny snowman with one piece of coal for a mouth.

And for it to have happened the *exact same day* as they'd finished recording series two. What a coincidence!

Mervyn wondered if it *was* such a coincidence...But no. It was just an accident. Definitely. Mervyn's brain was getting affected by all this talk about his 'sleuthing'. His suspicious nature may have caught Bernard with ray-guns in his pockets, but to start assuming foul play at every ancient dog-eared tragedy? He'd just look stupid.

He read on.

> Anyway; Sheldon was gone from the show, so Smurf it was. I unpacked the old Mycroft box of magic tricks. You'll be surprised how many succumb when I show them I've got nothing up my sleeve! I threw the lot at Smurf; getting him to drive me home after my car conveniently 'conked out' in the BBC car park... Letting him catch me au naturelle after I 'accidentally' got hold of his key and 'mistakenly' used his dressing room to

Mervyn was beginning to realise why Smurf was so angry. He scanned down the page, speed-reading Vanity's extensive 'box of tricks'. He was well acquainted with them himself.

> Nothing worked, would you believe! Gracious, was he slow on the uptake! Must be the thin air down there on the ground, makes their brains sluggish.
>
> Weeks passed. It was the last day of filming. It was the last day

before we broke for at least six months; maybe forever if we got cancelled. Well, desperate times call for desperate measures.

Early morning, and everyone was setting up cameras and stuff. I saw his little Styrax in the corner of the props area. It waggled one of its claw thingies, so I knew he was inside. So I hurried towards it. But damn and blast my luck! I had to hide behind a pillar. Ace producer Nicholas Everett was leaning on it, going through the shooting script with Smurf. I could see Smurf's adorable little head poking out the back, and occasionally an arm came out, and pointed at bits in the script. Mervyn Stone our cuddly script editor

So Nicholas was 'ace' and he was 'cuddly' was he? Huh!

came over and had a quick discussion with Nicholas, and they put Smurf's hatch on for him. My goodness! If the props boys had seen them handle the Styrax, they would have been up in arms! It would have been an instant strike; lights out, all out, and they'd be standing outside round their braziers, waving their placards.

Anyway, they left Smurf alone, and finally I could make my move. Finally. In the organised chaos, I crept up to it and knocked on the back of the Styrax. My special secret knock reserved for other people's husbands and secret admirers. Knock knockity-knock!

No answer. Was he there?

'Smurf darling, it's Vanity. Are you in there? Because if you are, I'll huff and I'll puff...'

'Yes. I'm in here.'

'I've got something for you, sweetheart. Could you meet me in the

Suddenly, there was a loud knock at the door. Mervyn yelped and dropped the book.

Knock knockity-knock.

'Merve darling, it's Vanity. Are you in there? Because if you are, I'll huff and I'll puff...'

My God! He stared at the book as if it was bewitched.

He swallowed. 'Yes. I'm in here,' he said in a dry croak.

'They're looking for you darling. You're late for the fancy dress. I've come to escort you.'

He gingerly picked up the book and put it on his bedside cabinet – for further inspection.

CONVIX 15. EARTH ORBIT ONE:

8.00pm

EVENT	*LOCATION*
FANCY DRESS COMPETITION	Vixos Central Nerve Centre (main stage, ballroom)

CHAPTER TWELVE

Vanity swept down the hotel stairway, accompanied by Mervyn. To the more generous onlookers, she looked like a star in a 1940s musical. To the less generous ones she looked like Bela Lugosi gliding down the steps of his Transylvanian castle. Scuttling alongside was the thin-faced girl in the cardigan, never speaking, never more than three feet away from Vanity.

'I waited for you darling, and you never came. That was naughty.'

'Ah. No. Well you know what this place is like. I got waylaid by a fan who kept me busy.' *Well that was only half a lie, wasn't it?* he thought.

'Oh drat. And I had such a marvellous surprise for you too. Perhaps later.'

'Well... Thanks for dropping me a copy off, anyway.'

'Sorry dear? What did I drop?'

'Your autobiography. Didn't you?'

Her mouth twitched with amusement. 'I didn't darling. Well you *are* a lucky boy. Someone up there must like you. Don't get too shocked at what I wrote about you...' She swanned off, ignoring a gaggle of fans that had congregated in the few short seconds the three of them had been stationary, leaving a very puzzled Mervyn.

Evening fell like a shroud on the hotel. Mervyn watched the darkness cloud the windows of the foyer. And shivered.

The fancy dress beckoned.

Mervyn was back on stage in the ballroom, only this time the chairs had been moved towards the wings to create a bit of space and a large banner hung overhead. He was sitting with Nicholas and Smurf, behind a trestle table that had been glammed up for the occasion. It was covered in a white cloth decorated with cut-out stars covered with glitter. There was a vacant chair at the end, labelled 'Andrew Jamieson'.

Simon took to the stage, dressed in a hideous jacket and bow tie. 'How marvellous to see you both,' he oozed, addressing Mervyn and Nicholas. 'I always knew I could count on you two to show up.' He gestured off the stage. 'This should only take an hour, then you're free to do as you wish.'

Smurf crossed his arms, huffing. 'Did you see that? Completely blanked me. Charming. What am I, chopped liver? I thought I was only invisible *inside* the bloody costume.'

Simon didn't hear. He bounced up to the microphone. 'Hi everyone, I hope you're ready for a good time! The bar's been stocking up since February!'

There was a thin cheer from the audience that was intended to sound hearty and hard-drinking. It didn't.

'Now, I'm afraid that we can't seem to find Andrew Jamieson at the moment. But thankfully – and I'm sure you'll all agree she's being a super sport to step in at the last minute – everyone's favourite force-field operator... Katherine Warner!'

'Oh balls. Here she comes...' sighed Nicholas as she appeared onstage.

Katherine Warner had been an up-and-coming young actress in 1985, climbing the television ladder with a minor sitcom part here, a small role on *Triangle* there. She was originally considered as Arkadia, and she'd had several meetings with Nicholas in which he'd all but offered her the part.

Unfortunately, along came Vanity.

Vanity was also doing the same minor parts as Katherine, but she'd recently appeared in a Duran Duran video wearing little more than silver paint and a tiny thong. There were rumours of a relationship with Simon Le Bon, spread by Vanity's agent. Suddenly, every TV series wanted her to be in their casts just to cash in on the publicity. In the eyes of the Beeb bosses, Katherine was suddenly deemed not high-profile enough to front a prime-time BBC drama. Vanity Mycroft's star was in the ascendant, and the rest was history.

Katherine did eventually get a part in the show – a cameo as a Force-Field Technician in 'Day of the Styrax'. Mervyn remembered that some wag – he feared it was him – had said that if she put all her *Vixens* publicity shots together in a pile and flicked through them quickly, it would create an animation lasting longer than the time she spent on-screen.

Katherine blamed Nicholas for not having the gumption to stand up to the BBC and cast her, as she regarded herself – rightly – as the better actress. As her career failed to scale the heights of Vanity's, the bitterness festered; it was mostly directed towards Vanity for usurping her, but there was more than enough left over to vent at Nicholas for betraying her.

Nicholas made a jokey half-attempt to get under the table as she appeared. All the fans knew their history, of course, and some laughed at Nicholas's mock show of cowardice.

She sat down, shone a glittering smile at the audience, and hugged Nicholas to show there were no hard feelings. During the next round of applause she leaned over to the former producer and whispered. 'You could have stayed under the tablecloth, Nicholas. The colour of surrender suits you.' Nicholas laughed back as if she'd just told him the best joke in the world.

Simon continued. 'As most of you know, it is our custom each year to concentrate on particular eras of this show we all love. This year, for example, we're concentrating on series two... in particular "Day of the Styrax', which was, of course, recorded at Betchworth Quarry at Reigate on the 25th to the 28th of May 1987, and in the BBC Television Centre's studio 8 on the 11th and 12th of June 1987...'

One of the many, many, many things that made Simon so uniquely punchable was his assumption that everyone else had as much of an encyclopaedic knowledge about the show as he did. Mervyn could barely remember the damn story names, let alone some extra who'd played third non-speaking monster on the left 20 years ago.

Simon's hand flicked up to where the hastily made banner hung limply above them. On it were the words 'The Sheldon Ellis Memorial Fancy Dress Contest'.

'Now, I know Sheldon Ellis didn't work on that particular episode, being let go some three months before the recording of "Day of the Styrax".'

Nicholas moved uncomfortably in his seat.

'But it was during the last day of filming, the "wrap" party afterwards...' – his lips curled around the technical TV term, savouring it – 'that he sadly died in a tragic fire at his home in Epping.'

The fans in costume looked very sombre. A few squeezed out tears, which mingled with cyc-shadow and ran slowly down their powdered cheeks like tiny black slugs.

'Sheldon worked on the start of series two, a very popular member of the team,' Simon continued. Mervyn expected a disbelieving snort from somewhere along the table – he threw a sideways glance at Smurf, but he was remarkably restrained, his face inscrutable. 'But alas, he never got a chance to return for the climax.' He paused. 'And, because this event is dedicated to him, it's... ahem... going to be a wee bit shorter than usual!'

A profound silence fell across the room, curdling the atmosphere and chilling the blood. Simon's microphone squealed in pain at the appalling joke.

'Ahem... Now, by way of tribute, we *were* going to have on this very stage one of the Styrax he used; as a sort of guest of honour. Unfortunately it can't be here because it's indisposed.'

Laughter. At last. Simon gave a loud wink at Mervyn.

'Or should I say, It's *been* disposed. It's all piled up in bits in my room.'

More laughter; relief flooded through Mervyn's body. The fact that

Simon was making light of it eased the tension he'd been feeling. 'See you at the party afterwards!' Simon shouted, and disappeared from the stage. The fancy dress had begun.

When Mervyn watched the news, it always amused him that whenever they reported on a catastrophe or global threat they always used Wales as a measurement of disaster. It was always 'the hole in the ozone layer is growing by an area the size of Wales every year.' *What*, he thought, *would they do if Wales was laid waste? How would we know how disastrous it was? What would they compare it to?* He got the answer, when he judged his first fancy dress competition.

He now knew that should Wales crumble, the newsflash strapline would read: 'An area the size of a *Vixens from the Void* fan in a home-made costume has just been destroyed.'

A dozen contestants thudded into view, the stage lights picking up every lump and nodule of their strange asymmetrical bodies. Half were dressed in Vixen-style kinky boots, lurid basques and silver cloaks. If they were aspiring to approximate the look of the original actresses in their 1980s heyday, most of them weren't within a light-year. They were all far too fat, squat or scrawny to begin to look vaguely Vixenish. Large dimpled bottoms bulged out alarmingly from fishnet tights, straining against the netting like freshly-caught hauls of whitebait. Pale breasts lay quivering in their corset cups like raw eggs, too flabby or underdeveloped to fill them with any degree of eroticism.

Mervyn tried to assess them as they all stood in a row. The effect was like a fairground hall of mirrors into which had wandered an unlikely transsexual. If Mervyn was able to present an award for complete absence of shame or self-awareness, he would probably give it to the Vixen at the end, who was five-feet nothing and approximately 17 stone.

'Look at the state of them...'

'Relax, Mervyn,' sighed Nicholas. 'They're just having fun. It's a harmless pastime.'

'You won't say it's harmless if that one wins,' he jerked a finger at the largest. 'I hear first prize is the chance to sit on your knee.'

'Actually darling,' grinned Nicholas, 'first prize is to attend the celebrity breakfast... With *you* and Vanity.'

'Oh God.'

Two of the contestants were dressed in purple bathing caps and boiler suits. That fact was the reason behind the angry whispers exchanged between them.

'I didn't know you were going to be a Groolian!'

'Well, you didn't tell me you were coming as one either!'

'I didn't think I had to! What did you think that boiler suit was doing hanging in my shed?'

'Oh *yeah*! Now you say that, it's *sooo* obvious!'

They realised Mervyn was staring at them, and they froze, embarrassed smiles jammed on their faces. One pointed at what they were both wearing. 'Our costumes...' he stuttered. 'The same.'

'Ah.'

'Bit embarrassing,' said the other.

'Oh.'

'You must think us right 'nanas.'

'Noooo,' soothed Mervyn. 'Nonono. Not at all. In fact, I thought you'd come as a delegation.'

'Of course!'

'Oh yeah! '

'That's right! We're a delegation!'

They resumed their positions in the line-up, much consoled. 'We're a delegation,' they said to the immobile Styrax next to them.

As Mervyn ticked off the minutes in his head, he surveyed the ersatz Vixens. Well, there was one who didn't look too bad... In fact she looked very good indeed. She filled her corset in the best way possible – did he see a cheeky nipple poking its head above the parapet? She was a bit short, but her legs were shapely and the fishnet tights complemented them wonderfully. They didn't have the 'pair of large uncooked German sausages' look that the others did.

The girl glanced across at him and winked. Mervyn's blood surged. It was Minnie! She somehow managed to wriggle herself along the line-up so she was nearest the judges' table. She leaned over the desk towards him, so close that he suddenly found himself sporting a pair of earmuffs.

'Hi,' she hissed in his ear. 'I've been thinking about you.'

'Really. I've been thinking about you too.'

This wasn't a lie. He *had* been thinking about her. He'd been thinking: *oh dear, I think I've accidentally had sex with a lunatic fan trophy hunter.*

Because her cloak was acting as a miniature tent around his head, he was taking in great lungfuls of her perfume. He was feeling quite light-headed.

'Were you okay after the panel?'

Mervyn nodded dumbly.

'You went down pretty hard,' she breathed in his ear.

Mervyn's blood wasn't frozen any more. It had unfrozen and was surging towards his penis.

'I'm fine. You should have seen the Styrax,' he said stupidly.

'I'd like to see you going down hard again,' she hissed.

'Hoi!' said a voice. One of the other Vixens was pointing at them. Mervyn didn't know her name but for his personal identification purposes, he had written 'Quasimodo's sister' on his pad. 'She's talking to a judge! Is she allowed to do that?'

Confusion broke out on stage. Simon wasn't there. Morris's voice echoed round the room. 'There's nothing in the rules to say she can't.'

Order was restored and they picked a winner. Luckily it wasn't Minnie. It was a hefty woman who'd squeezed inside a Major Karn costume she'd made out of a traffic warden's uniform and some bike reflectors. Mervyn was impressed that she'd made an effort with the false moustache. Only to realise, on closer inspection, that she hadn't.

Smurf presented her with the award. Unfortunately, with Smurf being the size he was, the woman had to bend down further than 45 degrees so he could loop the plastic medallion around her neck. There was a heart-thumping 'thrrrp' sound, and the woman's trousers ripped open right along the seam, less than two feet from Mervyn's head. For the second time in a few hours, Mervyn had a female backside pointed in his direction, only this was twice as big, and adorned with knickers that had 'Where No Man Has Gone Before' written on them.

No fee is worth this, he thought.

Ever the gentleman, he whipped the tablecloth off the table like a conjurer (there the resemblance ended. At that very second, Nicholas had finished pouring himself some water, and placed the jug back on the table. Pens, notebooks and the water jug went flying) and draped it around the fan's ample hips.

Oh. That was interesting.

The disappearing tablecloth revealed something unexpected; he noticed that Katherine's hand was resting on Smurf's knee – only for a second, because it realised it was exposed and sped back to its owner – but Mervyn definitely saw it.

The competition over, the contestants all left, slipping on the water-sodden stage, all apart from the luckless fan trapped in his home-made Styrax. He couldn't move in any direction and watched helplessly as his comrades danced away, his plaintive cries for freedom drowned out by the strains of 'Hi-ho, Silver Lining'. The water spread around the base of the Styrax, reached the electrics, and the car indicator lights he'd lovingly put on his costume blew up. Thankfully, Morris was on hand with a fire extinguisher.

Mervyn hadn't noticed any of this. He was too busy looking around for...

Damn. She was gone. Again.

He circumvented the disco, skipping around gyrating youngsters who tried to engage him in a boogie, shouting questions at the stewards over the din. He should have asked her for her room number, damn it! He went up and down in the hotel lift, hoping when the doors pinged open he'd catch a glimpse of her.

At last! He saw someone down the end of the hallway. Yes, it was someone dressed in a *Vixens* costume, Arkadia maybe. Someone with a shapely bottom and nice hips. Someone who didn't look like a bunch of novelty balloons. It *had* to be Minnie.

He ran up to her, grabbed her shoulder. 'Arkadia' turned, the silvery visor pushed up and...

It was a young man. A young man in a *Vixens* costume. Of course. The only contestant apart from Minnie who had a half-decent figure. He'd been stalking a man's arse all this time.

'Hello Mr Stone! Gosh sakes, this is a surprise! It's Stuart. Remember me?' He gave a wave, and Mervyn realised with a shock that it was the boy who'd asked for his autograph this afternoon. The one with the updated *Vixens* episodes on his computer. 'Do you like the costume? I made it myself. I studied the original costumes because I wanted to make mine better. More elastic and run-resistant. And look! Real pockets! They didn't have real pockets in the original costumes. They were a bit ropey. Mine are better.'

Mervyn nodded and smiled and backed away down the corridor.

When he got back to his room, the door was ajar, the bedside lights on. Mervyn nervously pushed open the door.

Someone was draped over the bed, wearing a *Vixens* costume.

Thankfully, the someone was female.

'I must have picked up your spare key by mistake,' said Minnie. 'So I just let myself in.'

She stole my key and got into my room. His brain tried to hit the panic button, but his libido arm-wrestled it to the ground and made it submit.

'So I see.'

'Sorry,' she said.

Mervyn wasn't.

CHAPTER THIRTEEN

He drifted awake a couple of hours later, dimly aware of Minnie getting up, the sound of the shower blatting water into the bath, then he drifted away again.

He woke up again about an hour after. He blundered to his feet and took some of his little coloured pills, wary of being woken up by revving engines in the night. He allowed his vision to blur, smudging the fixtures and fittings of his darkened room into grey shapes.

The next thing he knew, his eyes opened in darkness. He'd been nudged awake as Minnie slid back into bed beside him, a comforting warm presence. He gave a welcoming grunt. Once again, her hands moved over him, manipulating him. *Awaking a sleeping giant,* Mervyn giggled inside his head. She got up and sat astride him, and his face was engulfed in rough material. *God*, he thought. *She's put the damn costume on again*. She bent down and nibbled his face hungrily, then he felt her hot breath tickling his neck, his stomach, and then...

Is she insatiable or am I just old...?

Don't answer that, he answered himself. Still, honour was at stake...

As he rallied for a second assault, he thought he detected an odd, chemical smell. *Must be the cheap hotel shower gel,* he thought.

Then he didn't think about it any more. The pills were still pulling him towards oblivion. He had to concentrate...

Mervyn was awoken at about one in the morning by an ugly noise from the car park. A car engine grumbling to itself.

'Whurrrrghh?'

Bloody BMW drivers.

He stuck a pillow over his head and tried to plunge back into unconsciousness, but the noise didn't go away. Surely by now the sodding car would have revved off up the M1?

He struggled out of bed, dimly aware he was now alone, and went to the window. He could hear voices, some of them shouting. He looked down.

Thirty seconds later, he was in his clothes and out of the door.

He collided with Smurf as he reached the hotel door, and they both charged into Morris and Nicholas who were already in the car park. Mervyn's shoes sloshed in shallow puddles.

The stink of petrol flooded the concourse, making them retch. From the hollow rumbling sound, it was obvious the Styrax Superior was practically running on empty.

A pipe ran from the exhaust and was wedged deeply into its side grille, held in place by a rag. Mervyn pulled at the rag and the pipe came away, exuding sickly fumes. Everything was cold and wet from the rain, droplets dawdling and slipping down the shell of the Styrax like tears.

Mervyn placed his hands on the shell of the monster, but it was wet and slippery and he couldn't get a purchase on the secreted door handle. Thankfully, the rag was dry and he foolishly dried his hands on it, forgetting about silly things like DNA and forensic evidence. He threw the rag in a puddle, covered his nose and mouth with his sleeve, gripped the handle with his other hand and pulled. The door exploded open and belched out a cloud of exhaust fumes.

Simon Josh tumbled out onto the concrete.

Dead.

For the third time that day, the fan's head hit the floor with an almighty 'thunk'.

CHAPTER FOURTEEN

Simon's tongue coiled against his cheek; his complexion dark and purple like a fat bruise covering his face. An empty whisky bottle was clutched in his hand.

Mervyn felt hysteria prowl up his neck and pounce on his brain. Nevertheless, he surprised himself by stepping over Simon's body and fumbling inside to turn the engine off.

Unfortunately, he turned the wrong key.

The Styrax lit up like a Wurlitzer, disco lights blazing and pulsing in the night. Futuristic sound effects blasted through hidden speakers, whooshing and bleeping and zapping in all directions. 'DEATH TO ALL PEDESTRIANS!' it boomed.

This was one of four phrases programmed to fire off in quick succession when activated. All, ironically and unfortunately, along the lines of death, killing and eradication.

'Turn it off! Turn the bloody thing off!' screamed Smurf, his hands clapped to his head.

Mervyn found the ignition and twisted it. The Styrax juddered and died, leaving the silence to sing in their ears. The lights in the hotel were crashing into life all around them.

There was an awkward moment. No one knew what to do next.

Mervyn started to move back from the Styrax, but Nicholas clutched at his sleeve.

'Wait a minute,' he hissed, peering into the Styrax. 'Mervy. Look. There... there's something inside...'

It was on the dashboard, carving out a white square in the gloom, and Mervyn groped towards it. He positioned himself awkwardly, holding on to the door and straddling Simon's twisted body so he could make a lunge at whatever it was. It had been fastened to the dashboard, and came away leaving a string of goo.

Blu-Tack, of course.

Mervyn hopscotched backwards into Nicholas's waiting arms. The object turned out to be an envelope with *VixEnterprises* stamped on it. Smurf peered under Mervyn's armpit to see what he'd found.

'A suicide note.'

'It might not be a suicide note,' said Mervyn.

'Most likely it'll be a letter to the hotel, asking for a refund on his room.'

'Smurf, please!' Nicholas snapped.

Mervyn opened the flap and pulled out a white slip of paper. He unfolded it and read it to himself. It was a beautifully handwritten note, explaining in three neat paragraphs that Simon had been depressed for some time about the futility of his life, that he hated his day job, that he only lived for the conventions, and that the rumoured new series of *Vixens from the Void* would inevitably lead to the BBC withdrawing the licence for his little world. He'd seen it happen to other shows like *Star Trek* and he didn't want to live with being increasingly marginalised and pitied.

'He committed suicide all right.' Mervyn slipped the note back in the envelope. 'He's signed it and everything.'

'Well he would,' Morris's voice rumbled, causing Mervyn to jump.

'What do you mean "Well he would"?'

'Well it's Simon, isn't it? If he was alive he'd be the first to tell you how valuable his autograph is now he's dead.' He scratched the scrubland on his chin. 'Does that make sense? Oh well. You know what I mean.' He nodded casually at the letter. 'If you don't mind, once the police have finished with it I'd like to have it for VixEnterprises. It might offset the losses from this year's con. I'll put it on eBay. It's what he would have wanted.'

They all nodded at the grotesque idea, more out of shock than anything.

'We ought to call the police,' said Morris at last. 'I'll go and tell the hotel what's happened. I'm sure they'll want to stop people coming into the car park.'

Everyone nodded again and Morris disappeared.

It was only at that point, when Mervyn was closing the Styrax door, that he noticed something else inside.

Something resting on the floor.

He looked round. Nobody was watching.

He scooped up the something gracefully in one low swoop and slipped it inside his pocket. He would examine it later.

'What the *hell* is going on out here?' They all turned. Bernard had hurried out of the hotel, his bony wrists and ankles poking out of a hotel dressing gown.

Nicholas fluttered. 'There's been a bit of an... incident. It's Simon...'

'Oh God, what's he done to my Styrax?'

'It's not what he's done to *it*... It's more what it's done to *him*.'

'What?'

Mervyn moved to one side so Bernard could see Simon's crumpled body.

'Is that Simon? What happened?'

'He's gassed himself with the Styrax exhaust fumes,' said Nicholas, calm and brutal in equal measure.

'Oh good Christ!' shrieked Bernard, his spindly legs propelling him to the Styrax. 'You mean it was left running? Without fuel? The engine – is it damaged?'

Nicholas rolled his eyes to the ink-black heavens. 'Such compassion...'

Prickly as ever, Bernard advanced on Nicholas. 'What did you just say, you old pouf?'

'Just admiring your priorities, Bernard old thing. They always said you'd step over the body of your mother to get your hands on a valuable piece of merchandise. Now's your chance to rehearse.'

Black clouds gathered on Bernard's face. 'Look, if he wants to end his short and worthless life that's his decision, but I took three months to make this thing, it's a piece of history and I've got a right to know if it's damaged.' He pulled the bonnet up and dived in to check the engine. 'After all, the little shit hadn't paid me yet, so to all intents and purposes, it's still mine.'

Mervyn suddenly realised he was shaking. 'I'm sorry, everyone, I've really got to go in and lie down.'

Nicholas grabbed his arm. He was shaking too. 'Of course you do, sweetheart. We should all go in and go to bed. We've all had a nasty shock.'

'I haven't,' snapped Bernard, slamming the bonnet and crawling under the chassis. 'I'm staying here to look over the damage. You can all sod off back inside.'

They all trudged dazedly back into the hotel, leaving two bodies sprawled across the tarmac. One alive, one dead.

CHAPTER FIFTEEN

It wasn't until Mervyn got up to his room that he properly realised he'd woken up alone. Minnie had gone. The only evidence that she'd been there was that funny chemical smell and a war-torn bed.

He was too strung out to sleep. He pulled on a dressing gown over his clothes and watched events from his window. The police were obviously taken aback by the Styrax sitting there waiting for them. Mervyn knew by the half amused, half amazed expressions on their faces that some of the coppers had grown up watching them on television. Some made a point of sidestepping the front end, making morbid jokes about its killing potential, imagining it bursting to life and blasting them with its plastic laser cannons.

They placed the suicide note in an evidence bag. The Styrax was given a cursory inspection and secured in the hotel garage. Simon's body was taken away.

Is that it? Is that all they do? Mervyn's brain gibbered. *I suppose that's all they can do. What else is there to do?*

He looked at what he'd found on the floor of the Styrax. It was a very, very odd thing to find at the scene of a suicide. Either Simon was attempting one last joke at their expense or someone was playing very silly games with Simon's death...

Or Simon's death was a great deal more suspicious than it first appeared.

CONVIX 15.
EARTH ORBIT TWO:

9.00am

EVENT	*LOCATION*
CELEBRITY BREAKFAST VANITY MYCROFT MERVYN STONE Katherine Warner	The Slug Mines of Krell (hotel restaurant)
'DEMONS OF THE OUTER DARKNESS' **EPISODE SCREENING**	The Catacombs of Herath (video lounge - room 1024)
VIXENS FROM THE VOID: WOMEN IN SCIENCE FICTION **EXPERT PANEL** with Graham Goldingay, Larry Perkins, Craig Jones, Darren Cardew	The Seventh Moon of Groolia (room 1002)

CHAPTER SIXTEEN

The hotel restaurant was peppered with *Vixens* fans, distinctive in their swollen T-shirts and unwise shorts. Mervyn was hunched over his 'continental' breakfast. He felt groggy from his pills and the disconnected feelings that came from delayed shock. He didn't feel ready to face anybody this morning.

Unfortunately, this particular morning happened to be the morning of the celebrity breakfast.

For Mervyn, who was not a morning person, celebrity breakfasts were the grimmest part of the convention.

Mervyn stared at his croissant. Its soft yellow semi-circular shape seemed to resemble a smile. It grinned mockingly up at him.

Their table was separated from other attendees by little golden posts threaded together with a scarlet rope; the type usually put up at film premieres and royal visits. Whether it was there to stop unauthorised fans sneaking on to the table, or Mervyn making a break for it wasn't clear.

What kind of twisted mind would charge fans for the privilege of sitting next to a groggy old actor/writer/director in the early stages of a hangover?

Oh yes. The dead kind.

'Where is she?' asked John the Stalker for the eighth time. 'She should be down by now.'

They were meant to be seven; four fans and three 'celebrities'. In theory, anyway. Vanity hadn't turned up, and it was left to Mervyn and Katherine Warner to charm the fans and keep the event star-studded. As Mervyn was just a writer, and Katherine was barely in the show for more than a minute, they weren't doing too well.

Mervyn had fleetingly encountered all the fans present, so he was at least on uncomfortable nodding terms with them. The fan who kept going on about Vanity's absence was John. John was the strange greasy fan from yesterday's autograph session; the one with the binary brain from whose clutches Mervyn had been rescued by Minnie. He was still wearing the same T-shirt from yesterday; which depicted the improbably-designed superwoman. The smell wafting from him was almost as powerful as the woman's physique.

The others, Helen, Derek and Bob, were from last night's fancy dress party. Helen was the large woman with the interesting knickers who had won, and Derek and Bob were the two Groolian ambassadors who hadn't. Scrubbed of their purple make-up, the boys looked extremely nondescript – one squat and round and with heavy glasses, the other with a long horsey face dominated by a drooping nose that pointed towards his toast.

Hefty Helen was distressingly under-dressed, with her planetoid-sized bottom crammed inside a shiny leather skirt that looked like a whole herd of cows had been sacrificed for its construction. She wore the unwisest crop top Mervyn had seen in his life. Her stomach oozed out from underneath it; lumpy, wobbly and white like someone had upended a bowl of rice pudding on her midriff. Her nose, tongue and ears now sprouted an alarming number of metal objects. It made her look part Frankenstein's monster, part curtain rail.

'I'm sure she'll be down in a minute,' said Katherine tersely, also for the eighth time.

'Yes. But where is she?' John the Stalker pleaded. Despite his agitation, John's voice kept to a flat washed-out monotone.

'They don't always turn up you know,' bubbled Speccy Derek (Mervyn was using his special memory technique to remember which fan was which, hence 'Speccy Derek', 'Big-Nose Bob', 'Hefty Helen' and 'John the Stalker'. He was quite pleased about coming up with that last one).

'Oh yes, it's quite common that stars don't turn up to celebrity breakfasts. Very common, in fact,' agreed Big-Nose Bob.

'But she's in the programme,' said John the Stalker, faintly.

Oblivious to his slackly worried face, the Groolian pair continued. 'This is the seventh celebrity breakfast we've done,' Speccy Derek boasted. 'Last year we lost Samantha Carbury. Don't know why. Probably woman's problems. But we still had Noel Griggs and Jenny McLaird on the table. They were great. Really funny. Best ever.'

'Don't forget the one in 2002,' chided Big-Nose Bob. 'Roger Barker was a no-show, but we had that American from *Stargate: Miami Beach*. He was hilarious.'

'That wasn't 2002.'

'I beg to differ. It was 2002.'

'No it wasn't. It was 2000.'

'It was 2002. He'd left the show, remember? If you recall, Derek, he was bitching about the networks and the producer and talking about all his exciting projects he'd got lined up.'

'No, because if *you* check *your* programme guide, Robert, he'd already returned to the series in 2002 as his own clone.'

'Oh yes. That's an affirmative. You're quite right. My bad, Derek, sorry.'

'Gracious in defeat as ever, Robert. The neutral zone is thus restored.'

Their skirmish over, the two friends relaxed in their chairs. There was a blessed moment of silence, before the inevitable drone from John.

'But where's Vanity? I only paid for this so I could watch her eat.'

'Well...' Mervyn mumbled, shepherding a reluctant grin round the table. 'Never mind. It's still nice with the just the six of us.'

'I didn't pay for this. I got this for winning the fancy dress,' Hefty Helen growled. She jabbed Mervyn with her gaze. 'Come on, talk, be interesting. I'm not sitting here to watch you drink tea.'

'Well... what do you want me to talk about?' Mervyn smiled through gritted teeth.

'I dunno. Think of something.'

'Well... Do you have any questions? What would you like to know?'

'I'd like to know where Vanity is,' whined John.

Katherine's eyes rolled with weariness. 'Oh for heaven's sake, be quiet. She's not coming. All right?'

John blinked furiously. 'She has to. She was in the programme.'

'This is just typical of her,' Katherine spat, warming to a theme. 'Thinks she's the big star but doesn't have a professional bone in her body.' She humphed. 'Plenty of professional boners, of course, but no professional bones.' Mervyn gave her an askance look as if to say; *there are children present!* 'Oh, don't look at me like that, Mervyn. The fans know all about her. Snuffling around, gathering titbits all these years. They probably know more about us than we do. Can't keep anything from the fans, Mervyn, you know that.'

John the Stalker looked at Katherine as if he'd noticed her for the first time. 'Are you upset that Vanity hasn't turned up?' he asked her.

'Not exactly.'

'You look upset. I am too. Did you buy a ticket to meet her? I did.'

'Hardly,' she snorted.

'Oh. Did you win a ticket? Were you in the fancy dress? Were you the one inside the Styrax?'

'No I didn't win the fancy dress and I didn't buy a ticket,' said Katherine, frostily.

'Oh I see. Look, this is the *celebrity* breakfast table. You see that rope there? If you haven't got a ticket you should eat your breakfast at one of the undesignated tables.' He leaned confidentially into her space. 'You *could* be sitting in Vanity's special seat. That's probably why she hasn't turned up yet.'

Mervyn saw a pulse throb in Katherine's neck. 'Gosh. Where are my manners?' he babbled. 'I'm sorry, I have been a bit quiet. I'm not at my best at the moment. I'm a bit frazzled. It was a bit of a rough night for me. As you probably heard.'

The two boys nodded sagely. 'We get you,' winked Big-Nose Bob, making a 'glug glug glug' sign with his hand.

'We didn't see you in the bar,' said Speccy Derek. 'Mind you, that doesn't count for anything.'

Big-Nose Bob gave a crooked grin. 'God, it was a wild night.'

'Tell me about it. I nearly forgot my room number.'

'No, I wasn't in the bar,' said Mervyn patiently. 'I was actually in the car park – with Simon.'

There was a collage of blank looks from around the table.

'Don't you, um, know what's happened?' Mervyn asked. They shook their heads.

Mervyn recounted the events of last night. Telling the story out loud actually calmed him down, and he was relieved to see his hands had stopped shaking.

There was a profound silence around the table. They looked at him, their mouths agape.

'Wow.'

'That was great.'

'Is that a new anecdote?'

'Of course it is, you grexnix. He said it happened last night.'

'Wow.'

'A new anecdote. Brilliant. And we're the first to hear it.'

'That's great, Mr Stone. I think that's your second best car park story ever.'

Katherine gave Mervyn a *What can you do?* look and sipped her coffee. 'Yes it's terrible isn't it? I can't believe he would do a thing like that. It must have been a ghastly shock to find him like that.'

'Oh, it was, believe me.'

'I bet. I know Smurf was absolutely knocked sideways by it. He told me – when I passed him in the corridor this morning.'

Nice save, thought Mervyn.

'Oh...' said Big-Nose Bob. 'You mean after you came out of his room after having sex.'

Mervyn felt a fine spray of coffee on his face as Katherine spluttered.

'What?'

Big-Nose Bob seemed oblivious to the monumental embarrassment he'd just initiated. 'Oh, as you said, you can't keep anything from us fans,' he said happily, raising his voice over Katherine as she coughed into her napkin. 'We get to know everything sooner or later.'

It was an innocent boast that sounded uncomfortably like a threat.

'Well we're not perfect, are we Robert?' said Derek, tapping his elbow. 'After all we didn't know about Simon's death, did we?'

'Ah. But we're the first with the anecdote. And that counts for a lot.'

'Too blummin' right,' said Derek, and then he lurched upright in his chair as if a woman had placed a hand on his knee. 'Oh my God! The Loughborough posse went for a pizza last night, so they won't have heard. I've got to go and tell them.' He wiped his chin on a napkin, got out of his chair and headed over to spread the anecdote.

CHAPTER SEVENTEEN

Mervyn entered the foyer, which was already buzzing with people. Morris was by the reception desk addressing the stewards. Minnie was among them, her eyes darting in his direction while trying to listen to what Morris was saying. Morris was explaining how he'd laminated some of the schedules on cardboard, attached a string and persuaded the hotel to let them hang them over light fittings and picture hooks.

Mervyn saw Smurf sitting on a sofa and plonked down beside him. 'Everyone's being so flippant. Isn't anyone shocked by it? I mean, Simon thrived at these conventions. He lived for them. How could he... just... you know?'

Smurf shrugged. 'Don't tear your hair out for the likes of him. Simon wouldn't have been the slightest bit bothered if it were the other way round and it was you who'd topped yourself. He'd probably act like nothing'd happened; prop you up to try to get you to sign a few autographs before you started to smell.'

'Yes, I know all that, but even so.'

'Anyway, who cares? You didn't like him, did you? No one did.'

'No, of course I didn't like him. He was an irritating two-faced snide little creep. I don't know why I'm so...' He frowned. 'No, I know. I do know. Perhaps it's because I feel a bit responsible.'

'What?'

'Well. If I hadn't taken my pills perhaps I would have woken up quicker and got to the Styrax before he suffocated. I'm always such a light sleeper.'

Smurf laughed. 'Merv! Once a script editor, always a script editor. Always going through the story with a fine-toothed comb. No one, no matter how mental, is going to blame you for Simon's death.'

Morris sidled up to them and handed Mervyn a card. 'Someone left this for you. Wants you to be available to answer some questions.'

Mervyn's hand went numb as he read: SC STUART COULSON METROPOLITAN POLICE and the address of the local police station.

Oh God, they know I took evidence away from the scene. Who told them?

Mervyn made his excuses and left.

CONVIX 15.
EARTH ORBIT TWO:

10.00am

EVENT	*LOCATION*
'DAY OF THE STYAX' REMEMBERED VANITY MYCROFT RODERICK BURGESS Katherine Warner	Vixos Central Nerve Centre (main stage, ballroom)
'EXPIRATION POINT' **EPISODE SCREENING**	The Catacombs of Herath (video lounge - room 1024)
AUTOGRAPH PANEL JOSEPH McANDREW TIM WARNE BRYCE CAMPION RICK AMORY	Arkadia's Boudoir (room 1013)
PHOTOS NICHOLAS EVERETT	Transpodule Chamber (room 1030)
NEW VOIDS **AUDIOS EXPERT PANEL** with Graham Goldingay, Fay Lawless, Craig Jones, Darren Cardew	The Seventh Moon of Groolia (room 1002)

CHAPTER EIGHTEEN

A few minutes later, Mervyn was in a police station surrounded by sludge-grey walls. As with most cop shops, the reception area was covered with unhelpful posters shouting at the public – who'd come into the station after being mugged, burgled or swindled – to 'Watch out! There are muggers, burglars and con artists about!'

He was shown into a glass-fronted office. After about five minutes, a young man with straight blond hair and round John Lennon spectacles entered. He sat on the other side of the desk and bent low over his notes. 'Thanks for coming Mr Stone. I really, really appreciate it.'

Mervyn was in a state of panic. The thing he'd taken from the Styrax was still in his jacket pocket, screaming to be discovered. He stared and tried to answer; his jaw moved, but his lips failed to reciprocate.

'Egh.'

The man opened a slim black folder and inspected the contents closely. 'Before we start, may I just ask you a few questions?'

'Agh,' Mervyn went. He nodded madly to emphasise that 'agh' was his current word for 'Yes'.

Wait a minute. He's not taping us. Surely he should be taping us. And why aren't we in an interview room? Oh right, I get the picture. I know the score. I wrote for The Bill, *mister. It'll just be a few friendly questions and then he'll introduce me to his superior officers, Superintendent Rubber Hose, Chief Inspector Sock Of Sand and Detective Chief Inspector Open Stairwell.*

'Right. Okay now...' said the man.

'You're not taping us.' Mervyn blurted. 'Shouldn't you be taping us? I think that's what you're supposed to do. Aren't you?'

'Oh. Of course.' The man looked a bit taken aback, but nevertheless pulled out a tiny dictaphone. 'Right. Okay. Now...'

'Sorry, that's not good enough. I want a proper recording machine. A big one. And I want to be in a proper interview room. With a table. And an ashtray.' Mervyn didn't smoke, but he felt like asserting himself with some demands, and that was all he could think of at the moment. The policeman's eyes narrowed. He looked almost surprised.

Ha. I've got him, thought Mervyn gleefully. *I know my rights. He doesn't know who he's dealing with. I once successfully contested a parking ticket AND I got a refund on my poll tax.*

'Okay...' The man stood up and dutifully showed him down the stairs, along a corridor and into a tiny room with a bare table dimpled with cigarette burns. They started again.

The man closed the door, sat opposite Mervyn, and reopened his file.

'Right... Where was I...'

'You need to turn on the tape recorder.'

The man turned on the tape recorder.

'O-kay,' said the man. 'Now. Questions... Ah, here we are.'

Here we go, thought Mervyn. *I just saw it there and took it. It was just an impulse. I didn't think it was important, honest.*

'So, Mr Stone. Where do you get your ideas from?'

'Agh?'

The man took 'agh' as a sign that Mervyn was offended by the question. He scrabbled in his notes. 'Okay. Sorry. No, forget that. Sorry. That's a dorky one. Oh yeah. Ah! You know the episode "The Burning Time" by Marcus Spicer? From season four? Is it true you wrote all of it except the title? Because that would make a lot of sense –'

'Erm...?'

'Oh – waitwaitwait no – here's one. Now this is a good one. You know in "Beware the Ides of Mars" in season two? When Arkadia and Vizor take the Styrax shuttle from Chevron and it took *two days* to get back to Vixos? How come next season in "The Enigma Factor" it took the Vixen Flagship *Hyperion* two *whole weeks* to get from Vixos to Chevron – on *full* imperative drive? I mean, was that some kind of clue to a special stardrive the Nemetides were keeping secret? Because that would explain why they never appeared when we saw the Styrax prison planet in the episode "Prison Planet", wouldn't it?'

'What?'

'Cos if they had a stardrive, they could have evacuated and left the galaxy when the Styrax invaded the empire, couldn't they?'

'*What?*'

The policeman looked up from his folder, and Mervyn realised that the face grinning at him was one he'd seen not so long ago. The hair had been spiky, and there had been no spectacles, but it was definitely him.

It was the fan who'd asked for his autograph yesterday morning.

They continued the interrogation in the police canteen. Not as brutal as Mervyn expected, but all in all, it was one of the tougher fanzine interviews he'd endured.

Stuart Coulson plonked two coffees, a KitKat and a broad grin in front of Mervyn. 'I know you're very particular about your coffee. Best I can do, I'm afraid. Thanks for answering all my questions. It's going to be a great article. I'll send you a copy of *The Vix* as soon as it's finished.'

'So... Stuart. You're a policeman.'

'Yes. For my sins. Sort of.'

Mervyn looked at the card he's been given. 'SC Stuart Coulson. You're a superintendent chief?'

'Special constable, actually. I got the cards printed myself.'

'And you're at the convention.'

'That's right.'

'Are you undercover or something?'

'Nope, it's just a hobby of mine. Just having fun.'

'"Just a hobby"?'

'Yes.'

'And the fishnets and basques and capes and thigh boots?'

'That's just cosplay.'

'Cosplay?'

'Costume play.'

'What does that mean?'

'It means I was just having fun.'

'Because you do hear things. About policemen... You know... Masonic stuff.'

'Nope. As I said, just having fun.'

'Sure you're not undercover? I won't tell anyone.'

Stuart shrugged amiably, as a way of avoiding saying 'I was just having fun' again.

Mervyn took another daring sip of his coffee. 'So. You didn't bring me here to arrest me then.'

'Oh no. Whatever gave you that idea?'

Mervyn stared hard at Stuart. Stuart finally realised what the stare meant. His eyes spun and his mouth dropped open, like a fruit machine paying out.

'Oh. Right. The message I left. It should have been a bit clearer?'

'Do you think so?' Mervyn's sarcasm was so thick it could have been used to resurface motorways. 'But you didn't bring me here for an interview for your fanzine, did you? You could have done that at the hotel.'

'No. I mean yes. I mean no, I didn't bring you here for that. You see... I believe that Simon Josh was murdered... and I want you to help me find the killer.'

'I see.'

God cranked up the ambient noise. All of a sudden the clink of cutlery and whoosh of cappuccino machines grew to deafening levels.

'What makes you think that?' Mervyn asked.

Stuart moved his cup with the palms of his hands. 'Firstly, before I tell you why I think that... I want to say something. When I got into

Vixens restoration, sprucing up the effects, I kind of got obsessed about making little things right, you know? First it was a dodgy laser blast, then a dodgy spaceship, then I moved on to dodgy neighbourhoods, and dodgy people.' He grinned. 'Yep. It was down to you that I wanted to become a policeman.'

Mervyn looked doubtfully at the special constable. He suspected that Stuart's colleagues wouldn't thank Mervyn for inspiring the young man to go into the force.

'And let's not forget,' Stuart continued. 'You're a detective too! It *was* you who worked out that Bernard Viner was stealing all the props from the studio...'

'Oh, don't remind me. If I hadn't done that, Bernard wouldn't have held a 20-year grudge against me.'

'But don't you see? You have a classic detective brain! You could be so useful to me.'

Mervyn considered this. 'So tell me... Why do you think Simon was murdered?'

'It was his face. It was purple.'

'Fair enough.'

'He was sitting in the Styrax, he had a hose from the exhaust and he died from carbon monoxide poisoning.'

'Okay...'

'He died of carbon monoxide poisoning and his face was *purple.*'

'Yes? *And?*'

'Carbon monoxide poisoning causes the face to look flushed red. Simon's face should have looked ruddy or blotchy, because of the exhaust fumes, but it *wasn't*. It was bright purple – and do you know why it was purple?'

'Go on.'

'It was purple because he was wearing purple make-up.'

'What?'

'Exactly! Just cheap purple face-paint. I mean, the type of stuff kids use on Hallowe'en. When they want to dress up as scary creatures and terrify you on the doorstep.'

'Yes. I never quite understood that. I always thought that if small children wanted to dress up as something that *really* terrified me, ideally they should dress up as small children.'

'And Simon had a purple bathing cap in his pocket. Which I think we can guess means he was going to the convention's fancy dress disco. I mean, hardly the action of a man about to commit suicide, is it?'

'Must he have been going?' Mervyn didn't see the connection.

'Come on, it's obvious! He must have been planning to go to the fancy dress as a Groolian ambassador.'

'Of course he was. Obviously.' Mervyn was starting to find Stuart's geekish alter ego rather amusing – or at least, he was enjoying watching the part-time policeman and the full-time fan fighting for control of Stuart's brain.

'I mean... That's all you need to get yourself up as a Groolian ambassador. Purple make-up and a bathing cap.'

'And that's why you think he was murdered.'

'Yes.'

'Okay. Here's another question. Why are you asking me to help you? Calling in an amateur detective is a bit 19th century, isn't it? Why aren't you and your flat-footed mates ransacking the hotel and taking statements?'

Stuart fiddled with his cup, watching the coffee swirl. He was studiously avoiding Mervyn's eye. 'I... haven't told my superiors about my suspicions. They think he painted his face in some bizarre ritual that sci-fi fans go in for.'

'I see. Sitting in his Styrax with his face painted purple. Like a Viking in his longboat, or a Pharaoh being buried with his death mask on.'

'Exactly. Well the thing is... I'm only a special constable, and if I told them about my fancy dress theory I don't think they'd take me entirely seriously.'

Understanding dawned. 'Oh I *see*. You don't want to walk into your boss's office and say "Excuse me, I happened to be at the scene of the crime dressed in a lycra leotard and thigh boots, and I believe my extensive knowledge of an obscure science fiction show from the 80s might shed some light on a possible murder."'

'Exactly. They're still ribbing DS Perryman for coming out of the ladies with her skirt tucked in her knickers, and that was five years ago. If they ever found out about me being at a science fiction convention *and* dressing up as female star warrior I might as well emigrate.' Stuart looked up at him, his eyes wide, cute and imploring, like the God Of All Puppies.

'I was hoping we could solve it. Just the two of us. If you help me solve it, it would be... amazing, wouldn't it? What do you think?'

'Well, let me think,' said Mervyn.

He thought.

'I think,' he said at last. 'That if you don't put me in a car and take me back to the hotel in the next five minutes, I'm going to call a lawyer and sue the police for intimidation.'

It was Stuart's turn to go 'Agh'. He'd got whiplash of the brain. This was not the response he was expecting.

'Now, if you could arrange for a car to take me back to the hotel? I have an autograph session at 11 o'clock and I don't want to be late,' said Mervyn.

They went down in the lift, sharing a deep, uncomfortable silence. Or they would have if the lift hadn't had radio pumped through its speakers. Classic FM was playing the *William Tell* overture. Rather daringly, it was the gentle bit before the loud bit before the famous bit.

'I just thought you might be interested. I just thought I'd ask you if you wanted to help,' whimpered Stuart at last. 'I didn't think...'

'No, you didn't "think". I wasted my time coming to a police station, worrying what I'd done wrong because you "didn't think". Your sort never *do* "think". You fans always think we're up for anything, don't you? You take the fact that you can meet us at conventions, have a chat, share the odd drink and a joke as a sign that you own us, permission to drag us into any piece of nonsense you can dream up. The amount of mad schemes I've been roped into... Silly cabarets, weird charity records, embarrassing publicity stunts. There was one so-called "convention" I got invited to. It turned out it was a fan's tenth birthday party. I was asked questions about my career by six kids eating trifle while his mum served me cups of orange juice. I was on after the magician.'

'Oh. I can see that might have been a bit... well.'

Mervyn was starting to get quite heated. 'It happens time and time again. Did you know I was out of work for a year and a half after *Vixens* finished? *A year and a half!* Everyone assumes that a writer who devises and script-edits a TV series is too grand to be a jobbing writer any more – so the phone just stops ringing. Then – hallelujah – my agent gets a request for me to work on a "major film project". I travel 90 miles out of London with dollar signs floating in front of my eyes only to find myself in a car park in Peterborough with two ten-year-olds, a camcorder and a Styrax made out of eggboxes.'

'But... We did *pay* you!'

Mervyn stared incredulously at Stuart. 'What?'

Classic FM got to the loud bit before the famous bit.

'It was a really good fan video! We made several improvements on the original monster designs! Our Gorgs were brilliant!'

'Oh it was *you*, was it? Terrific! I might have known!' The lift opened, and Mervyn exploded out of it, throwing his arms wide in despair.

'But... This is murder!'

'But don't you see? That makes it worse! You're talking about murder and you're still treating it as an opportunity to play games!'

The desk sergeant ran up to them with a piece of paper. 'Excuse me, sir. Are you Mervyn Stone?'

'Yes. Can I help you?'

'There's a woman who's turned up at the front desk, says...' he checked his bit of paper as if he didn't believe it the first time. 'Says she's your alibi for last night.'

'My what?'

'She says...' he 'ahemed' like an old fashioned bobby from an Ealing comedy, '... that she and you were "at it like rabbits on Viagra-flavoured carrots all night, so there's no way you had the opportunity or the energy to murder... um... that little tick, Simon Josh."' Another 'ahem'. 'And there's other details she's mentioned. A costume of some description. And other things consented to, in a room in the Happy Traveller hotel.'

'Where is she?'

'She's just gone to the ladies on the first floor,' said the desk sergeant. 'She should be down in a sec.'

They waited.

'You see what you've done?' Mervyn glared at Stuart's stricken face. 'That's one of the stewards up there. A charming girl. Because of *you* she's interrupted her day and come here to rescue me. Because of *you* she's had to admit to a night of passion with an old fossil like me because she thinks I'm under arrest. I can't imagine what I'm going to say to the poor girl about why I'm really here...'

The doors to the lift opened with a huge piping fanfare.

Classic FM had got to the famous bit.

'Darling!' said Vanity Mycroft.

'Agh?' said Mervyn and Stuart.

CHAPTER NINETEEN

Vanity surged forward and hugged Mervyn. His face was impaled on her cheekbone, and he could feel his ear being scorched by the tip of her cigarette. She pulled away and looked searchingly into his shocked face like a mother checking a son for chocolate smudges.

'Darling, you look like a ghost. What have the bastards done to you?'

Mervyn just stared at her numbly.

She glared at the desk sergeant. 'Listen darling, I'm not leaving without him. I'll chain myself to the railings if I have to.' Vanity leaned on the front desk, a long finger jabbing at the woodwork.

'We haven't got any railings, madam.'

'Then I'll chain myself to *you*.'

The desk sergeant looked most alarmed at the prospect.

'It's all right, Ms Mycroft. It's all a misunderstanding,' said Stuart hastily. 'He's free to go.'

Vanity didn't even recognise Stuart. Because he hadn't fancied her, he'd completely slipped under the Mycroft radar.

'Hah! Come on sweetie, the car's outside. Let's get back to the hotel.' She bundled Mervyn towards the exit. 'Is that it? Are you done with him?'

'Oh yes,' said Stuart, cringing into a corner.

She rounded on the desk sergeant. 'He doesn't need bail, at all? Aren't you going to tell him he can't leave the country or something?'

The sergeant looked her up and down. 'I wouldn't dream of denying him that option, madam.'

'Well?'

'What?'

Vanity's sports car roared around the M25 and back to the hotel. The top was down and the noise of the engine was deafening.

'Did you like my surprise?'

'What?'

'My surprise, darling!'

Vanity's hair was gripped by the wind, and it leapt crazily in the air as it struggled for freedom. Mervyn's normally al fresco hairstyle was blasted behind him into a severe back-comb.

'Oh yes! Very good. What surprise?'

'Darling! Me in your hotel room dressed in my old costume! What other surprise could I be talking about?'

'Oh yes!' he muttered. 'Very good!'

'Romping around hotel rooms with dear old Mervyn, like many a location shoot of old. You certainly took me back, darling...' She smiled wickedly at him, taking her eyes off the road for a handful of heart-stopping seconds. 'Well, not just back. You took me in every direction you could think of, you naughty man...'

'What?'

'Don't pretend you can't hear me Mervy, I thought the costume held up rather well. A couple of frayed edges here and there and a torn lining... But at our age one expects a few frayed edges and torn linings, doesn't one, darling?'

They approached the turning. Her hand gripped the gear stick, fingered it, and with little warning or clutch, wrenched it back with unbearable force. There was a groan of pain from the gearbox, and the engine responded. *I know how it feels*, thought Mervyn.

'Just as well I was with you. I could see them mentally slapping the cuffs on you. Thank your lucky stars I was waiting to pounce on you last night. I said to that oaf Morris, "Bollocks to my fucking panel," I told him. "I'm off to the police. There's a man's liberty at stake," I said. "Let Katherine fill in for me; let her tell her single anecdote 200 times until they can all recite it backwards." The car screeched into the hotel car park, narrowly missing Bernard's backside as it poked out of the Styrax Superior, and ploughed into a parking space. The engine died, shuddering gratefully as it did so. 'Right. I'd better hop into the shower. I can still smell you on me, darling.'

Mervyn's face squirmed with embarrassment.

Waiting for them in front of the hotel doors was the thin-faced girl in the cardigan. The one who went around with Vanity. The one who *always* went around with Vanity. The girl was starting to make Mervyn feel uncomfortable.

Vanity slammed the car door closed with incredible force. 'It's a bit disappointing to be honest. I was hoping they'd admit me for evidence. Dust me for fingerprints or something like that.' She cocked an eyebrow. 'Anyway, don't worry. Your alibi is completely watertight.' They entered the hotel and she turned to him with a grin. 'Unlike the costume. Another challenge for the dry cleaners.'

Mervyn was left in the foyer, dazed.

A question was sliding around his brain. *Why did Vanity assume he'd been called to the police station as a murder suspect?*

The answer was simple.

Only because she'd never believed it was 'suicide' for a second.

Only because she'd instantly assumed Simon had been murdered.

CONVIX 15. EARTH ORBIT TWO:

11.00am

EVENT	*LOCATION*
INSIDE THE CRAB **INTERVIEW** PAUL CHESTER-ALLEN	Vixos Central Nerve Centre (main stage,ballroom)
'THE MADNESS OF MAGAROTH' **EPISODE SCREENING**	The Catacombs of Herath (video lounge - room 1024)
AUTOGRAPH PANEL MERVYN STONE ANDREW JAMIESON BOB AND BARBARA BRAINTREE	Arkadia's Boudoir (room 1013)
HOW TO BLOW UP EVERYDAY OBJECTS 1 **WORKSHOP** BERNARD VINER	Hyperion Bridge (room 1010)
PHOTOS VANITY MYCROFT	Transpodule Chamber (room 1030)
VIXENS FROM THE VOID: WHAT MAKES A MONSTER **EXPERT PANEL** with Graham Goldingay, Fay Lawless, Craig Jones, Darren Cardew	The Seventh Moon of Groolia (room 1002)

CHAPTER TWENTY

Mervyn was almost having a nice time.

Things had settled down in his brain and, to his profound surprise, he'd managed to meet lots of fans who were very normal; polite, intelligent, friendly folk who just happened to like an old TV show and had come along for a good time and see friends. He'd forgotten how fun some aspects of conventions were, and how he'd missed people asking him intelligent questions about his work. He even shared a drink with one or two, as he expounded in great detail about why he thought modern television was rubbish. He laughed as memories of the show popped back into his head, and because his drinking buddies had studied every aspect of the history of *Vixens* they were able to laugh along with him. It was a very civilized way to spend a long weekend. He could only guess what would happen if football fans tried to hold conventions. For a start, the hotel wouldn't just be worried about Blu-Tack coating their fixtures and fittings...

He remembered something that had slipped his mind during his seven years away. It was so often the guests who gave the impression that they were superior, more mature than the fans that clustered around them, but in fact it was the fans who had more perspective about examining the entrails of a long-dead TV show. It was the guests who deluded themselves into imagining themselves still huge stars. It was the guests who, more often than not, used conventions as an excuse to regress into behaving like infants.

Cue Andrew Jamieson.

'*You did what?*' Andrew shrieked. The fan who'd just asked for his autograph jumped in surprise.

Initially, Mervyn felt profound shock at the realisation he'd accidentally slept with two women in the one night. Then testosterone-fuelled exhilaration flooded through him; he was soon desperate to tell someone (anyone) who might appreciate his conquests. Unfortunately, as that required finding someone both male and heterosexual, the candidates were few.

'Seriously?' spluttered Andrew Jamieson.

That was the last thing Andrew said for five minutes, as he couldn't draw breath for giggling. Mervyn knew he'd made a mistake in telling him.

'It's an old story,' Andrew said at last, wiping his streaming eyes. 'You go to bed with a gorgeous young piece of skirt and wake-up with some raddled old baggage. Happens all the time when I'm out on the piss.'

'She's not exactly *ruddled.*'

'Well, yes, I admit she's not exactly smelling of catfood and wee yet, but it's only a matter of time –'

'Of course!' Mervyn slapped the table with the flat of his hand.

'What?'

'It makes sense. There was a smell last night, when she was in the room, I just couldn't place it...'

'Catfood and wee?'

'Mothballs,' said Mervyn. 'From the costume she was wearing. It's her old costume. I *knew* I smelt it from somewhere.'

'Very well deduced Mervyn – still got your detective mojo, I see.' Andrew placed his hand on Mervyn's shoulder. 'I want you to promise me something...' He looked directly in Mervyn's eyes with mock sincerity. 'If you do ever decide to tell La Mycroft you'd shagged her and didn't even *realise...*' His pudgy face twinkled with mischief. '... but the only way you *might* have deduced it was from the stink of mothballs...'

'Yes.'

'Please, please, *please* let me be there.' Andrew plunged back into uncontrollable giggles.

Apart from Andrew's choked titters, the writer's autograph session (Mervyn, Andrew, and the scarily chirpy husband-and-wife team of Bob and Barbara Braintree) was a quiet affair. It reminded Mervyn of the study rooms from his university days; hushed and deserted, with only dry coughing and the lonely scratching of a pen to puncture the silence.

'Hi.'

He looked up. It was Minnie.

Again.

Oh dear.

'Hi.'

'I can't stop, I'm stewarding Bernard Viner's "How to Blow up Everyday Objects" workshop,' she burbled breathlessly. 'Just thought I'd say hi...'

'So you said. Hi.'

She leaned over the table and hugged him. As she was standing and he was sitting, he found his face embedded in her bosom. Instead of being aroused, Mervyn felt awkward, compromised. He was being laid claim to in public by a virtual teenager. He felt like a teacher who'd had an unwise affair with a demonstrative pupil and was paying for it at a parent's evening. Minnie didn't seem aware of his discomfort.

'Oh shit, have you heard about Simon? I can't believe it. I mean, I thought he was a dickhead, but even so...'

'Yes, it's really terrible. Minnie, you remember saying something about Simon...'

'Sorry, gotta go. If Bernard blows himself up and I'm not there, we might get fined by the hotel.' She pushed her face onto his and gave him a clumsy kiss on the cheek. It brought home to Mervyn once again how young she was. She hissed into his ear in a conspiratorial way. 'I've left my bra in your room. I'd better go and get it back sometime...' She stood up and raised her voice. 'See you at lunch?' And then she was gone.

Now that was embarrassing. Some of the autograph-hunters were grinning at him. He wondered if they'd shared her bed too. He felt as if an invisible wall between him and the fans had been switched off and anyone could get to him.

Mervyn didn't want to stay in this miserable room any more. Sod it. He hadn't signed a thing in 20 minutes. He was going. Let Morris dock his fee, if he wanted.

He looked across to see Andrew, whose eyes were bulging with amusement. Andrew gave a huge cartoon wink, and held two thumbs aloft.

Back in his room, he wrote a list of whys.

WHY

1) ... would anyone kill Simon?
2) ... would Bernard sell Simon his beloved Styrax?
3) ... was Roddy so scared of Simon?
4) ... did someone leave me Vanity's autobiography?
5) ... did Vanity assume Simon had been murdered?

He looked at it long and hard. He hadn't made a 'why list' since...

Oh yes.

Since he'd been the script editor of *Vixens from the Void.*

He used to make a 'why list' in the margins of scripts (usually Andrew Jamieson's coffee-stained efforts. Reading his drafts was a unique experience. His characters barely kept the same motivations, the same names – or even stayed the same sex – throughout the script). He found it the best way to understand what was going on, to order his thoughts and get his mind to worry away at a story until it made sense in his head.

What he had in front of him was a story; a story that his script editor's mind told him didn't make sense. There was something about what had happened earlier that morning that seemed... wrong. Like it didn't fit. But he couldn't work out what.

Oh yes. And there was what he found in the Styrax. That was odd too. He took it out of his pocket and wrote:

6) ... were there TWO suicide notes?

The note he had found on the floor was quite different to the one the police had taken away in their evidence bag. It was crude, rushed. It said:

It's when your memories are at their happiest that it's time to say goodbye.

Below it was a signature – barely. It was so illegible it was more like a spasm. But Mervyn could make out an '***S---***' and a '***J---***' at the beginning of the two squiggles purporting to be a first name and surname. But it was a completely *different* signature to the one on the letter he'd found on the dashboard.

The special constable was a bit over-zealous, perhaps. But it didn't mean he was wrong about Simon's death. And if Mervyn did look into it as well, well... it might make the convention a bit more bearable, wouldn't it?

He hadn't been a writer for ages; he knew that, deep down. The manuscript on his computer was just an electronic placebo that helped him feel better, to help him convince himself that his artistic integrity was alive and well. No, he knew he wasn't a writer. What shocked him was the realisation that he was no longer a script editor either. Years of fans applauding his yarns and asking him to sign *Vixens* scripts, books and video sleeves didn't make him a script editor; it just made him *feel* like he was still a script editor.

All the stories he'd worked on, they were all old. He'd finished them off long ago; trimmed, finessed, shaped and nibbled at them with his typewriter until they made sense. And not just the mouldering *Vixens* scripts that had been made, broadcast and largely forgotten by the wider world. The behind-the-scenes anecdotes too, had been sorted and polished until they shone with immaculate structure, tone, pace and coherence.

Old stories.

He was slowly becoming aware that, at long last, a new story was forming under his very nose. One that wasn't shaped or polished or finessed yet. There were bits missing; there were huge parts that weren't clear or plain didn't make sense.

It doesn't have a final act, said Mervyn, *it isn't even half-finished; it's just a beginning with footnotes.*

What a script editor needed was a new story to sort out.

'Who knows?' he said out loud to himself. 'If this all goes well, I might even get a book out of it.'

CHAPTER TWENTY-ONE

When Mervyn entered the convention's makeshift office on the ground floor, Morris was sighing deeply. The source of Morris's annoyance was obvious. It was large and smelly, and filled most of the tiny office.

'Vanity Mycroft didn't turn up to the celebrity breakfast,' droned John the Stalker.

'I'm sorry to hear that. I hope she's not ill,' droned Morris back.

'Yes. I hope she's not ill too.'

'So if there's nothing else...?'

'I didn't get what I paid for.'

'What didn't you get?'

'The celebrity breakfast.'

'But you went to the breakfast.'

'Yes I did. Vanity didn't turn up.'

'So you got what you paid for.'

'No.'

'But you had the breakfast?'

'Yes.'

'So...'

'Vanity Mycroft didn't turn up to the celebrity breakfast.'

The conversation had obviously been chugging round in circles for some time. With Morris's low, rumbling voice alternating with John the Stalker's flat monotone, it sounded like an ordinary argument but played at half-speed.

'I've told you, we don't do refunds if one of the stars can't make it. You still had two celebrities on your table. We can't guarantee a specific celebrity will turn up. I'm really sorry about that.'

'That's all right. I'm sure she had her reasons.'

'Good.'

'But she didn't turn up.'

'Yes. You said. Quite a few times. I can't do anything about that now.'

'No. You can't. Because the breakfast is finished.'

'It's now midday, yes. I guess it's finished.'

'Yes. Vanity never turned up for it.'

John the Stalker stood there blinking furiously. His brain was telling him that Something Must Be Done, but he wasn't getting anything more specific than that.

'So if there's nothing else...'

'No. I don't think so.'

'So if you could leave. Now? Please?'

No movement from John the Stalker. Morris finally cracked. 'Look, I'll see if we can work something out. Give you a little something. We'll not call it compensation, we can call it a little something for you being so understanding.'

A brief silence while the proposal was downloaded and processed.

'Okay.'

'Great.'

'What do I get?'

Morris's eyes cast desperately around for inspiration, finally alighting on the corner of the room.

'Wait a minute...' he went over to it.

There was a photocopier in the corner of the room. On it was a large grey lump. It looked like a huge mouldy sandwich. He placed it in John's meaty hands with great ceremony. 'Here you go. A priceless item of memorabilia. A genuine piece of recently destroyed Styrax.'

John the Stalker looked doubtfully at the crumbling piece of detritus. 'It's a bit of papier-mâché.'

'But it's a very *special* bit of papier-mâché. It used to be a Styrax. It's a piece of history.'

John still showed no signs of leaving.

'Look, you just hold on to that, and we'll get Vanity Mycroft to sign it for you. How about that?' Morris said.

'I got her autograph yesterday.'

'All right, we'll get her to put some lipstick on and kiss it. Mark it with a big smooch.'

This seemed acceptable to John. He left, clutching his new prize.

Morris let the air go from his lungs. 'Finally.' Barely seeming to register Mervyn's presence, he took a pile of papers over to the photocopier and started to feed them in. Almost immediately, the photocopier jammed with a high-pitched squawk. Morris's shoulders slumped in resignation. 'Eight pence a copy, and they give us a photocopier that jams on every third sheet. I'll just have to ask someone very nicely to print the revised schedules on their computer printer.' It was only then he said. 'Now, Mervyn. What can I do for you?'

Mervyn was so surprised that he almost forgot his lines.

'Oh. What? Oh yes. Morris, I don't suppose you could help me – you'll think me an old fool but do you know what? I seem to have lost my name tag.'

Morris's massive head swivelled up from the dead photocopier. 'The spares are all packed up in Simon's room, I'm afraid.'

'Simon's room? Really.' Mervyn already knew this. He'd asked another steward about ten minutes before.

'Yeah. I've left his room as it is for the moment. I'm going to clear it out on Sunday when we leave.'

'So they're in Simon's room? Damn and botheration, that's a bit inconvenient. I feel a bit naked without a name tag. People will think I'm not a guest. They might not let me into hospitality.'

'Oh I'm sure the stewards will recognise you.'

'Morris... I'm a *writer*. No one recognises me.'

Morris digested the logic of this and found it made perfect sense. 'I haven't got his key. It's with his personal effects, and I haven't got them back from the police yet.' Morris groped in his leather jacket. 'I'll tell you what, I'll write you a letter.'

'There's really no need...'

Morris was scribbling on the back of a leaflet now. 'No, you're dead right. If any of the stewards stop you, this letter will let them know that you're famous.'

'Look, why don't I get a member of the hotel to go up with me, open the door and retrieve another name tag? It would only take a minute. I mean, it's only on the third floor...'

'Fourth floor. Best not really. There's valuable props in there.' He flicked a look at Mervyn as if to say, *you are one known as Prop Killer, you must be kept away from the rare, the valuable and the breakable at all costs.* He handed the scrap of paper to Mervyn. 'There you go.'

'Thanks so much.' Mervyn wandered off, thrusting the paper into his pocket, where it nestled alongside Mervyn's name tag.

Fourth floor. Right.

Two minutes later, he was on the fourth floor, nodding awkwardly at the fans as they entered and left their rooms. He felt like a bit of an idiot, not knowing quite what he was doing there.

He was about to admit defeat and head back down when he noticed a folded newspaper on the floor, nestling against one of the doors.

Mervyn looked up and down the corridor. It was the only one left. He looked at his watch. 12.20. There's not many hotel guests who wouldn't pick up their paper by midday – either the occupant was sleeping off a very heavy night...

Or the occupant wouldn't be picking up his paper again. Ever.

He walked over. It was a copy of *The Daily Mail*. Well, Simon certainly seemed like a *Daily Mail* kind of guy. It must be his room. He pushed the door.

To his surprise, it clicked open.

It was Simon's room, no doubt about it – it was the waste bin filled with

Styrax fragments in the corner that gave it away. Mervyn felt a twinge of guilt when he saw the sad little heap of bits.

As Mervyn expected, Simon had used it as a makeshift office and command centre rather than a place to sleep. Piles of papers were neatly stacked on the desk by the window. Plastic name cards, folders and props were bulging out of colour-coded boxes arranged on the bed.

What Mervyn didn't expect was the large wedge-shaped chunk of evil robot squatting in the corner by the wardrobe.

Another Styrax.

He foraged through the boxes on the bed. Nothing much of any interest. Certainly nothing suspicious. Well, there was plenty of stuff that *looked* suspicious – ray guns, laser rifles, large swords with exotic bejewelled handles and one large egg-timer-type device with the words 'ELECTRON BOMB' inscribed on it.

... But nothing *suspiciously* suspicious.

The desk was more promising. Lots of papers. There were receipts for expenses, invoices from caterers and printers and photocopies of gushing correspondence to the stars requesting their presence. It didn't escape Mervyn's attention that the wording on the flattering letter he'd been sent asking him to attend was virtually identical to everyone else's. The phrases 'legend in fan circles', 'incalculable contribution to the show' and 'constant requests for your reappearance' were tellingly familiar.

Lying on the corner of the table was a pile of artsy black-and-white photos; the type actors put in *Spotlight*. On the top was a brooding picture of man in his 70s using the bare amount of lighting and deep shadows to look like he was in his 40s. Mervyn could barely see a bit of nose and a cheekbone in the gloom, but he knew who it was.

Samuel Johns. A fruity actor of the old school. He was a nice old cove, Mervyn remembered. He'd been the first Major Karn, way back in '86. He caused quite a headache after the first series when he suddenly upped and left the show and the part had to be recast as Roddy Burgess (Mervyn hated to admit it, but Roddy was an inferior replacement). Everyone assumed that Samuel, an actor with a distinctly average career, would have stuck with the show as long as possible. It irked the production team to change an actor midstream; but it was nothing compared to the annoyance of the fans at the time.

Samuel Johns: now where had he heard his name recently?

Oh yes. When he bumped into Simon in the corridor and sent his autographs flying. Simon said his autograph was very valuable...

Mervyn had a thought. He picked up the photo. On the white panel below the picture there were four dog-eared adhesive corners, the type used to fix photos in albums. Whatever had been fixed there had been ripped out in a hurry.

Mervyn pulled out the second suicide note, the one he'd found on the Styrax floor, and slotted it into place. It fitted perfectly.

It's when your memories are at their happiest that it's time to say goodbye. S--- J---

So now he knew. The 'suicide note' was written by Samuel Johns. Someone had rushed in here and ripped the autograph from the photo, thinking it would serve as a suicide note from Simon Josh.

For a suicide note, it was pretty rubbish. It was completely different from the elegent letter he'd found stuck to the dashboard. Why was one suicide note done so well and the other so crudely?

'You don't think searching his room might look a little... suspicious at all?'

Mervyn's body spasmed in shock. When he regained control of himself, he spun round. No one there. Whoever spoke wasn't in the room.

Not yet.

'Who's going to know? I'll be quick,' said another voice.

The owners of both voices were in the corridor outside. Both near, and getting nearer all the time.

The corridors of the hotel were long, straight and extremely overlit; there was no way he could leave the room without being seen. Mervyn gibbered. He tried to ask his brain what to do, but the ungrateful bastard seemed to have dived for cover already without so much as a thought as to what it was going to do with the rest of his body.

Hide! Under the bed? No. Too low, no room. Bathroom? Hardly. Wouldn't want to get found there. The wardrobe! No. The damn Styrax was wedged up against it.

Oh damn. Not *there.*

'Oh. The door's already open.'

Mervyn could hear the door thud against the wall as it was pushed open.

'You sound disappointed.'

'I needn't have bothered getting the key-card out of his pocket, that's all.'

Bernard and Nicholas entered the room. Or so Mervyn gathered from the sound of their voices. As he was looking through the grille at the front of the Styrax, all he could see were two hazy black blobs.

One of the blobs leaned against the wall and crossed its arms. 'You stole his card? My goodness. Old habits die hard, don't they?'

'Look, don't you have some pissing off to do?'

'I'll stay if it's all the same to you. Believe it or not, I'm here to help.'

'I don't need any help.'

'Yes you do, old stick, and we both know it.'

Inside his fibreglass cocoon, Mervyn tried to relax. It wasn't easy – the heat was unbearable. The papier-mâché plastered to the inside of the Styrax was designed so the operator wouldn't bump and scrape himself against the sharp edges of the wooden framework. Unfortunately, it also acted as insulation. He'd only been in the thing three minutes and he was being roasted alive. He was in severe danger of blacking out. *Heaven knows how Smurf and Sheldon coped after a day in one of these.*

The other blob came closer and morphed into Bernard. He was moving like a cat, keeping his back to the wall and flipping his little dark eyes around the room, as if he was expecting to be attacked by something in the mini-bar at any moment.

'Well get on with it, if you're going,' sighed Nicholas.

Bernard started searching the room. Papers cascaded from the desk and scooted along the carpet.

'What's this?'

'It's an envelope. It's addressed to you.'

'I can see that!'

'Well done.'

'Well go on, read it!'

There was a sigh from Nicholas as he took it and read it. 'It's nothing. It's just a letter confirming your appearance at StarCon next month, darling.'

'I knew that!'

'Of course you did.'

Bernard threw the envelope on the bed, stood up...

And looked directly at Mervyn.

Oh no...

Bernard's eyes danced across the Styrax. Mervyn shrank down as low as he could. He counted his lucky stars that he habitually dressed in black; any other colour and Bernard would easily have spotted him.

'Hey look, I made this.'

'You made all of them, dear heart.'

'Yeah, but this one's in good nick. Perhaps I can buy it off Morris.'

Bernard continued to stare into the Styrax. Behind him Nicholas looked through the papers on the bed.

'I can't see any evidence relating to your crime, dear heart,' Nicholas sighed. 'I think you're in the clear.'

'Good.'

There was a metallic rattle on the side of the Styrax, as Bernard fiddled with the latch that opened the back. Mervyn tried his best to ooze out of the holes in the bottom, but his body stayed stubbornly corporeal.

'Have we finished? Because of all people to be discovered with in a hotel room, your name comes slightly lower than bottom of my list.'

There was more rustling and clattering as Bernard moved around the room. Mervyn was crazy with curiosity but he daren't raise his face to the grille to see what was going on.

'One thing left to do then,' said Bernard.

Mervyn couldn't see what they were doing, but thankfully within seconds of doing whatever it was they *were* doing they left, their voices dribbling back down the corridor.

The 'ker-chunk' of the door shutting was the sweetest thing Mervyn had ever heard.

The 'ker-thunk' of Mervyn's head hitting the back door of the Styrax was a less welcome sound.

The hatch stubbornly stayed where it was. When Bernard fiddled with the latch he must have locked it. Mervyn considered smashing his way out, but that seemed far too drastic. He'd destroyed one of these things already, and the cringing writer within would rather suffer and sweat in silence than draw attention to himself. Long years of riding the Metropolitan Line had conditioned him for that.

It was getting stifling in this thing. The heat wouldn't usually be this bad, surely? He was becoming drowsy. His eyes fluttered and closed, and his head nodded down on to the Styrax panel that operated the guns, lights and arms.

He barely heard the 'whumf' that became a strange crackling that sounded like toffees being unwrapped. He didn't see the orange fingers of flame that tickled the rim of the waste basket.

There was only one of his senses that realised anything was wrong.

Could he smell... Was that smoke?

That was his last thought. Things got blurry; coloured shapes swam across his eyes, and then the world buggered off and left him in blackness.

CHAPTER TWENTY-TWO

He'd died and gone to hell, obviously. There was smoke, and flames, and shouting. All the usual hell stuff.

He should never have written that episode where the Vixens whipped men who were tied to crucifixes. Too late now.

An angel was talking. He could hear her quite distinctly.

Did they have angels in hell? She obviously didn't like it in hell. She was coughing. She didn't sound happy.

'Bloody hell, what's happened in here?'

'The bin's on fire!'

There was a clanking and thudding as someone stamped on the fire in the bin. Then a 'swoosh' as the taps in the bathroom were turned on.

'Get that thing outside!'

Mervyn woke up. His head had been knocked against the casing. He was being moved! Quite roughly, in fact. Mervyn looked out and saw three stewards inside the room grappling with him and shoving him towards the door. He was wrestled outside. The cold air blasted into the little holes in the Styrax, and he realised just how hot it had got in that room.

There was a limp hiss as the bin was doused.

'Who the bloody hell's done this?'

'God knows.'

'I'll let Morris know what's happened.' One moved off to the lift. The other two proceeded to shove Mervyn along the corridor.

'I don't know. First Simon kills himself, and then someone sets fire to his room.'

'Just not his day, is it?'

A bubble of laughter floated around the corridor. Mervyn almost joined in. He was feeling quite giggly.

The second voice sounded familiar. He peered out. It was Minnie. She was right above him, exerting herself sweatily, as she manhandled the prop towards the door. He could see from the way she was swaying alarmingly under her sweater that she still hadn't managed to replace her bra. If he died now, the last thing he would ever see were her unfettered breasts hanging over him, swaying and thwacking together like an adult-oriented executive toy.

This all added to his otherworldly state of mind. Not only was he woozy from oxygen starvation, his blood chose that moment to leave his head and charge down his body to power a raging erection. His head was soon swimming like a frantic dog in a pond.

Down the corridor he hurtled, and Mervyn found himself on his own personal acid trip. He marvelled at the carpet whizzing by underneath him; the many small ugly patterns blurring into one extremely fat ugly pattern. It was most exhilarating.

'Did you hear something?' said Minnie.

'What?' said the other steward.

'I thought I heard someone going "Wheeeeeeee!"'

They wheeled him into the main hall, in front of the stage on the extreme left – exactly where his descending backside had destroyed the other Styrax. He was recovering his wits fast, and tried to hiss at Minnie for help, but she and the other stewards scampered away before he could make himself heard.

He was alone again. Everyone had gone to lunch. The only company he had were rows of empty chairs, the tackily ostentatious décor (plastic chandeliers and silver flock wallpaper), and a strange-looking robot creature about ten feet to his left.

A Maaganoid. That was new – it hadn't been there before.

The Maaganoids were a race of robots they'd introduced in the final season as a nemesis for the Styrax. It wasn't one of Mervyn's better ideas. He reasoned that, just as the Styrax were a type of supercar that had got out of control, the Maaganoids were a form of robot traffic control from the same planet, and that they had also developed their own intelligence. Speed cameras were a novelty in 1992, and the logic of making such a hated new device into a race to combat the Styrax seemed to make sense.

Unfortunately, the idea had two major drawbacks. First, the concept was just too comical for the audience to swallow. It conjured up memories of the *Monty Python* sketch with vicious 'Keep Left' signs. Second, and more importantly, there was a problem with the design. The Maaganoid had a huge triangular head, on which was mounted a telescopic eye like a camera lens. The head was perched on a tall column, which tapered down to large round base on which there were two round, stubby apertures from which guns or grasping claws could emerge.

In short; it looked like a penis. A monstrous strap-on wanger for a gigantic porn actress. A six-and-a-half-foot stiffy with huge bloated testicles that spat laser bolts, with the camera-like eye mounted in the head looking like a rather gruesome cock stud. It wasn't surprising that they became known among the production team as Maa-gonads. They looked obscene, sounded stupid, and kept toppling over on the set. It was safe to say that, had the mythical season eight happened, the Maaganoids wouldn't have made a return appearance.

So here he was, sweating slowly into oblivion, in a papier-mâché-filled iron maiden with only a huge fibreglass cock for company. He knew certain colourful individuals in television who'd pay for an experience like this, but at this particular moment the attraction eluded him.

'90 degrees wrong, 120 degrees crap,' he muttered to himself.

'What?' said a voice.

Mervyn fell silent.

'Who's there?' The voice seemed quite near.

Despite the heat in the Styrax, Mervyn suddenly felt chilled. Someone had heard him. Someone else was in the hall with him.

'Hello? Hello? Who's that?'

Whoever it was, they didn't sound like they were going to forget they'd heard him. Too late to lie low now. He'd just have to brazen it out.

'Hello?'

'Hello?' Mervyn replied.

'Mr Stone?'

'Is that... um... Stuart?'

'Yes. It's me. Where are you?'

Thank heavens. Special constable Stuart might be a bit weird, but Mervyn was sure he could rely on him to be discreet.

'Listen, Stuart. You see the Styrax by the stage?'

'Yes?'

'I'm stuck in there.'

'You're what?'

'I'm stuck inside the Styrax.'

'Oh.'

'It's been sealed.'

'Um... Is that a Vanity Mycroft sex thing? I don't want to intrude.'

'No. You wouldn't be a life-saver and undo this thing? I'm getting steamed like a haddock in here.'

'Um... I'd love to. But... I can't at the moment.'

'What? What do you mean "can't at the moment"?'

'Sorry.'

'What do you mean you "can't"?'

'Um...'

'You're not blackmailing me, are you?'

'What?'

'Not a form of police persuasion, regarding our little "chat" at the station?'

'Gosh, no!'

'Sure it's not a subtle "I'll let you out but only if you agree to play

Holmes and Watson with me" kind of thing?'

'Honestly, no, really. It's not that at all. It's just that... Erm... You see the Maaganoid by the stage?'

'Yes?'

'I'm stuck in there.'

'You're what?'

'I'm stuck inside the Maaganoid.'

'Oh.'

CHAPTER TWENTY-THREE

There wasn't much to say after that. Mervyn was speechless.

Unfortunately, 'speechless' wasn't a word in Stuart's vocabulary. There were loads of other words in his vocabulary, however, and he was determined to use every one. He droned happily away inside his prick-shaped prison; having his childhood hero as a captive audience was too good an opportunity to miss.

'Gosh, the inside of this Maaganoid is a bit ropey. Cheap and nasty. The one we made for our fan videos was much better. We didn't have to lag the insides with papier-mâché to stop the sharp edges jabbing into the operator. Gosh, this is a funny situation isn't it? I mean talk about coincidence! I mean, even when Elysia and Professor Daxatar crash-landed on Prendulum Major... and they'd crashed on *the same planet* where Medula had been hiding since the second assault on Chevron! That wasn't as much of a coincidence as this! I mean, my gosh that was a coincidence! Talk about contrived! Um... Not that I'm saying it was a bad thing, Mr Stone, but I do actually address that plot hole in my fan video. We remade it shot for shot, except we inserted a scene where the magnetic core of the planet that dragged them down was the reason why Medula was hiding there, because it was the only planet in the galaxy that Vixos sensors couldn't penetrate. So we made it a bit better than the original, if you like. I really wish I could show you my improved version...'

'Perhaps if we ever get out of here you can.'

'Really? Gosh, you'll be so impressed. We've made so many improvements on the original you would not believe it. We corrected all the things you did wrong at the time, you know, just little things, Mr Stone –'

'Please, call me Mervyn. If we're both going to sit and suffocate together, then we might as well use first names.'

'Okay Mr S– Mervyn.'

'And Stuart, perhaps you can bear in mind that sometimes fate is stranger than anything we can imagine,' said Mervyn testily. He was getting tired of this 'improving on the original' stuff. He was very aware of the shortcomings of the old series, but he didn't like the shortcomings rubbed in his face by someone who was, after all, supposed to be a fan. 'As you say, the fact we're here is a coincidence. Coincidence *is* something that can happen in drama, and coincidence is just as valid as anything else. You don't have to explain *everything*.'

'That's just an excuse for sloppy writing.'

'No it's not. Because life's like that. Coincidence. You said it.'

The Maaganoid went silent, thinking. 'Well not really... because we didn't get here randomly. After you left I thought, "Okay, I'll do a bit more investigating." You know, poke about a bit, see if anyone was acting suspicious, maybe get some evidence to convince you that my suspicions are correct. Anyway, I thought I'd hide in the Maaganoid because they were keeping it in the convention office where everyone was coming and going, and I thought that would be an excellent place to hear a few unguarded comments. So I crept in and hid myself inside.'

'And someone fastened the catch, trapping you inside?'

'Exactly.'

'And then they wheeled you in here.'

'Exactly. Just like you. You were investigating, just like me. Because you think Simon was murdered too. So it's not a coincidence, really.'

Mervyn closed his eyes wearily.

'Mr Stone – Mervyn.'

'Yes?'

'I don't wish to alarm you, but the gas canister under your seat – the one that powers your flame gun? I think it's leaking. I can hear a hissing noise coming from your Styrax.'

'No. That's just me. Sighing.'

'Are you sure? Because I can hear the noise a lot.'

'No. Just me. Sighing. A lot.'

'You see, it's not random at all. We're both investigating.'

'I suppose.'

'And I'm glad you are. You're very good at it. Catching Bernard Viner like that. I mean, however you did it... You know... You've never told us how you caught him.'

'Told "us"?'

The Maaganoid seemed to blush. 'The fans.'

'I didn't really want to talk about it.'

'Oh I understand. I quite understand. There are some things that should be kept private, and that privacy should be respected. Absolutely. Discretion is a much underated virtue. I mean, when Arkadia told the House of Mistresses that Major Karn died like a hero when in reality he'd hadn't, that was quite noble, but a bit odd, because if you think about it, they'd have known what he'd done anyway through the Osmosis Focuser that transmits soldiers' dying thoughts into the central – Mr Stone, are you sure you don't want to check under your seat?'

'No.'

'Because it's a very loud hiss.'

'It's fine. Really.'

'Right. His thoughts should have been transmitted via the Osmosis

Focuser – unless someone intercepted them and beamed them somewhere else, which would explain that weird bit in series five when Medula knew what happened on Spartus despite not being anywhere near it at the events of the time. I actually took those plot errors and did something with them. I took the original footage, got some actors and revoiced it, matching the lip movements exactly, saying that the Osmosis Focuser didn't exist, and it was a lie designed to instill loyalty in the Vixos troops. Much more neat, don't you think? And then I took footage –'

'*Okay!* Okay... Would you like to know how I discovered it was Bernard who was stealing from the studio?'

'Gosh, would I?' The Maaganoid wobbled excitedly. 'I'd be thrilled in the extreme.'

'Well it looks like we're not going anywhere, and I'm entertaining a faint hope that if I do tell you, you might stop talking for five minutes, so... All right. But this goes no further. I've done enough to ruin his life without the details finding their way into some photocopied fan rag.'

'I promise I won't tell. I swear.'

'All right... Well, let me think... It all started during filming at TV Centre. It was a hectic day. Not enough bodies on set, as usual... Not quite as bad as the last day of filming series two after that bloody general election, but still pretty bad. Anyway, one of the Styrax got damaged. The paintwork got chipped when it ran into a wall or something, and Nicholas wrote a note for Bernard to fix it urgently. He would have told him personally but things were getting very fraught. He fixed a Post-it note on his desk in his workshop and rushed off. The next thing I knew there was uproar on the floor. They'd started filming again after lunch, but when the Styrax got wheeled out it was still broken. Nothing had been done to it.'

'Wow. You mean the note had fallen off?'

'No. It was still there, in plain view on Bernard's desk where Nicholas had stuck it. Naturally Nicholas was furious with Bernard – didn't understand why he hadn't fixed it. Bernard was giving him all this flannel about being rushed off his feet that day, but that was nonsense.'

'Was Bernard bunking off somewhere?'

'No. He's just not that type. Bernard – well, he's unpleasant, rude, bad-tempered and a right pain in everybody's arse... But he's not lazy.'

'Then why?'

'It was only much later that I realised that his assistant had called in sick that day. That this was the first time I'd seen Bernard do any work on his own.'

'Then why didn't he fix the Styrax?'

'Only one possible explanation. Bernard couldn't read.'

'Couldn't read? *No!*'

'Yes. Couldn't read. He was illiterate... Or perhaps extremely dyslexic. I've never been particularly friendly with him, as you can guess, so I never had the guts to ask which.'

'But... How?'

'How what?'

'How could he get a job at the BBC? How could he even function on a show like *Vixens* and not be able to read?'

'Oh, there are ways. I did a bit of reading up about it. You'll be amazed at the things people who can't read do to try to keep their secret. Writing certain words on their sleeves so they can recognise them in everyday situations, "questioning" the fine print of documents so they can get someone else to unwittingly explain what's on them... And it was especially easy for Bernard. He originally came in as a freelance contractor because Nicholas liked his work on another show. He insisted on bringing in an assistant. His girlfriend. She must have explained all the paperwork to him.'

'Wow. That's just... Just... Wow.'

'Anyway, it was pretty obvious that's what was wrong – to me, at least. Nicholas just assumed Bernard had been playing silly buggers, so I didn't let on what I knew. I didn't want to get Bernard into trouble. Ironic really.'

'So when things started disappearing from the studio...'

'It took a while for me to cotton on, but I did start to suspect Bernard. A lot of the stolen stuff was just too specific; obvious valuable stuff was ignored in favour of props that collectors might be interested in...'

'Lots of people would know how valuable they'd be.'

'That's true. But these were props that we'd practically finished using, so they wouldn't be missed for days. None of the stuff went missing in a way that was inconvenient to, or made work for, the design department. So I thought it was one of them – and Bernard had been very vocal about being short-changed by the corporation.'

'Yes, I read about that. He was annoyed about designing the Styrax and you getting all that money for the Styrax merchandising and him getting... sod... all...' Stuart's flow of words dried to a trickle. The gigantic penis seemed to shrivel with embarrassment. 'I was just saying what he said in his interviews,' Stuart mumbled, lamely. 'I don't agree with it, necessarily.'

'Quite. Anyway, I thought it was Bernard, and as I knew he had reading difficulties, I decided to use that knowledge to test my theory. I got the pilot episode out of the BBC archive and left it in the production office.'

'*The* pilot episode? The unscreened one?'

'Yes, that's the one. I thought that, of everything we had, it would be worth the most to any collector.'

'Cor yeah... You could say that. I mean, before the BBC videos came out, I used to dream of seeing that episode... I remember at university someone got hold of this manky tenth-generation copy from a mate in this fan club in Exeter and we all squeezed into Nigel's bedroom to watch it, because he was the only one with a VCR. My goodness it was ropey. The special effects were even worse than the series proper. I've done that episode too, updated the ships, new gun blasts, improved it, added more effects, and as it was a third-generation copy, I've managed to get rid of the hiss–' Mervyn's Styrax hissed too, loudly and meaningfully. 'Sorry. Carry on.'

'Anyway... I left it in the production office. Only I didn't. I took the tape out *first* and *then* left the canister in the office – with a note on it which said something like "To whom it may concern. I would like to emphasise to anyone reading this missive that the tape within this case is not, despite appearance to the contrary, THE PILOT EPISODE OF *VIXENS FROM THE VOID*. It does however, contain within its confines a rather mediocre edition of *Blankety Blank*, which I'm reliably informed has little fiscal value to the myriad legions of *Vixens* fandom' – something like that. I filled it with big long words and put the important bit - 'the pilot episode of *Vixens from the Void*' – in big, heavy capital letters. To anyone else it just looked like some kind of incomprehensible practical joke; but to Bernard it must have looked like 'blah blah blah blah blah PILOT EPISODE OF *VIXENS FROM THE VOID* blah blah blah'. If it went from the office, I'd know for sure. And sure enough, last thing on Friday, it disappeared. I checked no one had cleared it away, and then I went to see Nicholas. Ten minutes later we were watching a security guard forcing Bernard to open up his car and Bernard throwing every expletive at us he could think of. We found the canister under a travel rug, along with two Groolian blasters and a laser probe from Professor Daxatar's toolkit.'

'Wow, that's amazing... Brilliant. You must have been so excited.'

'It was one of the worst days of my life. *He* was the one exposed as a thief, and I'd never felt so embarrassed.'

There was a long silence.

'Wait a minute Mr St– Mervyn... He was signing autographs, yesterday. I saw him.'

'He's learned how to do that. He's got his reading up to elementary standard. Were you there when he threw a fit about doing lengthy personal messages? Shouting that he's only prepared to do his signature and nothing else? That's why. He can copy out a few words, but not much more.'

'Wow. Just. Wow.'

CHAPTER TWENTY-FOUR

The conversation between the Maaganoid and the Styrax glided to a halt, save for an occasional 'wow' ejaculated by the Maaganoid.

Suddenly, Mervyn saw salvation. Salvation wearing tweeds, a cravat and a fancy waistcoat.

'Roddy! Major! Over here!'

The crusty old actor gave a start. He froze mid-amble. 'Who the devil's there? Show yourselves!'

'Over here! By the stage.'

Roddy wandered up, his eyes roving around the ballroom.

'Look, Major, I know this is a bit odd, but my friend – well, associate – and I are both trapped inside these things, and we'd really appreciate it if you could let us out.'

Roddy was listening, definitely. Mervyn was sure he could hear them. But the old actor's expression was one of benign disbelief, a half-amused, incredulous face that looked like it was all too used to the old hearing-voices-come-from-nowhere game.

'Major?'

He gave a slow grin; a wise, comprehending smile that wouldn't have looked out of place on a small boy on his first visit to Disneyland – meeting Mickey Mouse and noticing the mouse's face didn't move when it spoke. 'Don't you worry old chaps. You just sit tight. I'll just head off and organise a rescue mission.'

'No wait! You've just got to undo the latches!'

'Sit tight. I'll be back in a jiffy.' He disappeared from the room.

'Oh. Well, not to worry,' said Stuart brightly. 'He'll probably be back in a minute.'

'Somehow I'm not filled with confidence that we'll ever see Roddy again. He's not the sharpest pencil in the desk.'

'Wait!' said Stuart excitedly. 'I can see your latch from here. It's not been fastened properly.'

'It has. I can't get the hatch open – I've tried.'

'No, it's only been half-done. It's like those big latches you used to get on old-fashioned vacuum cleaners. The catch is in two parts. You pull the metal loop over a notch, then push the handle down so it locks with the loop fastened underneath. Yours only has the loop pulled down. The handle hasn't been locked in place.'

'I'm sorry, I don't speak Ikean. What are you saying?'

'Are you able to jiggle your middle?'

The lack of oxygen had made Mervyn a bit befuddled. 'You mean like a belly dancer?'

'The middle of the *Styrax.* If you jiggle the door, you might free the loop.'

Mervyn jiggled, and kept on jiggling until his arms were aching. The loop rattled enticingly but the hatch stayed stubbornly in place. He finally gave up. 'That's it. I can't do it any more.'

'That's it!' shrieked Stuart. 'When you let it fall back just then. The loop's free. It's not under the notch anymore. Just ease the hatch open... slowly.'

Mervyn did so, and the door creaked open. He hauled himself out of the Styrax like a swimmer breaking the surface of the water, his nostrils gaping as they sucked in the cool air. He wobbled over to the Maaganoid. He released the catch and Stuart appeared, making similar grateful gasping noises; he wobbled about rubbing his legs and then stood there for a long time, his hands on his knees, staring at the carpet.

He pulled himself up and looked at Mervyn, who was lying across three seats in the first row, hands on chest, nose pointed at the ceiling. Stuart jerked a finger at the Styrax. 'Did... phew... did you notice how the insides of those monsters are padded with papier-mâché?'

Mervyn didn't answer, he just nodded and gave a breathless thumbs-up.

'That's what makes them so hot. All that newspaper. Have a look.'

'No thanks. I'm well aware.'

'Oh. Ah... huf...' Stuart straightened up. 'Okay. Good. Thank heavens we're out of there. Now we can investigate properly,' he said.

Mervyn stared at him disbelievingly.

'See you in your room in half an hour,' Stuart hollered cheerily, and ran out of the door.

It was only after he'd disappeared into the depths of the hotel that Mervyn realised he hadn't actually told Stuart his room number.

CHAPTER TWENTY-FIVE

If Mervyn and Stuart had bothered to hang about a few more minutes, they'd have seen Roddy Burgess coming back into the main hall. He walked up to the stage, and wrestled the back off the Styrax. He peered into the sweaty interior.

Nothing. No one in there.

Just as he thought.

'I know your game, you foul robot fiend,' he growled, backing away. 'Both of you. Don't think I don't know what you lot did. Your leader killed that quisling Josh. Very clever to lure him inside like that. Not that I blame you chaps, of course. But I know your sort. One's never enough for you, is it?'

The Styrax and the Maaganoid didn't answer. Roddy tapped his forehead and gave a sly look.

'So you think you can pull the wool over the old Major's peepers? Pretend to have an old chum trapped inside, give out an SOS, and then get me to come near you on a "good Samaritan" mission, and what then? It'd be lights-out for the old Major, wouldn't it? Fiendishly clever.'

He made to leave, pausing at the door. Then he pointed his finger at the Styrax and cocked his thumb. He made a clicking noise in his cheek, taking an imaginary safety catch off.

'Just to let you know, I'm wise to you chaps. The Major's watching you hawkishly, just like the proverbial. So just watch it.'

CONVIX 15. EARTH ORBIT TWO:

2.00pm

EVENT	*LOCATION*
'DAY OF THE STYRAX'REMEMBERED JOSEPH McANDREW TIM WARNE BRYCE CAMPION RICK AMORY	Vixos Central Nerve Centre (main stage, ballroom)
'WINGS OF THE WARLOCK' **EPISODE SCREENING**	The Catacombs of Herath (video lounge - room 1024)
HOW TO BLOW UP EVERYDAY OBJECTS-2 **WORKSHOP** BERNARD VINER	Hyperion Bridge (room 1010)
PHOTOS RODERICK BURGESS Katherine Warner	Transpodule Chamber (room 1030)
NEW VOIDS - FANVIDS **EXPERT PANEL** with Graham Goldingay, Fay Lawless, Craig Jones, Darren Cardew	The Seventh Moon of Groolia (room 1002)

CHAPTER TWENTY-SIX

So I found a little love nest for us! It was a stroke of genius on my part, if I do say so myself.

I suppose I should explain a bit more about the Styrax. I've mentioned it a lot, so I better had.

'What?' I hear some of you cry. 'What on earth is a Styrax?'

For those of you who don't know (those of you who became a fan of my work through my year on the hit soap *Memory Lane* or my critically acclaimed vodka commercials – and who've never even watched *Vixens from the Void* – lucky you!), the Styrax is this big nasty robot that's meant to be a kind of evil murderous supercar from the future.

Not as far-fetched as it seems –you should see the way I drive!

Anyway, we had lots of dinky little ones, like dodgem cars, and one bloody great big one, really huge, and the reason why it was so massive was because it was built around a real full-sized Mini Metro. Truly. It was evil, with glowing eyes on the outside, beige plastic and velour on the inside.

I mean, how perfect is that? The amount of times I've had a fumble in the backs of vehicles. When I was at RADA I had a rather naughty time with a well-known *Coronation Street* actor in his rather nicely upholstered Rolls-Royce. I must say I was more proud about doing it in a Rolls than doing it with a household name!

A Mini Metro's hardly as posh as a Rolls, I grant you! But you'll be surprised at the Rolls-Royce experience – there's not as much leg-room as you might think. A Mini Metro actually has surprisingly good back seats, quite wide, and a Rolls is very narrow – and as us girls know it's the width that really matters! So I thought it was worth investigating what the more economy-sized person was able to give me in the way of thrills – it felt right to try him out in an economy-sized car...!

Anyway, with all the bits and bobs they'd put on it, it looked bloody stupid, like a big fairground ride. But, it was clean, it was warm and most important, the windows were covered in fibreglass, so it was out of the way of prying eyes.

So everyone broke for lunch, and I crept inside the props room. I couldn't put the lights on because someone would have noticed and investigated, so I had to grope my way (which is easy for me – groping is my speciality, just ask anyone!) in the pitch black. I got inside and waited for my little lothario to make his presence

> felt. I didn't have long to wait. He'd managed to get in there before me! All of a sudden, I felt a pudgy little hand on my

Stuart stopped reading aloud. He coyly skipped to the end of the page.

> you know that most dwarves are double-jointed? Well take it from me, it's true! As for whether his bits were – ahem – 'in proportion' to his size, well it was too dark to draw a picture, but they certainly didn't feel small!
>
> He might have been small, but what he didn't have in stature he certainly made up for in stamina! I was starting to wonder if he wasn't a midget at all, just a normal-sized person who'd worn himself down to a frazzle with sexual athletics!
>
> I was so exhausted that I fell asleep, and when I woke up, I was alone. Not that I'm saying that Smurf was a 'love 'em and leave 'em' type. I guessed he'd gone back to work, filming the final scenes of season two in his robot monster costume. I'd already finished filming for the day, giving my all as the cruelly betrayed Arkadia that morning (darling, I was marvellous!)
>
> So I just lay there on the back seat, allowing my undercarriage to cool off, watching the world go by through the grille in the front, hoping to catch another glimpse of Smurfy.
>
> I must have slept for hours, because they'd finished filming for the day. And who would come back into the props room but Mervyn Stone? The lovely and talented script editor of VFTV. He was lugging stuff around because most of the lazy lot who worked at the BBC hadn't turned up for work that day (typical unionised types – don't want anyone else to do their jobs, but don't want to do it themselves), and the sight of a sweating and cursing Mervyn zipping in and out, grappling with boxes and bags, his lovely little bottom disappearing and reappearing like Tinkerbell's light – I can tell you, the old undercarriage was getting ready to be lowered again!
>
> I must tell you at this point that Mervyn and I have a bit of a history. You know the old showbiz joke, the one about the actress who was so stupid she slept with the writer? Well guess which stupid actress did exactly that! And let me tell you, I didn't feel stupid at all! It's true, though; bedding a writer is hardly a great career move, but at that time of my career I was so successful I could actually pick my bedfellows based on their parts, not on their ability to GET me parts! Those desperate days (see chapters 3 - 10) were long, long past, let me tell you!
>
> I was aching to grab him and drag him into my makeshift

boudoir, but he was never on his own. Nicholas was sitting there, dismantling a Styrax and packing away props in huge cases the whole time, while Mervyn zipped in and out carrying ray guns and bits of the set – and then soon enough they were both finished, and left. I was alone and

'Are you going to sit there and read all of it out loud?'

'Don't you want to read it?'

'Read it, yes. Listen to you read it, no.'

'I've read my copy three times already. It gives you a real insight into the chaos that the production team was going through. It's just mad. When we did our fan videos it was nothing like this. The producer and the script editor didn't have to lug boxes around.'

'Well, we shouldn't have either. If anyone saw me touching a prop they would have gone on strike. Thank God Vanity didn't mention it at the time.'

'All in all,' Stuart said smugly, 'our production was much more professional and efficient, and was all the better for it.'

Mervyn gave a long-suffering grunt. He'd already tuned him out.

Stuart had turned up ten minutes ago, breezing into Mervyn's room after being semi-invited in (meaning that Mervyn had opened the door to his knock and didn't immediately slam it in his face). Mervyn felt quite uncomfortable in Stuart's presence – not least because Mervyn had leapt into the shower to wash the smell of smoke out of his hair and skin and was wandering around self-consciously in a dressing gown, gathering up his clothes so he could get dressed in the bathroom.

There was another reason for his discomfort: Stuart had turned up in his *Vixens* costume. Mervyn could only guess what the room service might think if she wandered in to find a half-naked middle-aged man entertaining a young transvestite.

Stuart had started talking about Simon, listing possible suspects, but soon got on to his favourite topic of 'restoring' episodes until they were 'better than the original'. He even brought his laptop to show Mervyn some more computer-generated effects dropped unsubtly into the middle of old *Vixens* episodes.

Mervyn was surprisingly relieved. He didn't want to talk with Stuart about Simon's murder. Despite the young man's enthusiasm, and the fact he was a sort of police officer, Mervyn didn't feel right discussing it with him. He hadn't shared with Stuart anything about what happened in Simon Josh's hotel room; Bernard and Nicholas's break-in, the crude suicide note he'd found, or the fire in the litter bin. Thankfully, Stuart was now occupying himself reading Vanity's book.

'I can't believe she did all those naughty things in the Styrax with a dwarf.'

'That's Vanity for you.'

'It's just not right,' mumbled Stuart. 'Think of the damage she might have caused.'

'Oh, dwarves are sturdy little chaps...'

Stuart missed the joke completely. 'I *meant* to the Styrax. It's very irresponsible! I mean to say, you were there on the final recording day, filming the final scenes of the final explosive episode of series two when the Styrax took over the planet Vixos! She could have broken a bit off and ruined the season climax.'

'Not the most well-chosen of phrases, Stuart.'

'Nothing like that happened on the set of my fan videos. When we did ours no one had sex inside the props.'

'I'm glad to hear it.'

'This book is dynamite.' Stuart flicked to the inside front cover. His face fell.

'Oh. It's not signed. Why didn't you get it signed when you bought it?'

'I didn't buy it!'

'Oh, she gave you a complimentary copy.'

'No. That's the strange thing. It was just left outside my door in that jiffy bag. Vanity said it wasn't from her.'

'Was there a note?'

Mervyn allowed a look of dumb surprise to wander on to his face. 'Do you know, I didn't look. I was more worried about what she'd written about me.'

Stuart picked up the envelope and slipped a hand inside. 'There's something in here, it's a compliment slip I think, or... Oh.'

'What?'

Stuart pulled out an A4 sheet of paper. He unfolded it slowly and placed it on the desk. It was a photocopy of a newspaper which covered most of the page; a jagged and faded clipping from *The Daily Mail*. Bits of it were so denuded that the photocopying process had left blank fuzzy spaces on the page. Peering at it closely, Mervyn could just make out the date. It was from 1986. He could clearly read an excitable profile of the Duke and Duchess of York's wedding, alongside a picture of Prince Andrew and Sarah Ferguson displaying large shiny eyes and huge toothy smiles, like a pair of straw hat-wearing donkeys on a picture postcard.

But that wasn't all. Written across the newspaper, in fat marker-pen scrawl, was:

376 – 229 – 22
HANDS OFF – GINGER!
SAFE

Mervyn eyed it suspiciously, like he would a first-draft script from Andrew Jamieson.

The silence got too much for Stuart. 'Does it mean anything to you?'

'Nothing. Not a thing.' Mervyn examined it close up, turned it upside down, and finally held it up to the light. '"HANDS OFF – GINGER!" Who's "Ginger"?' Sarah Ferguson – she's got red hair...'

Stuart leapt up behind Mervyn and pointed over his shoulder, causing Mervyn to flinch involuntarily.

'Well... Have you got any connections with the royal family at all?'

'There was that one-night stand with Princess Margaret, but I don't like to talk about it.'

'You're being sarcastic, aren't you?'

'No. Not in the slightest.'

'Wow. Seriously?'

'No. I *was* being sarcastic. You see, when I said I wasn't being sarcastic just then? I was being sarcastic.'

'Okay... Well... Have you at least *met* any of the royal family, then?'

'No. Oh... yes. Well, sort of. I did fleetingly meet Prince Edward once. At a *Children in Need* bash at the BBC. The year the *Vixens from the Void* cast danced the Time Warp, from *The Rocky Horror Show...*'

Mervyn stared at the paper again, concentrating on the words, rather than the background. 'Simon Josh had ginger hair. Perhaps "HANDS OFF – GINGER!" was a warning to him?' Simon's face swam unbidden into Mervyn's head. The smug expression, the silly glasses, and most vividly, the huge tangle of bright red hair.

Stuart looked doubtful. 'What about the numbers?'

'A safe combination? It says SAFE. But safe numbers are normally one or two digits aren't they? These seem too big.' Mervyn shrugged. 'I still don't know why it was sent to me, though. And what's it got to do with Vanity's autobiography?' Mervyn turned the sheet over. On the other side was a tidy message in courier font.

Hello Mervyn.

Sometimes the memory cheats... I think Vanity's book has thrown all sorts of interesting things up, don't you agree? You know what they say... Can't keep anything from us fans! I think we should have a little meet-up; discuss terms for your NEXT appearance at one of my conventions. I'm sure you'll agree, and I'm thinking that perhaps you should accept a more reasonable fee next time. Hope that's okay.

See me? 8.30pm, room 1024.

Your obedient servant.
S. Josh.

'Oh my God. I don't believe it!'

Stuart snatched the paper from him and read it. He looked as stunned as Mervyn.

'Simon Josh is blackmailing you... from beyond the grave!'

CHAPTER TWENTY-SEVEN

'So do you have any idea how he was going to try to blackmail you?' whispered Stuart.

Mervyn and Stuart were exploring the venue Simon had suggested for his 'little meet-up' with Mervyn. But there was nothing interesting about room 1024. It was just another conference lounge, like the room they'd signed autographs in that morning. Bare walls. Carpet tiles. Spindly chairs. Fiendish blinds on the windows.

Their search was made difficult because it was in pitch darkness. In its other, more fantastical life, the room was 'The Catacombs of Herath', and it played host to video screenings of *Vixens* episodes throughout the day. It was usually the darkest, smelliest part of the convention. And this year was no exception.

'No idea.'

'Oh, you *must* have some idea!'

'Shhh!' A lump of something vaguely fan-shaped glared at them and put a finger to its mouth.

'I've done many things in life I'm ashamed about Stuart,' Mervyn whispered. 'As no doubt you and the other fans are aware. I'm sure they're all listed on a website somewhere.'

Stuart leapt to his feet. 'Right, let's go and see.'

'No, Stuart! The point I'm making is I've done lots of embarrassing things, but nothing that's so shameful I'd be willing to get blackmailed over it.'

'That time you got arrested for smashing that restaurant window?'

'Stuart...'

'Or the time that actress – Shelley Bolan – cited you in her divorce?'

'Stuart!'

'Shhh!' The lumpy fan made another noise, like he or she was slowly deflating.

Mervyn lowered his voice. 'They're not secret are they? How could he blackmail me with them if they're not secret?'

'Point taken.'

Mervyn got onto his knees and started peering under the chairs. 'Oh my God!'

'Shhh!' More *Vixens* fans raised their fingers like weapons and fastened them to their lips.

'What? What is it? What?'

'If the other chairs are like this one I could open a second-hand chewing gum shop.'

Stuart helped with the search, but there wasn't anywhere to look;

no drawers or cabinets or cupboards. They moved around, brushing their fingers along window sills and skirting boards and raising their feet in an exaggerated fashion to make sure they weren't standing on evidence. They looked more like mime-artists practising a moon walk than amateur sleuths conducting a search. Once or twice they moved in front of the screen, to cries of anguish from the dimly lit figures on the chairs.

Mervyn crawled under a table, only to find Stuart had crawled in from the other end. He was trapped.

'So what made you suspect foul play?'

'What?' Mervyn was getting a little tired of this Scrappy Doo made flesh.

'Simon's death. What made you first suspect? It wasn't the purple face was it?'

'No it wasn't the purple face.'

'So what made you suspect?'

Mervyn had no intention of telling Stuart about the second suicide note. He groped for a story. Any story that sounded plausible. 'Well... It was the oily rag the murderer used to stuff the pipe in the window of the Styrax.'

'What about it?'

'It was bone-dry.'

'What?'

'It was dry. Everything else was wet; the ground, the Styrax, the inside of the grille, even Simon Josh's hair and shoes. But the rag was dry.' Mervyn was warming to his theme; he realised the rag *was* dry. His 'story' sounded terribly plausible. Had it been tucked away in his subconscious and he hadn't realised?

He continued: 'If Simon was prepared to kill himself and then got in the car, the rag would have been wet too. The only way Simon could have done it himself was to sit in the car, wait until the rain stopped, leave the car, get the dry rag out, put it around the hose and then gas himself. But what man in that state of mind waits for the rain to stop to kill himself?'

Stuart's mouth fell open.

'A more likely explanation is that Simon got into that Styrax when it was raining, dead drunk, and someone else came along later, after the rain had stopped, and wedged that pipe into the grille with the rag.'

Stuart looked at him, mouth open still. Respect had given away to amazement.

'Wow... you *are* good!' he said loudly.

'Shhh!'

Despite himself, Mervyn smiled in the darkness.

Mervyn crept out and made to leave, but the glowing screen in front of them transfixed Stuart. The episode 'Wings of the Warlock' was coming to an exciting bit.

'Just look at that,' he tutted. 'Look at those giant bats. You can see the wires on them. They're not very lifelike'

'Well... What did you expect?'

'Just something better, really. The technology of the time was perfectly capable of doing computer-generated bats, you know.'

'Stuart, that stuff was way, way beyond our budget. That was strictly the privilege of Hollywood sci-fi movies.'

'No it wasn't!' he said loudly. '*Star Trek Next Gen* did it! They weren't a movie! Not then!'

'SHHHH!'

This time the noise came from everywhere in the gloom.

'Come on,' said Mervyn. 'Let's continue this fascinating conversation outside.'

They crept out of the Catacombs of Herath, leaving the creatures inside to munch on crisps and drink alcohol in a way that was almost – but not quite – lifelike.

They emerged into the light. Mervyn took in lungfuls of fresh air.

'You should have a look at my version of "Wings of the Warlock". Two years ago I removed all the wires from the giant bats. Then I removed the giant bats, and put in my ones instead. Then I removed the catacombs because it looked just like bits of scenery and put in my versions. Then I –'

'I get the idea, Stuart.'

'So what shall we investigate next? Let's try and work out what those numbers mean.'

'Actually Stuart, I think it's best if we split up and investigate separately.'

'Oh.' Stuart looked hurt.

'Yes, we can both pursue separate lines of inquiry and we can both meet up...' *Don't be too specific.* '... at some point... and then we can pool our information.'

'Oh.'

'You'll be far better doing your own investigation without me getting in your way.

Stuart walked sadly to the door, then he turned. 'Are you being sarcastic?'

'No.'

There was a long, agonising silence. Stuart stared, aghast, at nothing in particular, and turned his sad eyes to Mervyn. 'Were you being sarcastic just then, when you said "no"?'

'No.'

'Oh.'

'And I think if you're going to investigate, you should lose the costume. Detectives need to be slightly more inconspicuous.'

'Oh. You think it's too –'

'Yes.'

From the look on Stuart's face, it was obvious that he wished Mervyn was being sarcastic. 'Okay. I'll get changed. See you later?'

He disappeared miserably into the corridor. Mervyn watched him go, feeling like he'd just drowned the Andrex puppy in a toilet.

No time for guilt. He had several lines of inquiry to pursue.

He looked at his schedule. It was five to three. Someone was just finishing their second 'How to Blow Up Everyday Objects' workshop of the day.

CONVIX 15.
EARTH ORBIT TWO:

3.00pm

EVENT	*LOCATION*
MY TIME AS A FORCEFIELD TECHNICIAN Katherine Warner	Vixos Central Nerve Centre (main stage, ballroom)
'KNIGHTS OF THE LONG KNIVES' **EPISODE SCREENING**	The Catacombs of Herath (video lounge - room 1024)
AUTOGRAPH PANEL VANITY MYCROFT	Arkadia's Boudoir (room 1013)
HOW TO WRITE VIXENS ANDREW JAMIESON	Hyperion Bridge (room 1010)
PHOTOS JOSEPH McANDREW TIM WARNE BRYCE CAMPION RICK AMORY	Transpodule Chamber (room 1030)
NEW VOIDS - ROLE-PLAYING GAMES **EXPERT PANEL** with Graham Goldingay, Fay Lawless, Craig Jones, Darren Cardew	The Seventh Moon of Groolia (room 1002)

CHAPTER TWENTY-EIGHT

'You! What do you think you're doing here?'

'I just wanted to talk to you.'

'Don't come any closer, you bastard! I'm not afraid to use this!'

'That's a washing-up liquid bottle, Bernard.'

'It's full of vinegar and bicarbonate of soda. I shake this baby... and we go up together!'

The stewards panicked and rushed to disarm him. He watched helplessly as they took his washing-up liquid bottle away, his lip poking out petulantly.

'I want that back, you know,' he called after them.

'I want to talk to you,' said Mervyn.

'Well Mervyn, I don't want to talk to you. Funny, that.'

'Look, talk to me, and I won't press charges.'

'What charges?'

Mervyn was taken aback. Had he forgotten already? 'When you punched me? When you knocked me off the stage and left me with a bruise the shape of New Zealand on my cheek, and one the shape of Australia on my bottom?'

Bernard blinked. He'd been feeling so self-righteous after he'd punched Mervyn, it hadn't occurred to him that he could get into trouble for it. 'Oh. You don't want to press charges?'

'No. I just want to talk about why you sold the big Styrax to Simon.'

Bernard started packing his equipment away. 'I don't want to talk about it. Especially not to *you*, of all people.'

'"*Me*, of all people"? What does that mean?'

'Work it out.'

'So, it was about you stealing.'

Bernard stopped, muttered 'fuck' under his breath, and carried on throwing his equipment into a box.

'Should you really chuck gunpowder around like that?'

'It's not gunpowder,' he muttered. 'It's coffee. Mix it with sweetener, light it with a Bunsen burner and you get a flame-thrower.'

'Oh.' Another awkward silence.

'Bernard, talk to me! This is more important than some old grudge.'

He continued to ignore Mervyn.

'Fine. There's a policeman somewhere in this convention. I suppose I'd better find him and talk about filing an assault charge against you.'

'Yes, of course you bloody would. You just get what you want and you don't care how you get it. More blackmail. You're no better than Simon.'

'Right. We've got somewhere. It's about you stealing, and Simon blackmailing you.'

Bernard muttered 'fuck' under his breath again; he finished packing his box and then sighed. 'All right, if you must know, he was blackmailing me... thanks to you!'

'Me?'

'You, you arsehole!'

'Why is it my fault?'

Bernard sighed. 'Because he found out I stole the Styrax I sold him.'

'The one I crushed?'

'Yeah.'

'When did he find that out?'

'When you crushed it.'

'Oh.'

'Yeah. Oh.'

Mervyn could have made the point that when he had crushed the Styrax he had been propelled in its direction by Bernard, but he resisted. At least Bernard was talking. 'How did he work it out?'

'Bloody fans! They know everything, don't they? There was something written on the inside of the Styrax that *he* said gave him concrete proof that it was the Styrax we'd used for the end of series two, the final day's filming on "Day of the Styrax".'

'The one that got... "mislaid".'

'Yeah,' spat Bernard. 'That one. I was owed something, Mervyn! You got yours, oh yes, you made sure of that! I just wanted mine!'

'If you choose to work on staff, then those are the breaks,' Mervyn snapped, weary of saying it for the umpteenth time. 'You gain security and you forgo intellectual copyright. Do you think I've not been in jobs where I've signed away my royalties for a salary?'

'I made that stuff with my own hands! A lot of it was just going to get thrown into a bin anyway!'

'And a lot of it wasn't!'

'Okay, I was wrong! All right? I admit it. Wrong, wrong, wrong! I stole stuff. I was wrong and I lost my job. I paid for what I did! I paid for it and I deserve to have it forgotten. But these bloody fans don't, do they? They don't forget a bloody thing! I do not deserve to have the whole pile of crap dug up and placed on my head again after all these years!'

'So what? Simon was...'

'He was threatening to sue me for it, or have me arrested for passing on stolen goods. He hadn't decided. But he wouldn't do either if I...'

'Oh, of course.'

'You guessed it. The sod wanted my bloody Styrax Superior. He's *always* wanted it.'

Mervyn allowed the air to escape from his lungs. He was almost starting to admire Simon for his sheer ruthless chutzpah. He had been quite an operator. A Styrax operator. He smiled at the thought.

'What are you smiling at?' snarled Bernard.

'Nothing.'

'Oh yes you are. You're smiling. You're laughing at me. I know what you're thinking. "Why didn't old Bernard check the inside of his Styrax for writing that might incriminate him? Hmmm. Oh yes, that's right. Poor old Bernard can't read very well! Oh har, har, har! How ironic!" Well fuck you, Mervyn!'

'Simon had evidence that you stole the Styrax? Is that why you broke into Simon's room?' A thought struck Mervyn. He'd completely forgotten what happened in Simon's room after they left. 'Is that why you burnt the bits of the Styrax in the bin?'

Bernard stared at Mervyn. It was the wrong time to ask that question. 'You've been spying on me, haven't you?'

'No I haven't!'

'Yes you have, you've been spying on me! You're investigating me again! Can't you just leave me alone, you bastard?'

'Gentlemen...' Nicholas was standing in the doorway, one hand on his lapel, the other tucked into his waistcoat. '... There is a crowd of people out there waiting to hear Andrew Jamieson talk about how to write for *Vixens from the Void* in this room. Naturally, he's late...' The former producer strolled in, patting Mervyn on the back. 'Of course, thanks to you and your raised voices, my old loves, the crowd has grown even larger. An even greater number of people are now waiting to hear Andrew's Jamieson's guide to being a writer. I hope you both can live with the guilt.'

Nicholas had defused the situation. Thank heavens.

Bernard glared back at Mervyn, tucked his box under his arm and blundered to the door. 'I'm done here. Leave me alone.' Then he was gone. Mervyn could hear him snapping sulkily at the fans waiting outside the door. 'Careful!' he shouted. 'I'm carrying everyday objects! I might explode at any moment!'

Nicholas now rested his hand on Mervyn's shoulder. 'Come on, my old love,' he said gently. 'Let's have a bite. Hotel restaurant?'

'Have we any choice?'

'None.'

'Hotel restaurant it is, then.'

CHAPTER TWENTY-NINE

The restaurant of the Happy Traveller wasn't bad. It had an unpretentious menu of steak meals and fish dishes, all served up with steamed vegetables and/or curly French fries, neatly divided into tiny bowls. Mervyn could see why they liked having conventions here; the menu seemed to cater for those with a touch of autism. It was quite quiet too; there was only one other table occupied by a few fans, well-behaved enough to be satisfied with a few perfunctory nods and smiles from him.

In years past, it had been customary for Nicholas and Mervyn to dine together at least once every convention – a chance to pull up the drawbridge for an hour and isolate themselves from the madness swirling around them. Mervyn instantly relaxed.

Nicholas offered him an insanely generous glass of what was described in the wine list as 'The Traveller's Tipple', but more closely resembled 'The Motorist's Mouthwash'. Mervyn declined, electing instead to gulp down pints of iced water to quieten the roaring in his throat caused by smoke inhalation.

'Good God, Mervy! I know I've just offered you a glass of the most execrable hotel red; a combination of Vimto and sulphuric acid which would shame a motorway service station, but there's no need to start drinking *water*! Has the world gone mad?' Nicholas suddenly looked perturbed. He drummed his fingers on the table, and cleared his throat. 'Mervyn old love, I hate to break this lovely ambience of cut-price conviviality, but I do need to say something that might shock you...'

Mervyn looked expectantly at Nicholas. *Here we go. He's going to tell me Bernard murdered Simon.*

'There's someone hiding in the plastic aspidistra behind us.'

Mervyn looked over. A couple of leaves parted.

'Hello,' Nicholas said, 'Dr Livingstone, I presume?'

A young man looked at Mervyn through the undergrowth. He held a finger to his lips, begging for anonymity. Mervyn had no intention of playing along.

'Stuart!'

Stuart stood up reluctantly, and Nicholas saw the strapping young man clearly for the first time. The former producer straightened up and gave a winning smile, unconsciously mirroring Vanity's behaviour. 'Goodness me, are you the hotel gardener? Can I be your Lady Chatterley?'

'Excuse me a minute, Nicholas. Sorry about this.' Mervyn escorted Stuart out of the restaurant.

'Have you deduced the murderer yet?'

'No. Go away.'

'But I've changed out of my costume.'

'It doesn't matter. We're still investigating separately.'

'Are you interrogating Nicholas Everett?'

'No I'm having a late lunch.'

'Oh.'

'Go away Stuart. Go away and conduct your own investigations, and allow me to pursue mine.'

'Oh. You are questioning him? Subtly?'

'If you like.'

'Okay! See you later, Mr St– Mervyn.' And Stuart bounded happily away.

Mervyn returned to the table where Nicholas beamed at him.

'Sorry about that. Never start a conversation with a fan. You suddenly become their best friend.'

'Don't worry about it, petal. The worst thing about these wretched conventions is they always manage to find a hotel in the middle of bloody nowhere. No little bistros down the road, no rustic country pubs to escape the masses. There's nowhere to go. You're a prisoner for three days, at the mercy of these buggers.'

Mervyn nodded, wearily.

Nicholas's eyebrows knitted together. 'Do I know that young man? Oh yes! He took an autograph off me, and then proceeded to tell me where exactly I'd gone wrong with the making of our little show.'

'That sounds like Stuart.'

'He said we shouldn't have used colour separation overlay for the spaceship shots in part two of "Assassins of Destiny", because it didn't match up with the other model spaceships we had in part one.'

'You did explain there were two different directors for the episodes, one of whom was Guy Hollis, who gave a shit, and the other being Ken Roche, who didn't?'

'I tried, old love, I really tried. But he told me I should have used one director for the whole story, that doing it like that was a bit ropey and a bit sloppy. I could have debated with him for hours about the pressures we were under, but I have a life.'

'Did he show you his "remade" versions that were much better?'

'He attempted to, petal, but I faked an attack of the vapours and got three stewards to carry me out.' He looked at Mervyn. 'So talking of being at the mercy of these bloody fans... I heard you and Mr Viner talking about Simon and his nasty blackmailing ways. Well more shouting than talking. Could hardly miss it, old love.'

'He told me you were helping him cover up the evidence. Burning the bits of Styrax.'

'Guilty as charged. Yes I was.'

'Thank you Nicholas. I appreciate your honesty.'

'Well darling, I'm sure you would have done the same. Simon was not a very nice man, and it didn't seem fair on poor old Bernard.'

'It was very philanthropic of you.'

'As I've said to you before, Mervy, Bernard isn't a bad person. He's just been dealt a dud set of cards. Also, Bernard is not an ace in the literacy stakes, as you know, so I was helping him retrieve the documents for the Styrax Superior, and having a quick sift through the papers for any incriminating evidence. It saved some time for the poor bugger.'

'Evidence of Simon's blackmail, and evidence that Bernard sold him a stolen Styrax.'

'Quite.'

'Evidence for anything else?'

'My dear old love. What else could there be?'

'You know what I mean.'

'My mind's a blank, Mervy. Enlighten me.'

'Simon's dead, Nicholas. His death seems awfully convenient.'

Nicholas put down his glass and stared at Mervyn over his spectacles. 'Mr Stone... Are you, perchance... sleuthing again?'

Mervyn didn't say.

'How super! Am I a suspect?'

'Now why would you say that?'

'Come on, Merv. Share your suspicions.'

'Well, possibly...'

'Well, possibly? That's not the detective way, Mervyn! You forget, I did produce a few Aggie Christie adaptations for the stage, so I do know the drill. You must stand up now and point a quivering finger at my startled face and shout "J'accuse"!' Nicholas lunged across the table, pushing cutlery on to the floor. He grabbed Mervyn's arm and clutched his own chest. 'Grill me in the Happy Traveller grill, sir!' he cried, oozing histrionics. 'Rake me over the coals like the tupenny-ha'penny lowlife I am! Tell me why I should have murdered this fiendish fan!'

'Well...' croaked Mervyn lamely. The other diners were turning around to look at them. Irritated glares raked Mervyn like searchlights. He was so embarrassed, he felt like joining the pieces of cutlery under the table. Mervyn's brain scrambled for a reason. 'Well... well...'

'Come on Inspector! Spit it out!'

'I... I was just thinking back to how cross you were about Bernard selling the Styrax to Simon. I just thought that might have been very irritating... How it ruined that tour of *Vixens* exhibits you were planning.'

'Me sir?' squeaked Nicholas, affecting an outrageous cockney urchin accent. 'Me kill someone fer that? Just cos someone sells somefink that don't belong to me? I mean, I'd likes to 'ave it in me exhibition, so help me, squire, but strap me, guv, could you see me doin' away wiv a bloke cos of one mouldy exhibit in a tour of the 'ome counties? Bit of a long shot, ain't it sir? Hardly worth risking a life in clink, ain't it? So help me! Gor blimey guv, I never heard the –'

'Nick! Please! No more of the accent! I beg you!'

Nicholas reverted to his normal voice. 'Unfortunately, what you haven't factored into your investigations, old love, is that this little event wasn't even going to go out in my name. I was selling the business. To Simon, would you believe?'

'Simon?'

'Yes, even he.'

'But how could he –'

'Oh, he was able to afford it. The autograph-and-whiskery-anecdote business might be dying on the vine, but his personal fortune from his corporate training stuff was quite handsome. Unlike him. There is no limit to the amount of money businesses are willing to spend on training their staff to say "please" and "thank you".' Nicholas swirled the wine in his glass and tapped his nose. 'So you see, old duck, it was in my best interests to keep him alive. In my mind, Josh meant dosh.'

'So you were going to sell up? What were you going to do? Retire?'

'Lawks no. Back to my first love, love. I've got a post as a part-time radio producer, which I start next month.'

'So with Simon gone, your plans to sell have all gone a bit pear-shaped.'

'More aubergine-shaped. The sale has merely been postponed. I'm sure there will be plenty of people with deep pockets willing to buy up the company, it's a nice little going concern.'

He went back to studying the dessert menu. 'Black Forest Gateau... Now will they dig out a fresh one...' he nodded at the sweet trolley. '... or will they liberate the one that's been slowly dehydrating in its glass prison since the morning? I'll take a chance...'

Nicholas smiled at Mervyn with deep and genuine affection, and Mervyn felt profoundly idiotic.

'Can I give you some advice, sweetie?'

'Of course you can. I've always respected your opinion.'

'You've gone native, dear. You're thinking like a fan. Do you seriously believe anyone here will commit murder over an old Styrax? Look at me Mervy. Would I? Really? For a tour of props meandering around the home counties? Would Bernard? Really commit cold-blooded murder to prevent Simon calling the police and shopping him for selling stolen goods? Does that make any kind of sense?'

'If you put it like that, then no.'

'Who on earth would kill over a mouldy old prop?'

'No one but an obsessive fan,' said Mervyn gloomily, 'and the only one sufficiently obsessive to do that is currently lying on a slab somewhere with a bright purple face.'

'Exactly. There are others with very good motives to kill Simon. Forget about Styrax.'

'All right, what other motives are there, to want Simon dead?'

'Mervyn, you don't have all the facts.'

'That's definitely true.'

'What you don't realise is the extent of Simon's blackmailing ways.'

Mervyn looked wide-eyed at Nicholas. 'You mean... you too?'

'Oh not me. Any skeletons got goosed out of my closet years ago.'

'Then who else?'

'You've noticed Roddy Burgess acting oddly, I take it?'

'Oh yes!'

'I'm sure Simon had something on Roddy. But I'm sure old Roddy's harmless; just like Bernard. But not everyone takes being blackmailed lying down, so to speak...'

'Meaning?'

Nicholas leaned back and pitched his face to the ceiling. His waistcoat bulged, threatening to decapitate the shiny buttons running down his front. Meshing his fingers together, he rested his hands on his stomach and his cufflinks clinked together as if they were proposing a tiny toast. 'Did you know that Simon received death threats?'

'From whom?'

'I'm probably not the best person to tell you this. You'd better ask Vanity.'

'What! Vanity sent him death threats?'

'I think you'd better talk to her.'

CHAPTER THIRTY

Mervyn advanced along the corridor to Vanity's room, mentally preparing himself.

Even though he was a detective of the strictly amateur kind, he was still investigating a murder. He was determined not to get sidetracked by any of the patented Mycroft distraction techniques; all that eyelash-fluttering, crotch-tickling and sexual-intercourse-having that managed to exploit his congenital weakness (a congenital weakness in which, ironically, his genitals featured prominently).

Why did Vanity rush to provide me with an alibi this morning? She jumped very quickly to the conclusion that Simon was murdered, and that I was being arrested for it. Almost too quickly. Did she feel guilty about the idea of me being arrested for a crime that she had committed?

Knock knockity-knock.

There was a pause, a scuffling and then a click.

'It's open!'

Mervyn pushed open Vanity's door.

The first thing that hit him was the mess.

The second thing that hit him was a bra. It hung around his neck like a fat black vampire bat.

The diva of the convention circuit was pulling clothes out of the wardrobe and hurling them around the room. Mervyn realised she was attempting to aim them in the general direction of a furry suitcase made from the skin of some near-extinct animal.

Something else landed on him. A pair of stockings rested on his face, and gave him a huge drooping moustache.

'You're in my line of fire, Merv. Unless you want to walk out of here a transvestite I suggest you move from the target area.'

'What are you doing?'

'Going, darling. On my toes. Upping sticks. Showing a clean pair of heels. Over the hills and far away.'

'You're leaving?'

'Darling! Does it show?'

Mervyn stood there, watching bemusedly as the suitcase slowly filled up with frilly things, lacy things, little leather things held together with shoelace and elastic.

'But... You can't.'

'Just watch me darling. You'll be surprised how quickly this pert little tush can move. I could leave a Vanity-shaped hole in that wall if I wanted to.'

'But what about your fans?'

'Bollocks to them. It'll be so much easier on them and me if I retire quietly and become some dowdy little spinster who crochets mittens.'

'But... Don't you enjoy being here...?

Vanity pierced him with a stare. 'I did once, but as the decades start to fly by it begins to lose its lustre.' She gestured around the anonymous hotel room, at the plastic kettle garlanded with sachets of coffee and milk, the mute television, the desk with the 'Welcome all Happy Travellers!' note still on it. 'Is this my life, darling?' she said. 'Cash handed to me in envelopes? Travelling from one shitty hotel room to another? There's a word for girls who live like that, and I'm tired of realising how much it applies to me.'

She resumed the hurling of unmentionables about the room. Mervyn decided to jump in with both feet.

'Is this anything to with Simon's death?'

Vanity stopped mid-hurl. 'You think I'm upset about that little ball of snot? Hardly. I've stepped over better corpses than him in my line of work. Running away blubbing because an odious little man gasses himself just isn't me, darling.'

'That's not what I meant.'

Vanity rested her hand on her hip. It was obvious she was waiting to see what he did mean.

'I know Simon was odious,' muttered Mervyn. 'I've also heard that Simon was very good at being odious in a... particular way. And he was odious to you. In that... particular way.'

'Ah. I see.'

Vanity stretched wearily on the bed, breasts straining against her insanely tight sweater, eyes and nipples staring vacantly up at the ceiling. Then she sat up, cross-legged, and plunged her face in her hands. There was an 'Oh God', squeezed out from behind her fingers. Finally, she allowed her face to resurface, wiping it with the back of her hand, dragging it across her cheek. He was surprised to see genuine tears glinting in the corners of her eyes. 'Yes. He was blackmailing me, darling...'

Vanity stared defiantly at him. She'd smudged her make-up, but had managed to do even that artfully. The lines of lipstick and mascara careered crazily across her cheek, like the tangled skid-marks of tyres feeding into a motorway pile-up.

'... But I didn't kill him, if that's what you're thinking. Oh God, I've wanted to wring the little shit's neck a few times, I don't mind admitting it.' She groped for her packet of cigarettes on the bedside table.

'I don't understand. How can he have any hold over you?'

Lighter. Drag. Exhale. Smoke.

'You mean I'm not the kind to keep skeletons in the cupboard? That's true.' She sighed. 'It wasn't me I was worried about. Well, not just me. It was my daughter.'

'Your...?'

'Daughter. Yes. You must have seen her darling. In the autograph hall?'

'Oh yes, I think so.' The thin-faced girl with the cardigan. The one who followed Vanity around. It all made sense now. 'I don't think I would have recognised her. You did show me a photo of her a while ago – a cute little toddler with a flower in her hair?'

'She's 19 now.'

'Gosh. 19... 19, eh? 19. You must have had her, well... 19? God. Certainly near the time we filmed the show.'

'Oh, Mervyn, you are so naïve. Why do you think I didn't return for series three?'

'Oh right. Oh. *Right*. I thought you were worried about typecasting.'

'Darling, that was my cover story! Actors leaving parts because they're worried about typecasting is a bigger myth than the Loch Ness monster! Surely all the years you've done telly you've realised that? No one leaves a part for "typecasting worries" unless they're some crazed bint from Sylvia Young whose daddy owns most of Norfolk.'

'So what about your daughter? What's the problem?'

Something appeared on Vanity's face that he'd never seen before. He realised it was embarrassment. 'I... never told my daughter from what circumstances she'd popped...'

'What circumstances were those?'

'Um... Have you had a chance to read my autobiography yet?'

'Only a bit of Chapter 13.'

'That's all you need to read.'

Mervyn's mouth opened and closed involuntarily. 'Ah.'

'Perhaps you'd better finish it.'

There were a good half-dozen copies of *Vixen to Fly* on the desk. She threw him one. He sat down on the bed, and dutifully read the rest of Chapter 13.

> As soon as they'd gone, I thought I'd be able to escape. Unfortunately, Bernard Viner came into the room.
>
> I'd never given him much thought before, because he wasn't much of a blip on the old Mycroft radar (I don't notice back-room boys unless they are pert and pretty and Bernard – well, Bernard just wasn't, take it from me). Bernard was the guy who made

all those bits and bobs on the set, he designed the monsters (probably got most of his inspiration looking in a mirror – rreow!). He also did the special effects – he was in charge of the on-set bangs and flashes (perhaps we had more in common than I realised!).

He took all the bits of the little Styrax out, one at a time; he took such a long time to load up his car! Then he came back, keys jangling in his hand. He was going to lock up the big Styrax – with me in it!

'Hoi! Stop!' I hollered, as I heard the keys turn in the lock.

He was very suspicious. Of course, he asked me what I was doing in there!

'I'm looking for my contact lens,' I said sweetly.

And he believed me. Of course you, dear reader, as my adoring fan, know I've got perfect vision, but he didn't know. He was completely fooled. Not much of a detective, not like my mate Mervyn Stone! (see Chapter 23).

Poor Bernard!

So I left the set with my dignity intact, and everyone packed everything away ready for the next season. But I couldn't stay on for the next season – for a very good reason! It was nine months after that fateful day that I heard the patter of tiny feet – and I don't mean having Smurf back for a rematch! I mean my darling daughter came into the world.

I won't deny it, I was worried in the weeks and months before she arrived – I did a bit of reading, and it turned out there was a 50% chance of my child developing dwarfism, or, as it's charmingly called in the books, achondroplasia, with all the bone, breathing and heart problems that go with it (I mean for God's sake, I wonder if these boffins realised how tactless they were being – giving a syndrome that affects short people such a long name?!).

Anyway, can you imagine what I was going through? The knowledge that your baby might not be 'normal'? I'm sure it's the worst ever agony for any woman. Certainly puts the odd leg wax and a few days of tummy ache every month into perspective, I can tell you. Not that I would have done anything about it! Oh dear lord, no. My miserable Catholic upbringing might be long gone, reduced to crossing myself before a doing a take and a residual fetish for dog collars, but there was nothing on heaven or earth that would have made me even think about getting rid of my little darling. Even so, the scan that told me everything was normal came as a blessed relief.

> I now have a fantastic daughter, who means everything to me, and it's to her I dedicate this book.

End of chapter. Mervyn closed the book.

'You see, I didn't tell her about any of that. When she was a little girl I spun her a romantic yarn about me being raped by a long-dead legend of the theatre during the Edinburgh Fringe.'

'I see.'

'You do?'

'This long-dead legend of the theatre being alive at the time, of course. Because you do hear stories about theatrical ghosts...'

Mervyn ducked as a shoe sailed past his head. 'Mervyn! It isn't easy for me to talk about this!'

'Sorry.' Leaving aside Vanity's idea of what constituted 'romantic', Mervyn pressed on. 'So you preferred not to tell her the truth? That's not like you.'

'Well, she was so young and starry-eyed. She reminded me of me when I was young.'

The mental image of the thin-faced girl in the cardigan swam into Mervyn's brain. He found it hard to imagine that Vanity could look at her and say 'Yes, I was once like that'.

Vanity continued. 'Anyway I left it at that. There never seemed to be the right time to say "By the way, darling, remember I told you that you were the product of me being ravished by a knight of the theatre when he was Malvolio to my Olivia? Actually I was being mauled by a midget in the back of a Mini Metro."' She sighed, and glided to the window.

It was obvious that being honest was not a condition Vanity was used to. Without a performance to sustain it, her face sagged. Little pouches of skin appeared on the sides of her mouth, and her upper lip puckered like an over-ripe tomato. If anything, the little signs of ageing and imperfections made her more attractive, not less.

'I see your problem. So Simon Josh knew and turned the screws? "Dazzle at my conventions or I spill the beans to little Miss Mycroft" – that kind of thing?'

'Exactly darling. That kind of thing. He didn't know exactly when it happened and who slammed the door on my bun-filled oven, but he knew for certain that I didn't get pregnant when I said it happened. And he made certain that I knew he knew. He was a worm, darling; but the thing about worms is they know how to dig. All those fans, they know so much and have so many ways of finding out – it's so difficult to keep things from them.'

'Oh yes. I know that.'

Vanity continued. 'He knew everything there was to know about the show, and he used that knowledge. He had all the trivia; names, locations, dates, stored in his head like a computer... He took an anecdote here, an off-the cuff remark there... He put them together, and suddenly he's ringing me up at *home*, darling, and I start getting offers I can't refuse. Oh, it's not blackmail in the strictest sense. Nothing the little bastard can be arrested for, it's more subtle and insidious than that...' She put her hand to her ear to represent a phone, and aped Simon's nasal voice. '"Vanity darling, I've got a little thing going on in Newcastle, and I wonder if I could trouble you..." Every damn convention and event I had to attend *for him*. And I was paid a bloody pittance. The little shit.' She blew air out of her cheeks. 'Anyway, that's all over now. I decided to end it.'

'How did you "end it"?'

Vanity looked surprised. 'That's what the autobiography's for, darling!'

'Your book? It seems a bit drastic, to tell your daughter in a book.'

Vanity's panda-eyes widened in disgust. 'What do you take me for, Mervy? The book was my ultimatum to myself. It was just to help me – to *force* me – to set the record straight. I told my darling girl *everything* before we came to this convention – *and* I told her about Simon and his little blackmail scheme.' She grinned savagely. 'After all my fears, you wouldn't believe how easy it was! I wish I'd done it years ago. My little girl wasn't bothered, in fact she was more angry on my behalf about the blackmail. She was all for caving Simon's head in with something sharp...'

Oh really?

'She was furious darling. Really. She's such a feisty girl. She sort of lost herself and sent Simon some very angry letters...'

Death threats.

'... But that's not important now. It's all over now, in the past.'

'And did you think to expose Simon's blackmail in the book?'

'The lawyers wouldn't allow it, darling. Anyway, Simon was very clever. As I said, it was all innuendo, all open to interpretation...'

Mervyn remembered the letter he'd got yesterday. Nothing in it was too obvious. The words could have been interpreted as a friendly 'hiya' and an opening for negotiations for the next convention fee. Very clever of him.

Vanity stood up, and her mask slid back on. 'Anyway. Regrets, I've had a few and all that...' She resumed stuffing her suitcase.

'Wait a minute... You can't go...'

'Why not, darling? I've thought very hard about it all morning – ever since I picked you up from the station. There's nothing to keep me here. I'm collecting my daughter, and I'm leaving.'

Mervyn was desperate. He had a new chief suspect, and she was being taken away by her mother. Right now. He had to do something.

'You can't go. What about me?' he heard a voice saying. He was shocked to find the voice was his.

'You, darling?' her face emerged from behind a pile of knickers.

'Yes. Ahm... It's a very big hotel in the middle of nowhere...'

She sashayed towards him. Mervyn found that he was being impaled against the wall by the points of her breasts.

'Look...' he said, 'there're no places to eat, no nice pubs around here. It would be unbearable to stay here without... Another friendly face.'

'Are you saying... that you would miss me, darling?' She started to absent-mindedly run her fingernail down his face, following the line of the bruise on his jaw. 'Are you saying you'll feel all lonesome without me here?'

Mervyn fastened a smile to his face. 'Now Vanity... darling... I don't even have to answer that, do I?'

'Well in that case... I think I might be... persuaded to stay...'

Mervyn's spirit wilted as he felt her arms encircle his waist. He was so damn tired. He'd been thrown off a stage, dragged to a police station, dragged back, trapped inside a Styrax, nearly burnt to death, forced to have sex twice in one night... And now...

Oh God.

The things he was prepared to do for this investigation...

CHAPTER THIRTY-ONE

There was a knock at the door.

The spell broken, Mervyn and Vanity stared at each other, dumbfounded.

There was another knock; louder, heavier.

'Oh my God!' Vanity hissed. 'It's my daughter! She can't find you in here!'

'What? Why not?'

'Think, darling! Think! She's already coming to terms with me putting out for a midget! I can't show her that the moment I arrive at a convention I start diving into bed with every Tom, Dick and Harry!'

'Thank you very much!'

'You know what I mean! She's got a temper on her that could stop a rhino! You have to hide!' She grabbed him by the scruff of the neck and forced him to the floor. 'Quick! Under the bed!'

Mervyn's head thudded against the bottom of the bed, and he howled in pain.

'Vanity! There's no gap under here! It's all bed!'

There was another knock. Very hard. It was very forceful – more an attempt to batter down the door.

That's her daughter?

'The wardrobe!'

She grabbed his collar, hauled him up and shoved him towards the wardrobe, opening the doors and pushing him in with one smooth movement. The doors slammed in his face, missing his large nose by millimetres.

Mervyn looked through the slats. Vanity had already composed herself, hair immaculate and ragged make-up removed. She was spreading a beatific smile of innocence across her face. It was beautifully done, he thought. A consummate performance. It seemed as though the years she'd spent appearing in grotty touring sex farces as her star power dwindled hadn't been wasted. She opened the door.

It wasn't her daughter.

'Why little man,' she trilled. 'To what do I owe the pleasure... again?'

Smurf pushed angrily past her and prowled across the room. He paced backwards and forwards feverishly, always with his eyes fixed on her, like a small yappy dog waiting for his owner to take him for a walk.

'Right. Let's have this out. Now.'

'Well *there's* an offer a lady can't refuse.'

'Oh shut up. You bloody know what I mean.'

Mervyn saw Vanity sit back on the bed, stretch her arm across the headboard and pose languidly. It wasn't just the hair and make-up that had been repaired. Gone was the emotionally damaged and rather vulnerable woman that just confessed her sins to Mervyn. She'd regrown her hard outer shell; her voice was once again the bored, affected drawl, the eyes now dry and flinty, mouth beautiful and full, ready to chew up and spit out anyone who inspired her displeasure.

'I want that libel out of your book. You're ruining my reputation.'

'Enhancing it, darling, enhancing it, surely. It's not as if I said you were rubbish...' The lighter flicked open again and another cigarette was produced. 'After all, you did very well in my league table in the appendix.'

'It's not true and you know it!'

He started pacing furiously again, this time next to the wardrobe. Mervyn could see his head bobbing back and forth. Now Smurf went purple. 'And your daughter's been following me about the convention again...'

'Our daughter, darling...'

'Stop it!'

'You can't blame her for trying to get to know her father, sweetheart...'

'*Stop it!*' Smurf was literally hopping up and down with rage. 'How can you lie to her like this? I've seen her watching me, looking daggers at me, all because of *you.* First thing this morning I opened the curtains, and who could I see out my window, staring up at me from the car park? I've been getting notes pushed under my door...

'She's upset her father is ignoring her, darling.'

'But... It's... Not... Bloody... TRUE!' Smurf clapped his hands to his head and howled. He looked like a cartoon character who'd failed to catch the canary and blown himself up into the bargain. If he had a hat, he would have thrown it to the floor and jumped on it. 'She's going to do something she's gonna regret, and it's gonna be your fault. It's freaking Katherine out. She and me, we were happy. We were getting along great until she got wind of what you'd put in your book.'

Vanity's head drooped to one side in mock-sympathy. 'Oh you poor darling. Can't she get over the fact you'd been with me first? That's a shame. I can understand how it must be upsetting for her. After all, once the understudy, always the understudy.'

'Don't say anything against her.'

'Of course, she was bound to end up with a midget. With her career, she's got to be used to small parts.'

He hurled a quivering finger in her direction. 'For the last time... I'm warning you... You'd better –'

Vanity had had enough. She stubbed her cigarette out, squishing it into a saucer with grim resolve. 'Better *what*, darling? What should I do? Rewrite my book? Stop it going out? Not possible, darling. Too late. The presses have rolled. There are a hundred thousand copies stashed in a grotty warehouse in Leavesden.' She looked condescendingly down at his angry face. 'So sue me! I'm hardly accusing you of rape or murder, darling, simply of being a jolly good shag and a fertile little munchkin. The publicity alone will generate enough extra sales to offset any costs...' She sashayed to the door and opened it. 'So if that's all... If you're a very lucky little boy I'll send you a free copy.'

'You don't know who you're messing with, you bitch. I'm going to get you – my way.'

'You're not going to bite my ankles are you, darling?'

'No, really, I'm serious. I'll sue. I'll take a DNA test and I'll sue. You do this to me, you'll be sorry. I sorted Sheldon out, and I'll do it to you.'

Mervyn almost fell through the wardrobe doors. *Sheldon? What did he just say about Sheldon?*

'Is that a threat?'

'Definitely. He crossed me. I got rid of him –'

Got rid of him?

'– and you'll be just as sorry. Remember what happened to Sheldon. That's your last warning, and don't you forget it.'

'Threats don't work on me darling. I've been threatened by aliens, robots and at least four ex-boyfriends; including an East-End gangster and a middleweight boxer. Empty threats from one of Santa's little elves aren't going to interrupt my beauty sleep.'

Smurf's feet pattered across the room. 'You'll be sorry. Just wait. Sheldon was sorry. You'll be too.'

Mervyn mind was spinning. Investigating one murder, had he just heard a confession to *another* one? One that everyone presumed was a tragic accident?

Is this what it's all about? he thought wildly. *Was Simon blackmailing Smurf too? About something he did in the past?*

'Why does it have to be *me*? – all the blokes you've – why do you have to *invent* shit like this? Why can't you just pull someone else out of your bloody closet? Someone like Mervyn, for example...' As he said this, he illustrated his point by gesturing towards the wardrobe; he pulled open the doors, revealing Mervyn sandwiched between two coats that Vanity had yet to pack.

Smurf stared at Mervyn, open-mouthed. 'Mervyn?'

Mervyn waved, feebly.

'Jesus Christ! Mervyn?'

Smurf slammed the wardrobe shut again and stormed out. The room shuddered as the door banged shut. The wardrobe doors were immediately flung open with the force.

'The coast is clear, darling...'

Mervyn expected to get yanked out by his lapels. Instead, Vanity slipped into the wardrobe and snuggled up to him.

'Well this is cosy... Mmm.' Mervyn felt something wet and slimy wriggle into his ear.

Mervyn wasn't in the mood. 'Vanity, what did he mean?'

'Mean what, dear?'

'What did he mean by "sorting out" Sheldon?'

'I don't know Mervy, I don't know what the nasty man was talking about, I'm not cwever wike you.' She was putting on her baby voice now; an ominous sign that sex was imminent.

'He must have meant something by it...'

'Who cares? He's like all little men – big temper, big talk, no action. He's harmless.'

Mervyn wasn't so sure. 'I have to go and talk to him.'

Mervyn tried to escape, but an arm lassoed his neck and dragged him back in. 'Not yet darling. You haven't persuaded me to stay yet...'

There was a sound; a 'harrumph' noise. Someone close by had cleared their throat very loudly and very meaningfully. Mervyn and Vanity both looked in the direction of the noise.

At the other end of the wardrobe, separated from Mervyn by Vanity's coats, was an attractive young man clad only in a shirt and boxer shorts, holding a pair of shoes, trousers and a jacket. Mervyn thought he looked familiar. He mentally dressed him, put a jacket and bow tie on him, and realised it was one of the younger receptionists. The young man gave a feeble smile and an even feebler wave.

Vanity was truly surprised. Her eyes were wide and her mouth had formed a perfect circle, as if she was auditioning to model for her own sex doll. 'Oh balls,' she said. 'I'd forgotten about you, darling. Mervyn, meet Jeremy, Jeremy meet Mervyn.'

'Hi.'

'Hello.'

'Jeremy's very good. Always willing to do that bit extra for favoured guests... He gave me a room with a *lovely* view.'

Jeremy and Mervyn both made their excuses and left.

CHAPTER THIRTY-TWO

Mervyn should have used the opportunity to ask Jeremy for a better room, but it didn't seem sporting to take advantage of a man running down the corridor with his shirt hanging out and his shoes in his hand. Besides, he wanted to talk to Smurf.

He saw Smurf in the hotel lift, jammed his foot between the doors and slipped inside.

'You traitor!'

'Smurf, calm down!'

'*Et tu*, Mervyn!'

'I wasn't having sex with her!'

'You've got scratches on your cheek!'

'That wasn't her. That was her coat-hangers.'

'Oh yeah?

'I was investigating!'

'Oh yeah?'

'She was confessing something very private.'

'Stop digging the hole, Merv, you're looking shorter than me.' The lift doors opened and Smurf strode out, heading for the room where he kept his Styrax.

'Smurf when I was in the wardrobe – I *heard* you.'

'What?'

'I heard what you said.'

'So? Do you blame me? She libels me in her book, and her daughter sends nasty threatening letters to me. Of course I said that stuff.'

'No. What you said about Sheldon.'

'What about Sheldon?'

They walked past another queue of expectant fans, waiting to have their photos taken with the star of *Vixens from the Void* wearing his Styrax costume. At the front of the queue was Hefty Helen, looking at her *Star Trek* watch and sighing. 'At last!' she hooted.

Mervyn was not to be deflected. 'You said you'd "got rid" of him.'

'Too right I got rid of him. Served him right. You know what he kept calling me? He was half an inch taller than me. Half a bloody inch! You know what nickname he had for me? "Small fry"! *Small fry*! The toffee-nosed half-pint fascist called *me* small fry! How can you be sizeist *and* a dwarf?'

The Styrax was set up in the corner of the room, a 'GONE TO LUNCH' sign hanging round its neck. A vulgar diorama of stars and planets was suspended behind it.

Morris was in the room, checking his camera. His massive head swivelled upwards. 'All right, Smurf. Mervyn... Stand anywhere, but don't go near the Styrax.'

'That joke's never going to get old,' muttered Mervyn.

'Shall I start letting them in?' droned Morris.

'Yeah, okay. Mervyn, if you'll excuse me... I'm working here.' Smurf took the sign off, and opened the Styrax with slightly too much force. The hatch bounced open and wobbled dangerously on its tiny hinges.

'But what did you mean by it?'

'What do you think I meant?'

'I don't know.'

Hefty Helen had entered the room, and was standing pointedly behind Mervyn, clearing her throat like a dying bull elephant. 'Excuse me!'

Smurf clambered into the Styrax.

'I don't know, so tell me. Did you get rid of him?'

'Yes.'

'So, what, you killed him?'

'What?' The back slammed shut.

'Are you saying you killed him?'

'Of course I didn't kill him.' Inside the Styrax, his voice was blurred and distorted, like someone speaking into a plastic cup. 'It was an accident. A fire at his house. Faulty wiring – plain and simple...'

'Can we get on?' thundered Helen. 'I've got photos with Bernard Viner and the Styrax Superior on the other side of the hotel. I've got to be there in ten minutes.'

'... accidental death. Tragic accident. Poor bastard...' There was an angry scuffling from within as Smurf wriggled around in the Styrax. 'Look, wait a sec. Mervyn are you still out there?'

'Yes.'

The back opened again and Smurf leaned out. 'Are you doing your detective thing again?' He gave a big grin. 'You've got the wrong end of the stick, mate. Look, when I said I got rid of him, I didn't "get rid of him". Not like that. What I mean was I "got rid of him" from the show. I was the one that shopped him to the BBC and got him sacked. You see, he hadn't taken his medical. He said the BBC was a socialist bureaucracy and that medical tests were Stalinist. Or was the BBC a Stalinist bureaucracy and medical tests were socialist? Whatever. You know how he went on. So he paid another dwarf to go along to do the medical for him...And guess who that was?'

'You?'

'Yep.'

'And they fell for it?' Mervyn remembered the horrors of his own medical – all that coughing and grabbing and standing there trouserless

– and wished he could have found a similarly crumpled writer to have stood in for him.

'Mervyn mate, there are *some* advantages to being like me and Sheldon. If someone three foot tall walks into your surgery and says they're Sheldon the Midget, you don't ask for their bloody driving licence. Anyway, spin forward a few years, and he's got a bit full of himself, a bit, y'know...'

'Big for his boots?'

A tobacco-stained chuckle came from within. 'That's a pretty nasty insult for us dwarves. We don't do big in boots. Anyway, he started dropping hints to Nicholas about me keeping booze in my Styrax. I mean! God, it was just one tiny bottle of whisky because it was so bloody cold in that quarry, but that bastard looked like he was going to shop me. Anyway, I thought, if he's prepared to do that, I'd better get in there first. It was him or me. So I grassed him up, and he got sacked. I got let off with a reprimand, cos Nicholas pleaded on my behalf, cos when it came to midgets to work the Styrax Sentinels, Nick was a bit short. *Short*, get it? In fact, I was the only midget he had left when Sheldon got the boot – he couldn't afford to lose both of us. So I stayed and he went. Sheldon would have understood. Him being a Tory. Survival of the fittest and all that...' There was another faint chuckle from knee height. 'Silly old Merv. Who'd want to murder him? Bloody hell, who's been fiddling with this? Why is my seat so low?'

Helen sighed impatiently. There was a hideous noise as Smurf began adjusting his seat. SQUEAKsquee. SQUEAKsquee. SQUEAKsquee. The lights of the Styrax switched on, and one of the clamps on the front extended and flexed itself.

'Did the claws wiggle just then?'

'Just the left one,' rumbled Morris.

'Bollocks. I thought as much.'

SQUEAKsquee. SQUEAKsquee. SQUEAKsquee. The single clamp wiggled again. SQUEAKsquee... SQUEAKsquee...

'If anyone interferes with my Styrax again, I'm *really* gonna to kill someone, and for the benefit of Mervyn out there, that's hyperbole. I'm not *really* gonna kill someone. All right, Morris, I'm ready.'

Helen stood sullenly by the Styrax. Morris readied his camera.

'Now smile...' said Morris. 'There's going to be a flash, so try not to blink...'

And then the Styrax exploded.

CHAPTER THIRTY-THREE

Mervyn was showered in bits of Styrax and, he realised, bits of Smurf.

He screamed, but couldn't hear his scream because he had no hearing left. He could see the vast rump of Helen poking over a shattered table and Morris lying awkwardly on the ground, still clutching his camera.

The Styrax was gone. Smurf was gone. Only the base of the Styrax remained, engulfed in flames. Foul-smelling smoke filled the room and the air turned grey and greasy.

'Smurf!' He hoped he'd said 'Smurf', but he didn't know for sure. He needed someone to lip-read his own mouth and report back to him.

The plumes of smoke were swamped by a big black cloud which surged into the air like an evil genie. Morris's huge body stood over him, filling his eyeline. Morris gallumphed over to Helen, yanked his ConVix T-shirt out of his jeans, bunched it in his fist and pulled it up to his face, revealing a generous role of belly fat carpeted with black hair. He buried his nose in the T-shirt with his left hand, reached out with his right and flipped Helen over his shoulder with surprising ease.

There was a greasy smell.

Like...

Like the smell at a barbecue.

Mervyn felt sick.

Then Mervyn watched the ceiling come towards him, and he watched it glide past. Morris was carrying him on his back.

He put Mervyn gently down outside. Mevyn lay there, dazed, and the big man knelt down and silently mouthed 'Are you all right?' to him, while humming a high-pitched note that never stopped.

Mervyn was going to answer, but he was staring disbelievingly past Morris's shoulder.

Through the carnage, through the burning, charred wreckage, the smoke and dying flames, he saw someone walking towards the inferno. Mervyn thought he was hallucinating, but there he was.

A man from the hotel holding a little bucket of sand.

The man upended his little bucket of sand on the raging carcass of the Styrax, and mopped his brow.

'Bugger,' he said. 'We're going to need a bigger bucket.'

CONVIX 15. EARTH ORBIT TWO:

4.00pm

EVENT	*LOCATION*
A PRODUCER'S STORY NICHOLAS EVERETT	Vixos Central Nerve Centre (main stage,ballroom)
'HYPERDEATH' **EPISODE SCREENING**	The Catacombs of Herath (video lounge - room 1024)
~~PHOTOS - WILLIAM SMURFETT~~ Cancelled	Transpodule Chamber (room 1030)
PHOTOGRAPHS BERNARD VINER & STYRAX SUPERIOR	Outside the spaceship (hotel car park)
AUTOGRAPHS RODERICK BURGESS	Arkadia's Boudoir (room 1013)
ACTION FIGURE ADVICE **EXPERT PANEL** with Graham Goldingay, Fay Lawless, Craig Jones, Darren Cardew	The Seventh Moon of Groolia (room 1002)

CONVIX 15. EARTH ORBIT THREE:

10.00am

EVENT	*LOCATION*
~~UNDER THE BONNET~~ ~~WILLIAM SMURFETT~~ Cancelled	Vixos Central Nerve Centre (main stage, ballroom)
~~'DEATH TO THE STYRAX' EPISODE SCREENING~~ Cancelled	The Catacombs of Herath (video lounge – room 1024)
~~AUTOGRAPHS~~ Katherine Warner Cancelled	Arkadia's Boudoir (room 1013)
REMEMBERING WILLIAM SMURFETT – Fan Panel with Graham Goldingay, Fay Lawless, Craig Jones, Darren Cardew	The Seventh Moon of Groolia (room 1002)

CHAPTER THIRTY-FOUR

After a quick examination from a doctor, Mervyn was pronounced okay. His hearing soon returned.

'Hi Mr Stone. I mean, Mervyn.'

Unfortunately.

Stuart sat down beside him, unprompted.

'Hello Stuart,' Mervyn said wearily.

Mervyn had watched the comings and goings for an hour from a chair tucked away in the corner of the foyer. He'd been sitting alone. Until now.

The police had started taking things seriously all of a sudden. They were all over the hotel last night, interrogating the guests. Both Mervyn and Morris had had a perfunctory little interview about the circumstances of Smurf's death. Mervyn started outlining his suspicions to the policeman, but slowly gave up. The police all thought it was terrorists; some religious fundamentalists who believed they were alone in the universe, and that anyone who strapped antennae to their head and pretended to be from another planet was being blasphemous. Mervyn's tale of autographs dressed up as suicide notes and multiple blackmail plots simply didn't interest them.

Morris was, as ever, his implacable calm self; in fact, he had asked the inspector if he could film their interview for the convention website – a suggestion which caused both Mervyn and the inspector to go bug-eyed with disbelief. The request met with a firm 'No'.

After their police interview, Mervyn asked Morris about Hefty Helen. The last he'd seen of her she had been sprawled lifeless on the carpet where Morris had dropped her, great patches of soot plastered to her face as if she had come dressed as a panda.

'Oh, she's fine. A bit shaken up, concussion... And she's got bits of Styrax embedded in her leg and arm and both cheeks of her bum.'

'Oh dear.'

'No, don't worry, she's fine with it. She already checked herself out of hospital. Doesn't want the shrapnel removed. She says it makes her more valuable. More of a collector's piece.' Morris gave a slow wink. 'We've got a date tonight.' He'd lurched off, thinking about his forthcoming evening of romance and of wooing a prime piece of merchandise.

Whereas the death of Simon was still officially 'just another nerd who couldn't take being a nerd any more', the death of Smurf was unquestionably murder, obviously premeditated. The story made it to the national newspapers. Tasteless headlines abounded: 'Pop goes the

Wee Will' was *The Sun*'s, *The Mirror* came up with 'Alien Blownapart' and *The Daily Express* crudely went with 'Shred Dwarf'. If Smurf was looking down on them now from above – and quite a novel experience if would have been for him to be looking down on anybody from above – he would have been most offended by *The Daily Star,* which had 'Small Fry'.

Reporters were now at the hotel, trying to gain access to the convention. Morris had stepped up security, asking his stewards to help the hotel staff by keeping a look-out in the foyer by the exits. Some stewards had gone way over the top, using the situation as an opportunity to don biker boots and black crash helmets, patrolling the foyer like royal guards from Vixos. This at least gave the frustrated paparazzi outside something to photograph.

The journalists' attempt to inveigle their way into the hotel were pretty pathetic. They'd hired cheap monster suits from fancy dress shops. One such reporter was at the reception desk now. The large purple hairy thing with horns sprouting out of its head was being interrogated by Morris.

'I tell you, I'm with the convention and I've locked my pass in my case,' it said.

Morris raised a sceptical eyebrow.

'Really. I have.'

'Oh yes, and you've come as... what, again?'

'A Krell.'

'And this Krell is from... which planet?'

'It's also called Krell. Everyone knows that. From the episode "Bride of Krell". It's the beast that Arkadia marries in series seven. She marries the Krell to gain access to the mines of Krell, where they mine Krellinine 60.'

Mervyn was impressed. The hairy thing was doing awfully well. Must have stayed up all night reading Vixipedia.com. It was still a futile attempt, though. Morris was just toying with the poor fool.

'Oh really? Series seven you say? So the production code for that story would be...?'

'Ah... seven.'

'Seven what?'

'Seven... G?'

'Nice try, Mr Journalist. Goodbye.'

The attendees were also taking it seriously now. Very seriously. One death was bad enough, but two deaths in two days had raised a few glitter-encrusted eyebrows. All the 'normal' fans, the nice affable types with jobs and families and Other Things They Could Be Doing were leaving early. He could see a family bustling to the entrance, bags in hand, checking out; a mum and dad and two small girls about seven years old who were dressed – somewhat scarily – as Vixens in knee-high boots, basques and lycra. Mum and dad went to the reception desk, which gave the two girls an opportunity to make a break for it and run around the foyer, bouncing on the seats and hiding behind the plastic pot-plants.

The parents finished checking out and shouted out to the girls. 'Medula! Arkadia! We're going!' The girls ran back to join them.

Mervyn didn't wonder what kind of parent named their children after fictional characters; he'd met enough young Leias, Romanas and Buffys in his time. He *did* wonder which girl was named after the good character and which one was named after the evil character... and whether it would have any bearing on how they grew up. Not for the first time, Mervyn felt uncomfortable about what he'd unleashed back in 1986.

So, the sane fans left. The others remained.

The interruptions for Simon's death were all very well as far as they were concerned, but this had been a guest for heaven's sake! They bitterly resented the remainder of the previous day's schedules being cancelled to make way for the police, and were completely thrown by the schedule changes for day three.

One by one, they ambled up to the timetable in the foyer, eyeballed the 'cancelled' bits written next to Smurf's name, made audible clicking noises with their cheeks (as if Smurf planned his own death just to spite them), and ambled away again. Some of them ambled in Morris's direction, complaining that the loss of Smurf's 'Under the Bonnet' panel had left a yawning hole in their convention experience, and could they have a partial refund please? This request was also met with a firm 'No'.

Stuart beamed at Mervyn. 'How goes the murder investigation?' he asked.

'Great!' said Mervyn. Sarcasm greased his voice. 'Look, I've discovered another murder.'

They watched as policeman carried out bits of exploded Styrax.

'It was a propane canister,' explained Stuart. 'Mr Smurfett used propane to juice his Styrax flamethrower. It wasn't very safe. It was even less safe when someone fixed an automatic pistol to it, tied the pistol's trigger to a piece of cord, and tied the cord to his seat, so when he raised the seat, it tightened the trigger on the gun, the gun fired into the cylinder and... well...'

Mervyn was glad of Stuart's inside information, but wished he'd go away.

Two murders.

His chief suspect was now his only suspect. A pattern was forming, a pattern about as subtle as the insides of an Indian restaurant.

Simon blackmailed Vanity. And was murdered. Smurf threatened Vanity. And was murdered.

Both had been threatened by the same person: Vanity's daughter.

What to do now?

Bernard's capture back in the 80s had been so easy. A quick word with the producer, and unsmiling men in shiny hats came to take Bernard away. But he couldn't just run up to the police and shout 'J'accuse!' this time. His theory was just a theory, born from circumstantial evidence. What to do? He had to get firm evidence on this woman. He had to find her, follow her, find out everything about her.

Stuart sighed. He seemed to be marshalling up his courage to speak. 'I knew, you know,' he said at last.

'What?'

'I knew.'

'What?'

'Back then. Back when *Vixens from the Void* finished. When you didn't have any work. When we got you to come to Peterborough. I knew you hadn't got any work.'

Mervyn stared ahead. 'I see.'

'Not that we didn't want a proper professional to write our script. I just knew, that's all. Fans do.'

'Of course they do.'

'It was... fortuitous. I mean, you were our favourite writer anyway, and you helped us, and we... um... helped... you.'

'I understand.'

'It wasn't charity, if that's what you're thinking –'

'Yes it was. But it's all right. It's... It was a nice gesture.'

'You weren't offended?'

'About giving me some work? How could any writer be offended by that? We survive through pity and charity at the best of times.'

'But it wasn't Hollywood, was it? Sorry.'

'No, you're right. It wasn't Hollywood, but it was fun, I must admit. Writing a film with practically no budget, it was a good exercise. Exercised the little grey cells. Something new to do – after all, anything's better than just fading away, dining out on past glories until you end up telling anecdotes about anecdotes...'

Stuart's face glowed. His eyes bulged with pride. 'That's what I thought. I think a lot of fans employ their heroes just to see them back in action again. Watch them working. Give them a bit of self-respect.'

'I think you're probably right.'

'Listen. About our murder mystery...'

'It's not a murder mystery. It's a murder. Multiple murders. I've told you, it's not a game. You must take it seriously.'

'Oh absolutely. I do. That's why I want to show you something.'

'Hey Dr Spock!' called a voice. 'Loser! Looo-ser!'

Mervyn blinked, startled. Someone was shouting at them.

'Having a good time with your mates, Stu?'

'Where's your scarf?'

Stuart cringed, curling up like a prodded woodlouse. 'Oh no. They've seen me.'

Mervyn looked in the direction of the shouts. It was two policemen who had been going round the hotel making enquiries.

'Oi! Batman! Where's your cape?'

Stuart gazed fixedly at a piece of air about a foot above nowhere in particular. 'Oh ha ha, Baz. Very funny.'

'Enjoying yourself?' Baz jerked a thumb at the doors of the hotel, where the Styrax was parked. 'Just give us the word and we'll confiscate it as material evidence. I bet you'd love to drive to work in one of those. You could zap villains in it.'

The other one was holding fingers up over their heads to simulate antennae.

'Beep, beep, beep! Oi, are you listening Stu? Beep beep beep! Where's your sonic screwdriver? Up your arse?'

The policeman who wasn't Baz had stuck pencils in his belt and pulled his trousers low to unleash a generous portion of lower cheek. He proffered his backside in their direction. 'Stu! Look! I'm a Rectoid from the planet Bumcrack!'

Stuart leaked a watery smile at Mervyn. 'My work colleagues. They don't like special constables.'

'Do you want to get out of here?' asked Mervyn.

Stuart whispered a heartfelt 'Yes!'

They got up and retreated into the hotel, the policeman yelling after them. It was only after the cries faded into the distance that Stuart was able to straighten up and breathe.

'Now, where shall we go?'

'I've got a place we can go. I think it might be useful.'

CONVIX 15. EARTH ORBIT THREE:

11.00am

EVENT	*LOCATION*
VANITY MYCROFT VIXEN TO FLY	Vixos Central Nerve Centre (main stage, ballroom)
'THE PANDORUS PARADIGM' **EPISODE SCREENING**	The Catacombs of Herath (video lounge room 1024)
AUTOGRAPHS RODERICK BURGESS	Arkadia's Boudoir (room 1013)
~~**PHOTOGRAPHS**~~ ~~Katherine Warner~~ *Cancelled*	Transpodule Chamber (room 1030)
HOW VIXENS PREDICTED THE FUTURE **EXPERT PANEL** with Graham Goldingay, Fay Lawless, Craig Jones, Darren Cardew	The Seventh Moon of Groolia (room 1002)

CHAPTER THIRTY-FIVE

The hotel's 'Business Suite' was a glass-fronted cubicle no more than eight-foot square with three computers crammed inside. It was occupied by a solitary businessman; he had come to do work, but his resolve had dribbled away and he was searching YouTube for home-made videos of American teenagers dancing in their knickers. As Mervyn and Stuart piled into the tiny room, he looked up guiltily, then collected his papers and left them to it.

'This is what I wanted to show you.'

He pulled out a dog-eared piece of rubbish, a small fat square of papier-mâché.

'I got this from Smurf's Styrax. It was part of the lining.'

Mervyn was shocked. 'Stuart! A man just got killed! This is no time to be taking souvenirs!'

'I wasn't taking souvenirs,' Stuart said, hurt. 'It's a clue.'

Mervyn looked closer at the papier-mâché. He could just make out the words of an article from a very old newspaper. It was gushing about the wedding between the Duke and Duchess of York. Just like the one on Mervyn's blackmail note.

Astonished, Mervyn took the blackmail note out of his pocket and held it against the papier-mâché. One article was from the *Daily Mail* and one was from *The Daily Telegraph*. They were both crumpled with age and glue, but they both had the same smiling wedding photos.

'What does it mean?' puzzled Stuart.

'It means that the insides of the Styrax were padded with papier-mâché made from old newspapers from 1986,' said Mervyn slowly. 'Which means I know what this weird blackmail note is. It's a photocopy of the insides of a Styrax.' He paused. 'And I'd be willing to bet real money on which one.'

'The one you fell on,' said Stuart.

'In my investigations, Stuart, I've discovered that Simon blackmailed Bernard. He claimed that he had proof that Bernard stole that Styrax. Proof that was *written inside it.*'

'Oh wow. And you're thinking that something else written on the inside of the other Styrax was proof of... something else? Something you could be blackmailed for?'

'But what?' Mervyn stared at his blackmail note again in frustration, Vanity's daughter momentarily forgotten. 'Why does it say SAFE? What do those numbers *mean*? Is it a safe combination? A compass bearing? A date? A password? A code...?'

'The galactic co-ordinates for a planet...?'

Mervyn threw him a look. 'Yes. Quite.'

'Well I did have a suggestion... Sort of why we came here. We could use the computers.'

'You're not going to show me more of your "improved" bits of *Vixens* are you?'

'No. Suppose we put the numbers into Google or something?'

Mervyn smiled. 'Stuart, that is a brilliant idea!'

Stuart glowed with the compliment. 'Thanks.' He went to the nearest computer, put in a password, and his hands skittered over the keys. 'Right. Here we go. Google. What are the numbers again?'

Mervyn looked at his blackmail note. '376... 229... 22.'

Stuart put them in and pressed return. Mervyn looked over his shoulder.

Stuart shook his head 'Most of it's all gibberish. Just websites full of numbers. I'll go on to the next page.' He pressed a key and scrolled down. 'Nothing.' And again. 'Nothing.' He did it again. 'I think this is going to turn into a long –'

'Wait... Look at that!' Mervyn's finger jabbed the screen. Halfway down the fourth page it had a link for the Wikipedia entry on the UK general election 1987. 'My God!' He leaned over Stuart's shoulder and clicked the link. 'General election 1987 – the results were... Conservatives 376, Labour 229, SDP–Liberal Alliance 22! Of course!'

'I don't understand...'

'Oh Stuart, Stuart, Stuart! Don't you get it?'

'What?'

'And I thought you were an expert in all things *Vixens*.'

'What? What?'

'The 1987 general election happened the day before our last day of filming on series two! The day Bernard stole the Styrax! The day described in Chapter 13 of Vanity's book! The day she had her wicked way with Smurf in the back of a Mini Metro covered in fibreglass!'

Stuart clapped his hands over his mouth, and gasped.

'The Day... Of the Styrax!'

CHAPTER THIRTY-SIX

'But what does it all mean?' said Stuart.

'Buggered if I know.'

Mervyn wandered over to the corner of the 'suite' and rested his arms on a ledge. He looked down, thinking.

Then something caught the corner of his eye.

Another panel session was finishing downstairs; fans were cascading out of the hotel ballroom. The suite's huge glass walls overlooked the foyer, and Mervyn could see a thin-faced girl clad in a pink cardigan, holding an armful of pens and photos.

Vanity's daughter.

She opened a loose-leaf file and scribbled something officiously in a margin. Snapping it shut, she tucked it under her arm. She pulled her pink fluffy cardigan across her scant chest, stretching the woollen bunny rabbits and ducklings on it into obscene positions. Her head twitched about, up and down the corridor, presumably looking for the lifts.

And then suddenly she was looking up at him.

She didn't just catch his eye, or flick a glance at him; she appraised him with a detached interest, as if Mervyn were a painting and she was an artist assessing whether he were finished. And her eyes...

Staring, unblinking, pale and grey.

And then, when she finished looking at him, she kept on walking.

Mervyn dashed to the door of the business lounge. 'Excuse me, Stuart, I've just remembered, I've got to be somewhere.'

'What about the numbers? What about the 1987 general election?'

But Mervyn was gone.

CHAPTER THIRTY-SEVEN

He ran downstairs. He couldn't see her.

No – there she was, at the other end of corridor. She was just about to turn into the dealers' room.

The dealers' room was the designated area for the sale of merchandise. Large hairy men who looked like they'd come out of prison only moments before smiled wolfishly as they took huge amounts of money off young people for – as far as Mervyn could see – no particularly good reason. It was like a funfair, but without the unpleasantness of going on the rides.

The place was very busy. He could see Morris moving around with a video camera, getting all the dealers to say 'Hi'. Most of them were surreptitiously removing the 'unofficial' merchandise from their stalls, making sure that Morris's footage didn't end up on *Crimewatch*.

Mervyn looked around and spotted her. She wasn't hard to spot; she was the only pink woolly thing in a sea of leather and crushed velvet. He watched her from the other side of the room as she flitted from table to table, examining bits and pieces with a leisurely lack of interest. He went up to a stall, trying to act casual by examining the T-shirts, models, keyrings and books, all the while keeping an eye on her.

'Take a good look,' the man sitting behind the table cackled, waggling a pair of caterpillar eyebrows.

He was large man; the bits of him that weren't covered with hair were covered with metal. There were so many studs protruding from his body the police could have thrown him across roads to stop joyriders.

Mervyn looked down and was surprised to discover a statuette of Arkadia in his hand, his thumb resting neatly over her left breast.

'She's completely anatomically correct, you know.'

'Really?' said Mervyn, concentrating on keeping the girl within his peripheral vision.

'Yep,' said the man, 'all the figures here are home-made and accurate down to the last detail,' he scratched a spiky chin. 'Which is ironic really... because four years ago I got cancer of the willy and had to have a penectomy.' He gestured at his array of little plastic men and women, arranged in a semi-circle as if waiting for the encore in a musical. 'So you see, I'm the only one at this table without any genitals.'

Mervyn made the kind of noise people made when they knew they should respond to someone talking, but had absolutely no idea how.

'Go on, have a peep.'

'What?' flinched Mervyn, expecting the man to stand up and unzip his flies.

'Have a look at her,' grinned the man, in the manner of a pantomime villain selling new lamps for old.

'I don't really...'

'Go on! Tell me what you think.'

Determined not to be intimidated, Mervyn turned it over. The figurine was dressed in a toga-like costume, so the material bunched up, leaving two plastic legs sticking up in the air.

'Oh yes. That's very, um, very. Um.'

The man winked. 'I bet you can't find anything wrong with that.'

A voice came from behind them. 'Oh dear, sir, I'm afraid you've asked the wrong man.'

Mervyn turned around. It was Andrew Jamieson, craning over his shoulder and peering down Arkadia's dress.

'This man, sir,' Andrew said to the vendor, slapping Mervyn on the shoulder, 'is the world expert on all matters Mycroft. Why, I can tell just by glancing at Professor Stone's aghast face that he is mortally offended at being subjected to such a blatantly inaccurate representation of the derriere.'

The man's off-white smile faded. 'Really? I did research. I bought the magazines specially. *Mayfair*, volume 28, number 6, June '93 – "Space Slut Special"'

'Pfff! Hopelessly out of date, as Professor Stone will tell you. Her left buttock is entirely wrong. It now has a tattoo of a dancing hippo on it. And as for the frontal area...'

The vendor snatched it off Mervyn and peered up its skirt, absent-mindedly scratching the area where his penis used to be.

'What's wrong with it? It ain't that bad, surely? I had a bit of a problem with getting the materials. I used the grass underfelt they use for model railways and I sprayed it black –'

'Hopeless. If you'd only read Professor Stone's papers on the subject, Ms Mycroft is the proud bearer of a Brazilian these days. All the most successful actresses have them. And you know why? Tell him, Professor.'

'Well, I really wouldn't know,' said Mervyn impatiently.

'They're neat, tidy, and most importantly they look like "Welcome" mats.'

Mervyn had had enough. He placed a hand over Andrew's mouth. 'Excuse my friend. He's on day-release from an asylum and I'm his doctor. He's under the insane delusion that he's funny and I have to humour him to stop him killing again.'

The vendor looked uncertainly at both of them.

Mervyn left the stall, Andrew waddling after him. 'What are you doing following that girl? I thought you had enough balls in the air without another one. Anyway, I wouldn't have thought she was your type.'

Mervyn spun Andrew round until they were nose to nose. He dropped his voice to a low and urgent murmur. 'She *isn't* my type. What do you know about Vanity Mycroft's daughter?'

Andrew grinned. 'I thought it was only a matter of time before you'd ask. She's a bit of a nutcase, frankly, so men – beware! Trouble at boarding school... Pushed a teacher through a plate-glass window, or something. Mum put her in the Territorial Army to teach her discipline. All she learned was how to strip a rifle and blind people with her thumbs. She only started coming to conventions in the last few years. Mummy finally convinced her there might be a few decent men in amongst the genetically challenged.' Andrew winked.

'Do you think she's capable of murder?'

'What kind of question's th–'

Out of the corner of his eye, Mervyn saw a cardigan festooned with bunnies and ducklings vanishing through the doorway.

'She's going,' he hissed. 'Can't stop. I want to see where she goes.'

'Merv! Wait a minute!'

But Mervyn was gone.

CHAPTER THIRTY-EIGHT

Mervyn hurtled up and down the length and breadth of the hotel, sure he had lost her.

... But she had gone all of ten yards to sit in the hotel bar.

He sat down in the other side of the bar to keep an eye on her, partially obscured by a sad-looking miniature palm tree, and tried to look inconspicuous. He realised after half an hour that the girl was never going to do anything exciting or remotely interesting. Ever.

He also realised that attempting to look inconspicuous in the middle of a convention where people had paid to see him was pretty futile.

'Afternoon, Stone...'

Roddy slumped down on a chair, next to him, neatly blocking his view of the girl. Roddy was a crumpled pile of tweed and paisley. He looked pale and unshaven.

'You okay, Major?' Mervyn was desperately looking over Roddy's shaggy white mane to see what the girl was doing.

'Couldn't be better, Stone. Working on strategy at the moment. Tactics. Getting a good measure of the enemy.'

'What enemy is that, Major?'

'The robots of course.'

This caused Mervyn to snap his attention back to Roddy. 'The robots? What robots?'

'They're after us. Crafty buggers. Picking us off one by one.'

'The Styrax.'

Roddy nodded furiously, his little glasses jumping on his nose. 'Josh owned them, and the little chaps steered 'em. Now they're all gone. You see what I mean, old chap? Josh. Gone. Both dwarf fellas. Gone. What's their plan? What's their robot strategy, I hear you ask?'

'What's their robot strategy, Major?'

'Good question that man. Haven't the foggiest. But they planned it all along, didn't they?'

'Who?'

'The robots. The Styrax. With Josh and the dwarves dead... that means they're free... free of their masters... free to do what they bally well want... with us!'

'Really?' Mervyn unconsciously edged his chair an inch or two away from Roddy. 'And what do they want to do with us?'

'Who's to say, old boy... who's to say? But I'll tell you this for nothing. They've killed me once. They're not going to do it again...' He popped his glass down on the table. 'I'll make sure of that...'

Mervyn looked up.

She'd gone!

He twisted his head around frantically, looking for her.

Roddy noticed Mervyn looking in all directions. 'Oh don't worry. They won't make their move just yet. They're biding their time.'

Where was she now?

The ladies' toilets. The door was still swinging, back and forth. An opportunity.

Mervyn headed for her table. There was a bag tucked under one of the seats; large, denim, covered with beads in an elaborate pattern. 'M. Mycroft' was stencilled untidily on the flap. *Right. Here we go.*

He opened the bag and looked inside, shaking it to see all the odds and ends. Hairbrush, lipstick, bottle of Chanel No. 5, presumably borrowed from Mum... Among the usual feminine clutter, he saw a book of autographs. Now that looked familiar...

'What are you doing?' trilled a voice at his elbow.

Mervyn flinched in surprise. It was Minnie. He was sort of hoping he wouldn't have to see her again this weekend; her demonstrative displays of affection in public were becoming a little embarrassing. 'How are things?' he asked.

'Not good. I'm bearing up. Trying to keep busy. Morris has me patrolling the back of the hotel, in case any reporters try to get in through the kitchens.' She was still staring at the bag in Mervyn's hands.

'Oh,' said Mervyn, realising. 'This isn't mine.'

'I know it's not yours. It doesn't suit you.'

Mervyn dropped the bag.

'Why are you looking at it?'

'You promise to keep a secret?'

Minnie traced her finger over her delicious bosoms. 'Cross my heart and hope to die.'

Mervyn steered Minnie to a quiet corner of the bar. 'I think Vanity's daughter has something to do with the deaths of Simon and Smurf. Or, I should say, the murders.'

'Really?'

'It all makes sense. Simon blackmailed Vanity – he gets killed. Smurf threatened Vanity, wanted to sue her over her book – he gets killed.'

'Really?'

'Vanity's daughter threatened them both... And now they're dead. Draw your own conclusions.'

'Sounds like a pretty devoted daughter.'

'Scarily devoted. Scary full stop. I heard she's done a lot of mad things. She's got more screws loose than the Styrax I fell on.'

'Oh my God. Really?'

The thin-faced girl emerged from the toilet. 'Oh God, she's coming back. Don't look. Or if you do look, don't make it obvious.'

Mervyn pulled Minnie behind a plastic aspidistra. Vanity's daughter glided in, not unlike a Styrax herself. Her unblinking eyes scorched the artificial foliage as they looked around.

Minnie looked slowly round, then she followed Mervyn's eyeline and giggled. '*Her?* She's not her daughter.'

In classic Styrax fashion, the girl went past them without looking in their direction and glided straight out of the bar. She didn't go to the bag. It was only then that Mervyn realised the girl hadn't been carrying a bag, only folders.

'She's Spooky Sandra,' said Minnie. 'She's the president of the Vanity Mycroft fan club. Follows Vanity around every con she comes to...' She craned her head in the other direction. 'Ummm... Ah! Look! *That's* Vanity's daughter...' She pointed.

Mervyn looked. Minnie was pointing into a large mirrored wall that made up one side of the bar. Mervyn could clearly see himself bent awkwardly over the pot-plant.

He could also see Minnie standing by him, finger pointing directly into her own reflection.

Pointing at herself.

'There I am,' she said.

Oh God...

180 degrees wrong. 180 degrees crap.

CHAPTER THIRTY-NINE

Mervyn leant against the table, clutching at the place in his midriff where his stomach used to be.

Everything started to move in slow motion, like a crash test film with Mervyn as the luckless blank-faced dummy flying through the car windscreen. Only this time the dummy just sagged limply onto a chair and waited helplessly for the inevitable impact.

Which never came.

Minnie just grinned at him.

'More screws loose than the Styrax you fell on?'

'Minnie I'm sorry, I didn't realise. I honestly didn't realise.'

'Don't worry about it.'

'I'm so sorry...'

'I SAID... DON'T WORRY ABOUT IT!'

Her shout was loud and unexpected. A lot of hotel guests looked up from their conversations.

She swung her bag onto her shoulder, too violently. It hit the wall and exploded in a shower of lipsticks, packets of tissues, tampons and condoms. Mervyn felt guilty, embarrassed and incredibly old.

'Here, let me...' Mervyn dived to pick up the bits. He picked up the autograph book; he recognised it now. It was the one he'd signed yesterday.

Minnie knelt too, and whispered in his ear. 'So what if I did kill them both? They deserved it. They crossed my mum. They hurt her.'

Mervyn went numb. 'But... One of them was your *dad...*'

'He wasn't my dad. Mum had four husbands. I never had a dad. Certainly not him. Don't ever tell anyone I killed them, or I'm going to have to kill you too. You're very lucky I fancy you, Mervyn, or you'd be dead now.' She grinned. A crooked, damaged grin.

She finished picking up her stuff, and walked off calmly, swinging from side to side, the bag slapping against her pert bottom.

Oh my God.

180 degrees wrong. 180 degrees crap.

After a good ten minutes staring into the mirrored wall at his own slackened face, Mervyn found the use of his legs again. He got up and lumbered away, too dazed to work out where he was walking to. He barely realised he was wandering back into the dealers' room – where he was greeted by Andrew.

'So to sum up, you accidentally slept with a mother *and* her daughter – in the one night?'

'I thought Minnie had returned for a rematch. I'd taken some sleeping pills. I wasn't fully compos mentis. It was an accident!'

'An accident? I've heard of Freudian slips, but that's ridiculous.'

'You knew, didn't you? Of course you did. You saw her hug me.'

'Well... I suspected. To be honest, I was a bit stunned when you got hugged by Minnie this morning, but I assumed that was the effect you have on most young women.'

'Oh my God. Oh... my... God. She's going to kill me. What am I going to do? What the *hell* am I going to do?'

'Don't panic. Help is at hand. You see him over there?' He waved at the vendor across the room, who gave them a cheery wave.

'Yes?'

'When they do find out, and one or other of them rips your dick off, don't worry. He's got catheters you can borrow.'

CONVIX 15.
EARTH ORBIT THREE:

1.00pm

EVENT	*LOCATION*
RODDY BURGESS **LEADING FROM THE FRONT**	Vixos Central Nerve Centre (main stage, ballroom)
'WAR OF THE VIXENS' **EPISODE SCREENING**	The Catacombs of Herath(video lounge – room 1024)
AUTOGRAPHS VANITY MYCROFT MERVYN STONE	Arkadia's Boudoir (room 1013)
~~**PHOTOGRAPHS**~~ ~~WILLIAM SMURFETT~~ *Cancelled*	Transpodule Chamber (room 1030)
BRINGING BACK 'VIXENS: WHO TO SEND YOUR LETTERS TO **EXPERT PANEL** with Graham Goldingay, Fay Lawless, Craig Jones, Darren Cardew	The Seventh Moon of Groolia (room 1002)

CHAPTER FORTY

Mervyn walked woodenly along the corridor; his legs moved, but he couldn't feel them. But they seemed okay on their own for the moment, doing the right–left–right thing under him.

Calm, calm, calm.

So he'd found the murderer.

And slept with her.

And the murderer's mum.

It could have been worse, but he wasn't sure how.

He ended up in his room, hiding. If he stayed under the bedcovers, no one would find him.

Knock knockity-knock.

That was his door. Bugger. So much for that plan.

Knock knockity-knock.

That was a familiar knock, he thought. *Oh God. It must be Vanity.*

Knock knockity-knock.

Oh God. Unless... Wouldn't it be ironic if her daughter had exactly the same knock as her...

'Mervyn? Are you in there lover boy?' shouted Minnie.

Oh God...

'I hope me being a murderer won't change our relationship at all.'

Mervyn stayed as silent as he could.

'I thought we could have some fun. I could tie you up, and you could be at my mercy.' She waited for an answer. Mervyn remained quiet.

'Some other time, then. If you're in there, Morris wants you for the writers panel. You've already missed one autograph session. Don't be late. Or I'll be very cross.' One last knockity – and she left.

He was sitting on a time bomb. There was going to come a time when Minnie or Vanity would find out that he'd slept with both of them. And then the third murder victim at this convention would definitely be him. His only hope was to get out fast.

Something was vibrating under the covers, jiggling like a freshly caught salmon under his buttocks. For a moment he thought one of the Mycrofts had left something interesting and buzzing in his bed, but then he remembered he'd put his phone on to silent during his last panel.

'Hello?'

A wash of sound. Low stertorous breathing, so close to the earpiece that it created a deep rhythmic whooshing noise in his ear. A blustery coastline making a dirty phone call.

'Hello?'

'Mr Stone, it's Stuart. Sorry to bother you.'

'How did you get this number?'

'Morris had it. He leaves his files in the office. Listen. Can you meet me? I think I've located some key evidence in our investigation.'

'Stuart there's been a change of plan. I'm not doing any more investigating.'

There was a huge pause, but not a silent one. The storm rushed into his ear again.

'What did you say?' Stuart asked.

'I'm leaving very quickly. Probably now.'

'But you're doing the writers panel in a minute. I was looking forward to that.'

'I'm sorry, but I've got to go. I've got an important thing that's just come up...' His mind scrabbled for a plausible excuse. It failed. 'Work.'

'Work? That's great! I'm really glad you have something to do. It's great to see you at work.'

Mervyn didn't know how to take that. 'Thanks.'

'But I do have important evidence. You might be interested. I'm going to the writers panel anyway, and then I'm going to the fancy-dress disco. See you there?' And then he hung up.

Mervyn realised he'd made a mistake. The best way to catch a murderer was to use a sympathetic policeman, of course. Find Stuart. That's right. Find Stuart and get him to get his policeman buddy' to arrest Minnie. That's a good plan.

He went to the writers panel, where he found Morris taking down redundant posters.

'Hi Morris. I don't suppose you've seen a young man anywhere? Called Stuart. He might be wearing a *Vixens* costume?'

Morris looked around at the sea of fans wearing *Vixens* costumes and just raised his eyebrows helplessly.

'Point taken,' said Mervyn. 'Oh well, I'll keep looking.'

'Don't forget you've got a writers panel in five minutes.'

'Of course. Where is it?'

'Right here.' Morris pointed at the door next to them. A sign on it said 'Writers panel'. There was already an expectant collection of fans clustering in a ragged queue, looking at him with awe. He was trapped.

He went into the empty room and sat at a long table facing the rows of chairs. No sign of Stuart.

The fans outside the door stared at him. Making sure he didn't try to escape.

CONVIX 15.
EARTH ORBIT THREE:

2.00pm

EVENT	*LOCATION*
NICHOLAS EVERETT **LOOKING BACK**	Vixos Central Nerve Centre (main stage, ballroom)
'OPERATION GENOCIDE' **EPISODE SCREENING**	The Catacombs of Herath (video lounge - room 1024)
PHOTOGRAPHS RODERICK BURGESS	Arkadia's Boudoir (room 1013)
WRITERS PANEL MERVYN STONE ANDREW JAMIESON BOB AND BARBARA BRAINTREE	Hyperion Bridge (room 1010)
QUESTIONS FROM THE AUDIENCE **EXPERT PANEL** with Graham Goldingay, Fay Lawless, Craig Jones, Darren Cardew	The Seventh Moon of Groolia (room 1002)

CHAPTER FORTY-ONE

In the hospitality room, the stewards were packing away for another year. They were removing the laminated schedules and trying not to singe themselves on the light fittings, while a steward was folding up struts and tripods, fitting them snugly into the padded security of a silver suitcase.

Minnie was there too, calmly working away. All trace of madness had been expunged from her face. She was her usual chirpy self again.

Morris entered and patted the video camera round his neck, like a St Bernard showing off a particularly fine barrel of brandy. 'Just filmed the dealers. They're not very good at smiling or sounding excited to be here,' he said. 'You wouldn't do me a favour, would you?' He gave the video camera to Minnie. 'Could you have a look through the footage to find any shots of Simon and Smurf? Perhaps I can put a "murder victim" package together, get some music under it or something.'

Whether Minnie thought that was a particularly tasteful idea or not, she took the tape without a word and left to go to the office.

After she left, a ghost of a smile played around Morris's lips for the first time at the convention.

At almost exactly that moment, Minnie's mother was in her hotel room, changing for the fancy-dress disco. She was pleased at how she looked in her old costume, so she thought she could try the same trick on Mervyn again.

Mervyn hadn't turned up at their last autograph panel. Well, he wasn't going to slip through her clutches as easily as that. They had had an interrupted assignation that she was determined they would keep.

Something was irritating her. Unusually, it wasn't something that was on her long list of regular irritations: fans, ex-husbands, her agent, younger actresses, magazines that didn't contain photos of her, and magazines that did contain photos of younger actresses. She had been tugging at her bra all day, trying to settle it into a position where it wasn't showing, but the bra wasn't having any of it; it was intent on peeping out of her low-cut blouse.

It was most odd – not least because she had her undergarments made especially for her. There was an exotic little shop in Portobello Road with a flame-red sign and provocatively dressed dummies in the window. Within its walls, pretty little men would crawl over her with tape measures, looping them around her bosom and hips and crawling up her thighs.

Anyway, enough was enough. She took off her blouse and peeled off the offending garment. It was too small as well. Large red marks decorated her body in a way she hadn't seen since she'd gone out with that drug-splattered pop-star with an appetite for erotic flagellation. She looked inside the bra and realised what the problem was. This was a full-cup bra. She always wore half-cups, to keep as much of her womanly flesh as visible as possible. Inside was a ragged and faded name tag, an old relic from a dozen boarding schools and numerous excursions with the Territorial Army. It bore the words 'Minnie Mycroft'. What?

Minnie levered open the screen of the camera and whizzed through the footage, guests and convention attendees jerking madly as they went about their business at high speed. Then she saw Mervyn and that other writer bloke, Andrew Jamieson, chatting in the dealers' room, their backs to the camera. She was interested. She wondered what they were talking about. She slowed the camera down.

'So to sum up, you accidentally slept with a mother *and* her daughter – in the one night?'

'I thought Minnie had returned for a rematch. I'd taken some sleeping pills. I wasn't fully compos mentis. It was an accident!'

'An accident? I've heard of Freudian slips, but that's ridiculous.'

'You knew, didn't you? Of course you did. You saw her hug me.'

'Well... I suspected. To be honest, I was a bit stunned when you got hugged by Minnie this morning, but I assumed that was the effect you have on most young women.'

'Oh my God. Oh... my... God. She's going to kill me. What am I going to do? What the *hell* am I going to do?'

Vanity couldn't work out why she was wearing her daughter's bra.

They didn't share a room. They hadn't even arrived at the convention together – the sulky little mare refused to drive there with her mother, using the predictable 'You'll just embarrass me mum' whine of teenagers everywhere. She'd travelled up by train instead.

Very odd. She threw her mind back over the events of the past few days. She definitely knew she wasn't wearing this bra during Friday's autograph session, because she hadn't been wearing one at all. That evening, before the fancy dress, she was positive she'd been wearing her beige half-cup instead of her black one because she didn't want her underwear showing through her *Vixens* costume when she ambushed Mervyn that night.

Oh that's right.When she ambushed Mervyn that night.

Oh yes. When she ambushed Mervyn.

That night. Oh.

CHAPTER FORTY-TWO

'Please forgive me,' said Mervyn.

He raised his hands.

'But could you all come down to the front please? There's not enough of us to spread out.' Mervyn only asked the dozen or so people to come closer so he could make absolutely sure Stuart wasn't one of them.

No. He hadn't turned up yet.

Mervyn sat in the middle as *de facto* chairman. The happily married writing partners Bob and Barbara Braintree dominated the south end of the table. Barbara was doing some knitting, Bob held the wool. At the north end, Andrew Jamieson had draped himself over a chair, arm propped up on the table, hand splayed in mid air, fingers curling around an imaginary cigarette.

The shape of these sessions would follow a pretty set pattern; someone would ask 'Where do you get your ideas?', that had them scratching their heads for five minutes (Andrew would say – only half-jokingly – that he stole his), and then some bright spark would ask Mervyn what a script editor actually did.

'Hmm... I've heard a lot of script editors use all sorts of analogies to describe the job; sheep-dogs rounding up sheep, head chefs running a busy kitchen, conductors of an orchestra... I usually see myself as the soldier in the regiment who throws himself on the live hand grenade when it gets lobbed into his trench – particularly when I was lobbed scripts from this bloke here on my right.'

Mervyn would then try to explain what he did, and as what he did usually involved clearing up Andrew's scripts, he usually used examples involving Andrew. The whole session would usually end with Mervyn and Andrew having a good-natured argument in front of a handful of attendees about who did what to whom.

'Andrew's scripts were always on the sketchy side. It was a case of "Here's a title, fill in the blanks later."'

'You're exaggerating, Merv.'

'Last time we went for a curry, he handed me his menu. I thought it was the second draft of "Prison Planet".'

There was a giggle around the room, which Andrew fed by pulling a mock distressed face. 'You wound me Mervyn, you really do.'

'I don't think you realised what you put me through. I used to wake-up in cold sweats. I must be the only person ever to have flashbacks about things that hadn't happened yet.'

'Don't believe you.'

'Five words, Andrew: "Demons of the Outer Darkness".'

'"Demons of the Outer Darkness" didn't need any work.'

'No, you're right. "Demons of the Outer Darkness" didn't need any work. Those five words on the cover I didn't have to change at all. It was the 6000 words on all the other pages that needed replacing. Namely because half the characters you'd written for had all died in the previous season.'

'Well I didn't have to watch the bloody thing as well, did I? That was your job.'

Mervyn addressed the tiny audience. 'Lady and gentleman, to sum up, the most important part of a script editor's job is to expect the unexpected.'

'There he is! That's the bastard!' Vanity was standing in the back of the room, in full *Vixens from the Void* costume, holding a quivering finger in their direction. 'That's the man who ravished my daughter! Calls himself a man of letters? Mad old lecher more like! Old pervert! And I have proof!' She was waving a bra in her other hand. The image of a vengeful Arkadia come to life, and wielding what appeared to be some kind of futuristic slingshot startled the fans.

Mervyn panicked and dived for cover underneath the table, wearing the edge of the tablecloth around his head like a burqa. Even though he was petrified with fear; he still noticed that at exactly the same moment he dived for cover, the *other* male members of the writers panel *also* hid under the table.

Arkadia charged into the room, knocking fans aside and upended the table, forcing Mervyn and the other men to scramble to their feet. He half ran, half crawled as he moved to the door. Vanity came after him, screaming obscenities. Burly stewards tried to rugby tackle her, but they were knocked aside too. Mervyn was near the door, finally, and dimly aware of the chaos exploding around him. He could hear Barbara Braintree shouting and screaming at Bob Braintree; the cosiest writing partnership in television was coming to an end behind him.

And then Vanity was there in front of him, throwing everything she could find on the desks, assaulting him with swearwords, pens and autograph books. Figurines and books rained down on him. A limited edition keyring caught him behind the ear and he went down, landing heavily on his knees. He knelt, ready for more punishment.

And then she wasn't there.

He looked blearily up, and saw that Andrew Jamieson had pinned Vanity to the floor in an extremely rare act of heroism.

'Get off me you... you hack bastard!'

'Go!' Andrew yelled. 'Run! Save yourself!'

Mervyn ran.

CHAPTER FORTY-THREE

He ran blindly to the lift, pressing the button, jabbing it repeatedly with his finger. The doors opened. He got in and waited for the doors to close, which they did with agonising slowness. And then the stiletto spike of a familiar *Vixens* 80s style knee-length boot wedged itself into the shrinking gap, causing the doors to judder and widen. Vanity had caught up with him. He was trapped. Why hadn't he just taken the stairs?

She got into the lift and slapped his face again and again, alternating hands like some bizarre alpine dance.

'You bastard Mervyn!'

'I'm sorry!' He sank slowly to the floor. 'I didn't know she was your daughter!'

'No excuse! How dare you prey on the young and innocent!'

'Vanity that's what I do! That's what we both do!'

'How dare you! You soiled my little Min! I'm going to kill you!'

'You dried-up old bitch!'

That was another voice. Just outside the lift.

It was Katherine Warner – angry and tear-stained, eye shadow creeping down her cheeks and collecting above her nostrils.

'Your bitch daughter killed my Smurf! You fucking bitches! You lied about him in your filthy book and you told her she was his daughter and she killed him for it! You couldn't leave us alone, could you! You couldn't let anyone be happy, miserable cow, you fucking bitch!'

Vanity had no intention of being talked to that way, even by a grieving girlfriend. 'She *was* his daughter, darling! If he'd dealt with it instead of denying it and trying to cover his undersized arse with you, she wouldn't have got so cross with him!'

'Cross? She *murdered* him, you fucking insane, deluded, dried-up old bitch!'

In Mervyn's experience, actresses didn't have face-to-face cat-fights.

Until now.

He had never seen the screeching, face-slapping, cheek-scratching, hair-tugging or blouse-ripping found in 1970s British sex comedies.

Until now.

Katherine went for Vanity, red nails drilling into Vanity's cheek. Vanity lunged and punched Katherine in the throat, grabbing her hair and yanking her head back. Katherine kicked out, winding Vanity and forcing her to join Mervyn on the floor of the lift.

Mervyn, meanwhile, had been planning his escape. He crawled on the floor between them, edging forward like a sniper. Fortunately, Katherine was half-in, half-out of the lift, and the doors were juddering apart as they detected an obstruction.

He got to his knees and scrambled out of the lift, striking the button for the top floor as he did so. Vanity and Katherine were too intent on screaming, snarling and tearing expensive bits of clothing from each other to notice his escape.

Thankfully, the lift doors finally closed, shutting them off from Mervyn and sending them hurtling up and away. The lift made further stops, showing its semi-naked contents to fans as it journeyed to the highest point of the hotel. Some were shocked; some took photos; some stuck their hands deep in their pockets and walked awkwardly to their rooms to think about what they'd just seen.

He took the stairs up to his room, huffing with the exertion and panic. He rammed his pass key in the slot and clawed open the door with shaking fingers. He hurled his clothes into his suitcase, slammed it shut – still with shirt sleeves and ties poking cheerfully out of the edges – and pulled it off the bed, dragging it to the floor.

And then his bedside phone rang.

CONVIX 15.
EARTH ORBIT THREE:

3.00pm

EVENT	*LOCATION*
COSPLAY DISCO	Vixos Central Nerve Centre (main stage, ballroom)
'ESCAPE TO FIRE' **EPISODE SCREENING**	The Catacombs of Herath (video lounge - room 1024)
HOW VIXENS FROM THE VOID IS BETTER THAN DOCTOR WHO **FAN PANEL** with Graham Goldingay, Fay Lawless, Craig Jones, Darren Cardew	The Seventh Moon of Groolia (room 1002)

CHAPTER FORTY-FOUR

Mervyn screamed, jumped a full three feet in the air, and dived for the phone, more to stop it making a noise than to find out who was calling.

Breathing heavily, heart jumping like an excited dog, he fell on the bed and put the receiver to his ear. 'Yes?'

'I know, Mervyn.' It was Minnie's voice. Flat. Cold. Threatening.

'What?' he gasped, barely able to form words.

'I know. About you and me... and my mother.'

Mervyn's heart stopped. He was dead. He knew he was, because he was definitely floating on the ceiling, looking down at his corpse.

All he could think to say was a 'No,' and a 'Listen, Minnie...'

'I'm coming to get you, Mervyn. Get ready to run.' Then a click, and the line went dead.

He threw the buzzing receiver on the table and grabbed his suitcase.

Mervyn ran.

CONVIX 15.
EARTH ORBIT THREE:

4.00pm

EVENT	*LOCATION*
COSPLAY DISCO	Vixos Central Nerve Centre (main stage, ballroom)
'THE BRIDE OF KRELL' **EPISODE SCREENING**	The Catacombs of Herath (video lounge – room 1024)
VIXENS FROM THE VOID: A DIFFERENT POINT OF VIEW **EXPERT PANEL** with Graham Goldingay, Fay Lawless, Craig Jones, Darren Cardew	The Seventh Moon of Groolia (room 1002)

CHAPTER FORTY-FIVE

He ran down the stairs and stopped, panting and sweating as he looked down at the foyer. It was full of people in costumes; half of them were dressed as Arkadia. He could walk straight into Vanity or Minnie and not even know it.

He wouldn't know it was them, but they'd know it was him. With his plain black jacket and trousers, he stood out like a goth at a glam rock concert.

Unless...

He had to get a disguise. If he wore a disguise, he could edge out of the door and they wouldn't spot him

'Hello Mr Stone!'

Mervyn cowered instinctively, but it was only Big-Nose Bob and Speccy Derek. They were once again in their purple make-up, overalls and bathing caps.

'Look, we're a Groolian delegation!'

'Just like you said!'

Mervyn grabbed Big-Nose Bob by the lapels and held a purple ear to his mouth.

'Do – you – have – more – of – that – purple – paint?' he enunciated, over the sound of Simple Minds singing *Don't You Forget About Me*.

'What?' said Bob. 'Right here, in my pocket, in case I need a touch-up before the smoochie songs.'

'Don't want to look shabby for the ladies,' said Speccy Derek.

'Come with me,' said Mervyn. He grabbed Derek with his other hand and dragged them to the lifts.

Inside the lift, Mervyn let go of them. They dusted themselves down and were getting ready to say something like 'What is the meaning of this?' Which was not easy when the person kidnapping them was a childhood hero.

Mervyn saved them the embarrassment. 'Someone's trying to kill me.'

'What?'

'Really?'

'Well, I tell a lie. To be specific, there's two people trying to kill me, but I think only one of them has actually murdered before and intends to kill me.'

'Really?'

'Wow.'

'I need your help. I'm going to be part of your delegation. Hope you don't mind.'

From the thrilled looks on Bob and Derek's faces, they realised they were on the verge of a new *Vixens* anecdote, one so huge that they themselves could tell it at conventions for the rest of their lives.

It was too risky to go back to Mervyn's room; Minnie was sure to have gone there first. They went up to the second floor and Derek's room. It was strewn with clothes, and a large inflatable Styrax was in the corner performing some kind of sex act with a blow-up doll. The doll had the name 'Medula' written on it in marker pen.

'Sorry about the mess,' Derek said lamely. 'Haven't cleared up properly since the Friday night.'

Mervyn went into the bathroom and coloured in his face furiously, making big heavy streaks of make-up. He was finished in minutes and then came out.

'Right, that's done.'

'You haven't done behind your ears.'

'I *said*... that's done.'

He ran back and forth across the room while Derek and Bob watched him in fascination, a piece of street theatre put on for their benefit. He wrapped a towel round his head, pulled the dressing gown off the door, put in on backwards and tied the belt tight. Then he rolled up his trouser legs. Not bad. He was starting to look like a Groolian. 'Have you got a swimming cap?' he asked.

Both Bob and Derek touched their heads nervously. 'Not a spare one, no'.

'Don't worry, I'll improvise.' Mervyn grabbed the hotel shower cap in the bathroom and rammed it on his head. He looked in the mirror. Not good enough. 'I can still tell it's me.'

Derek looked around and pounced on a pair of glasses by his bedside table. 'Try these dark glasses.'

'He can't wear those.'

'Why not?'

'Because Groolians have very poor eyesight. It said in "The Doomsday Sequence" that they have very poor eyesight and can't see in the dark. They wouldn't be able to see wearing dark glasses.'

'Look, it doesn't really matter...' groaned Mervyn.

'Okay, clever clogs, if they can't see in the dark, how did they go down that really dark tunnel in "Ship of the Stateless Ones" with no trouble at all?

'Well obviously the script editor was asleep on the job that day and he couldn't be arsed doing his...' They both realised they were in the presence of the script editor in question, and their argument dribbled away.

'Sorry,' said Derek.

Mervy popped the lenses out of the sunglasses and put them on. 'Satisfied?'

They nodded dumbly.

'I'll buy you a new pair, Derek. I promise. Just so long as I get out of here alive.'

CHAPTER FORTY-SIX

They left Speccy Derek's room, scuttling awkwardly, walking practically shoulder to shoulder. They would have looked very suspicious, but luckily everyone else in the hotel was doing his or her best to scuttle awkwardly too.

They were soon back in the foyer, where people spilled in and out of the main hall, laughing, drinking and chasing each other with clamps, mandibles and tentacles outstretched.

Mervyn peeled away from the group and sauntered up to the front desk. He waited impatiently for the people in front to hand in their keys and settle their bills.

A young couple settled their bill.

'Hope you enjoyed your stay,' trilled the receptionist.

The man behind them moved up, and after some heated discussion about how many massages he'd had, checked out too.

'Hope you enjoyed your stay,' trilled the receptionist, in exactly the same tone and inflection.

It was Mervyn's turn. 'I'm checking out,' he hissed, lowering his head to her ear.

'Of course, Mr...'

'Stone, Mr Mervyn Stone...' he muttered in a hoarse whisper.

The receptionist didn't take Mervyn's growl as an invitation to keep her voice down. She assumed he was putting on an alien voice. 'Of course, Mr Stone, I hope you enjoyed your stay,' she said loudly. She printed up a bill and handed it to him.

'I'm with the convention. My room is paid for by Mr Simon Josh.'

'Yes, he hasn't settled the account.'

'No, he wouldn't have.'

'Well I'm afraid he needs to. And according to the computer he checked out yesterday morning.'

'He actually checked out late the night before. He was the dead man who gassed himself in the funny space car outside.'

'Oh.'

'I'm sure, aside from being murdered, he enjoyed his stay very much.'

She gave him a look.

'You need to speak to Morris,' Mervyn continued.

'Morris who?'

'Well... I don't know his surname, but Morris should be handling things from now on.'

She looked sceptically at her screen. 'Okay... I've got a note here that

"VixEnterprises" are paying for the room. Mr Morris Campbell?'

'That's him.'

'... But not the extras. You have several movies on your bill that you haven't paid for.'

Mervyn cursed his filthy habits. He'd thrown everything in his case, including his wallet. He wrestled with the zips and pockets until his fingers grasped smooth leather. He sighed with relief, pulling it out and producing a credit card.

The receptionist was now looking at him directly. Up and down. Mervyn wondered why she was eyeing him in such a funny way. Everyone else looked weird. Why was she looking at him like that?

Then he realised that he was wearing hotel slippers, a hotel dressing gown, a hotel towel and a hotel shower cap.

'That's original,' she said with a smile. 'Most people just put that stuff in their suitcase.'

'Ha ha.'

'I'll let you have the shower cap, but we do sell hotel merchandise, should our guests wish to have a souvenir of their stay.'

Mervyn didn't want to strip in the foyer. He thought it might make him look conspicuous.

'Do you know what, I loved my stay so much, I want to walk out here covered in my hotel merchandise. How much is that?'

She told him. The terrifying sum would neatly dispose of half of his convention appearance fee.

Mervyn cursed. 'Okay. Okay. Put it on my card.' She typed in the extras, with agonising slowness.

Then she handed him his bill, and he was just about to pass her his credit card and key when he noticed a flash of orange out of the corner of his eye. He turned away from the desk to see someone dressed as Arkadia standing in the doorway of the hotel.

Facing him. Looking at him.

'Arkadia' wasn't short, fat or stumpy, so it could be either one of two people: Stuart or Minnie.

The figure strode directly towards him. Mervyn didn't feel like taking any chances. He retreated into the bowels of the hotel, the receptionist watching him disappear with wide-eyed curiosity.

'I've changed my mind. I'm putting this stuff back. Take it all off my bill...' he called to her.

He turned to go along the opposite corridor, only to see *another* 'Arkadia' marching directly towards him, looking grim and determined. One gloved hand was clenching and unclenching, twitching open and closed like a carnivorous plant.

Despite the mask Mervyn knew it was Minnie, and his soul leapt out of his body screaming, danced along his spine and crapped in his head. She was coming for him.

Mervyn ducked into the fancy-dress disco, hoping to lose her amid the alien life forms that writhed and jiggled in the semi-darkness. He weaved through, apologising when he stepped on a flipper or snagged himself on a tentacle.

'Sorry, sorry, pardon me, coming through...'

'Arkadia' dived in after him and was pointing at him and shouting. The hand was still twitching. Its owner was deeply unhinged. He doubled round and waded back out into the foyer...

... Only to come face to face with Minnie. She wasn't even in costume. She grabbed him with her powerful arms and dragged him into the tiny corridor where the cleaning ladies put their trolleys. There was no one around to see them.

CHAPTER FORTY-SEVEN

She slammed him into the wall. 'I said I was going to get you.'

Their noses were less than an inch apart. Mervyn's eyes watered as he tried to focus on her face. Now that he knew the truth, Mervyn could see that the family resemblance was insanely strong. Not that he was stupid enough to mention it. She had the mane of lustrous hair, the pointy aristocratic nose. The wide, mobile face that could flip from sardonic-smiley-sexy to sardonic-angry-sexy in a split-second.

She's so like her mother. It was so obvious. Some detective I turned out to be.

'Minnie, I didn't think it right to tell you...'

'That you slept with my mother after me?'

'Ummm. Yes.'

'The same night?'

'Yes...'

She stared into his face, searching his eyes, like a snake wondering where to strike first.

Then she kissed him, hard and long, on the mouth. Mervyn's lips felt dead, but he soon had no choice but to respond.

She finally broke away, pulling at his bottom lip with her teeth. She fixed him with a filthy grin. A grin just like Vanity's.

'No champagne. Well, at least you don't taste like Mother.'

'Agh,' said Mervyn.

Minnie let him go. His legs just about supported his body.

'Did I scare you?'

'Um. A bit.'

'Good. I like freaking people out.'

'Ah.'

'Beats the boredom, doesn't it?' She looked at Mervyn's ashen face. 'You're not going to die on me, are you?'

Mervyn straightened up. 'Not just yet.'

'I'm glad. I like you Mervyn.'

'I'm glad you do.'

She barked a laugh. 'Sorry for scaring you. As I said, I like freaking people out.'

'So I see.'

'I give them a bit of a scare. Most of them start scared, because at least they know I'm Vanity Mycroft's daughter. Unlike you...'

'Yes. Sorry about that.'

'Don't worry about it. It's nice to be hit on without thinking the other person's doing it to get a trophy.'

'Likewise.'

'Hey, we're very alike, you and me.'

Mervyn didn't think so.

'Anyway, I just wind them up further. Right up to eleven.'

'Was... was...' Mervyn struggled to get his breath back. 'Was that why you threatened Simon? And Smurf? To freak them out?'

'Yeah, and to freak out Mum as well. She deserved it, after all.'

'Well, perhaps she did – keeping the truth from you, about who your real father was. That must have been upsetting.'

She pulled a face. 'Not that. I've had four dads. I know how Mum can lie to everyone. I always guessed that bollocks about me being the daughter of Sir Bafta of Wotchamacallit was just that; bollocks.'

'Oh.'

'No, what *really* pissed me off was when she showed me my birth certificate.'

'Right.'

'Finding out my middle name was "Metro". I mean, fuck. Can you believe it?'

'Minnie Metro Mycroft?'

'Minnie Metro Mycroft,' she rolled her eyes. 'You see, our family have this stupid tradition of naming our kids after –'

'Where they were conceived.'

'Oh, you've read mum's book.'

'She told me.'

'So. I was named in honour of a desperate five-minute shag in a crap English car about the size of a wheelbarrow. Ha fucking ha.' She stepped back and folded her arms, one leg bent. It was a classic *Vixens* pose. Mervyn could almost have imagined it was a younger Vanity Mycroft, preparing for a publicity shoot. 'So I didn't kill Simon or Smurf, if that's what you're thinking. Though I'm flattered you thought I did.'

'Flattered? That's a crazy thing to say. Your own father's been killed...'

'He wasn't my father. As I said. I've had four dads. I didn't need any more, especially one that won't even admit it. He was no loss. Neither was Simon.' She frowned. 'Are you sure you're okay?'

'I'm fine.'

'Sorry, I got carried away. I might have done too much of a number on you. I would have left it at waiting in your hotel room last night, and the big hug this morning; made you think I was some nutty stalker for the whole weekend. That was funny. But when you told me you thought I was a mad murderer, I couldn't resist, sorry.'

'But... You did threaten Simon Josh?'

'Hell, yeah.'

'But he let you work at the convention!'

She looked at him pityingly. 'He didn't "let" anyone work at the convention. We had no loyalty to Simon. He was a twat. We work for Morris. Tell you the truth, I think Morris used me as a steward to wind him up. Morris likes stirring things up, from time to time.'

They walked out of the corridor.

'I've got to hand it to you, Mr Stone Ranger.' She grinned at him admiringly. 'How rampant and self-obsessed do you have to be to sleep with the wrong person and not even notice?'

Mervyn shrugged, and gave a weak smile.

'You're an interesting man, Mervyn.' She looked over the foyer, where pin boards and props were being taken out to waiting vans. 'Anyway, fun's over. Got to pack up. Maybe I'll see you before I go, yeah?'

'That will be nice.' Mervyn heard himself saying. He was his own worst enemy, and considering the enemies he had at that very moment that was saying quite a lot.

'I'll try not to scare you again.'

'Great.'

She suddenly growled and swiped a hand near his face. Mervyn flinched. She laughed and left.

He watched her retreating bottom with a mixture of awe, pity, lust and fear.

Then he started thinking about what she'd just said: *How rampant and self-obsessed do you have to be to sleep with the wrong person and not even notice?*

Then everything clicked. The story was complete, all in place.

He'd finished it.

He had to have another look at Vanity's autobiography. And catch the murderer, somehow.

Before the murderer struck again.

Someone tapped on his shoulder, making him yelp. It was Stuart. He was dressed in his Vixen costume. 'Why did you run away from me?' he said, hurt.

'Sorry. I thought you were someone else.'

'You have to come with me.'

'Why?'

'There's been another murder.'

CHAPTER FORTY-EIGHT

John the Stalker's room wasn't pleasant, even allowing for the dead body lying in the middle of it. A suitcase lay open on the bed. The T-shirt with the huge-bosomed warrior-queen was marinating sadly in the sink. The stench of body odour floated in the air like John's recently departed spirit, hanging over both of them.

John himself was lying on the floor behind the bed, his head caved in. Stuart and Mervyn stood over him. The blood had oozed out over the carpet and stained his beloved collage of photos, which was lying curled near his feet.

This was the second body Mervyn had come across this weekend (or the second and a half if he counted the bits of Smurf as a fraction) and he was surprised how quickly he'd got used to them. He wasn't shaking and his heart wasn't jumping in his chest. It was fast becoming business as usual.

He picked up the ruined collection of photos and placed it almost reverently on the desk. 'Goodnight, sweet prints,' he said sadly, to himself.

'Why would anyone want to kill *him*?' said Stuart, helplessly.

Mervyn looked around the room. 'The reason he died is probably long gone, by now...' Then he noticed what John was holding. 'My God. It's still here. That's why.'

He leaned across and pulled a battered piece of papier-mâché from under John's arm. 'Oh God, he's still warm. The blood's not dried either. He's not been dead long. Just minutes.'

That definitely took Minnie off the suspect list. She had been too busy chasing him round the hotel.

But he already knew she wasn't the killer.

Because he knew who the killer was.

Mervyn showed Stuart the piece of papier-mâché. 'He died for this. He was given this as compensation for Vanity not turning up to the celebrity breakfast. Morris got Vanity to sign it with a kiss for him.' Mervyn looked at the piece. 'I didn't expect it to still be here. He must have put up a hell of a fight for it.'

'Well it's "signed",' said Stuart, automatically, seeing Vanity's lipstick on one side. He realised what he said and blushed. 'I'm sorry, I didn't mean to say that.'

'No Stuart. You're exactly right. It *is* signed. With a special autograph. And that's what makes this cruddy old bit of Styrax worth killing for.' He turned the piece of papier-mâché round. 'There, you see? As we suspected.'

Stuart looked at the other side of the lump with something approaching awe. 'Gosh, yes.'

'I need to go to my room, and check Vanity's book,' said Mervyn. 'Then when I've confirmed my suspicions, we need to set a trap for the killer.'

CHAPTER FORTY-NINE

Back in his room, Mervyn divested himself of his Groolian ensemble, unrolled his trouser legs and tried to get the purple make-up off his face. The anecdotes had been right; it was bloody hard to shift. He finally scrubbed it away, but he was left with a pink complexion that made him look like he'd caught the sun.

Then looked through Vanity's book. He reread Chapter 13.

'Okay. I'm satisfied. There's only one person who can be the murderer.'

'Really?' asked Stuart.

'Oh yes. You see, I think Simon tried to blackmail two people last night. Me and someone else. I, of course, didn't know I was being blackmailed. The other person did know, and did something about it.' He waved the book. 'And from this chapter, there's only one other person it could be.' He sat on the bed. Stuart looked at him.

'So what now?' the young man asked.

'I don't know.'

'Oh.'

They sat there for a while, not saying anything.

'Well, in this situation...' Stuart said slowly, 'you'd normally find a quiet place, confront the murderer, throw your deductions and your evidence in their face, and watch them crumble and admit everything.'

'I do know the drill, Stuart. But this is a new thing for me, confronting a murderer. Perhaps it won't work out like that.'

'Oh, you'll be brilliant!'

Mervyn wasn't so sure. 'But what happens if things get nasty?'

'Hey, why don't I hide in the wardrobe and film it with my digital camera? If anything violent happens, I'll leap out and save you.'

'That sounds like a plan.'

Mervyn rang another room in the hotel. 'Hello. I'm ringing to let you know I've come across some information... Let's just say I've got a piece of Styrax here in my room. I think you know what I'm saying... Don't come the innocent... Fine... Then I'll just have to go to plan B, and hand what I have over to the police, tell them what I know... I think we should talk about it.'

There was a longer pause as he listened to the response.

'What do you mean "Why?" I've got no career. The only money I can rely on is dwindling royalties and convention appearance fees. This is the first one I've done in seven years and I didn't like it very much. I was hoping you'd help me so I never have to go to another one, if you catch my drift.'

He put the phone down and looked at Stuart. 'Five minutes,' he said.

Stuart gave a thumbs-up and climbed into the wardrobe.

Mervyn felt queasy. The knock knockity-knock at the door sent his stomach into cartwheels and it was all he could do not to run into the bathroom to vomit.

He opened the door.

'Come in.'

CONVIX 15. EARTH ORBIT THREE:

6.00pm

EVENT	*LOCATION*
THE MAJOR'S LAST SALUTE RODERICK BURGESS Goodbyes and farewells. See you next year!	Vixos Central Nerve Centre (main stage, ballroom)

CHAPTER FIFTY

ConVix had a tradition. In the final minutes of every convention, before all the guests waved goodbye from the stage, there was a final interview with the elder statesman of *Vixens from the Void*, Roddy Burgess, asking him whether he'd enjoyed the convention and inviting him to 'dismiss the troops' for another year.

The ballroom was full, packed with attendees holding their coats and suitcases, ready to go home or – which was more likely – on to another convention in another dingy part of the country.

Roddy himself sat in a comfy armchair on stage, facing the one where Simon had usually sat. This time, Simon's chair was occupied by Morris. The wedge-shaped Styrax Sentinel and the penile Maaganoid were still there, flanking them like silent sentries.

'So, Major,' rumbled Morris. 'Have you enjoyed your convention?'

What usually came forth at this point was a jumble of bluff military nonsense, about how the rations were splendid, his billet was comfy, his batmen were well drilled...

But not this time.

Roddy just sat there and grinned.

CHAPTER FIFTY-ONE

The person Mervyn had deduced to be the murderer came into the room.

'What's this nonsense about?'

Mervyn showed them the lump of Styrax. It was getting very tatty now, falling apart in his hand. 'Stop pretending. I can't believe you did it. I can't believe you killed Sheldon.'

'I beg your pardon? I did no such thing.'

'I know what happened back in 1987. Back on the last day of filming.'

There was a dismissive sniff. 'You only *think* you know, Merv, darling...'

'Oh I know. The evidence all started coming out the day before yesterday, thanks to me. When I fell on that Styrax and smashed it to bits. This was written on the inside.'

He flipped it round, displaying the numbers '376 – 229 – 22' and the words 'HANDS OFF – GINGER!' and 'SAFE' on the other side, scrawled on a crumpled article about Prince Andrew and Sarah Ferguson squished into the papier-mâché.

'The minute Simon Josh saw this, he knew what it meant. Because Simon was a fan, and of course, fans know everything.' He pointed to the 'SAFE'. 'This doesn't say "safe" at all. What it is is an autograph.' He looked at it and grinned wearily. 'Obvious, really... The one thing that Simon would know better than anyone is how to recognise the autographs of stars from *Vixens from the Void*.' He pointed at it again. 'And "SAFE" is actually the autograph of our long-dead Styrax operator, Sheldon Algernon Forbes-Ellis.'

CHAPTER FIFTY-THREE

'But inspector!' Nicholas spread his hands and engaged his most winning grin. 'Lawks a-mercy! Midgets wrote on the inside of their Styrax every single day. They got very bored sitting inside their little cocoons for hours on end. It's a fact of life, dear heart. I'm sure their opinions about me were also luridly documented on the inside, and many tasteless limericks about Vanity. Stripe me pink, I've no notion where you're going with this, and I ain't got a clue how this makes me a murderer, cor blimey, me old guv'nor.'

'Please Nicholas, no more cod cockney. This is serious.'

Nicholas fell silent.

'You're right, Nicholas. Midgets wrote on the insides of their Styrax every day when we were filming. It was like prison; they used to mark off the hours and write rude graffiti about each other. But this graffiti was special; it was written on the day after the 1987 general election – three months *after* Sheldon got sacked. I presume "HANDS OFF – GINGER!" was a reference to our red-haired leader of the opposition, Neil Kinnock. Sheldon was a ferocious Tory, I'm sure he was delighted that the Labour Party had failed to get in yet again.'

He pointed to the numbers. 'I thought at first these numbers were a combination to a safe – after all, they'd been written right under the word "SAFE". But of course, they're not are they? It's the result... 376 seats for the Tories, 229 for Labour and 22 for the SDP–Liberal Alliance. A result which, unless Sheldon was clairvoyant, could only have been known to him on the 12th of June; the last day of filming. And he shouldn't have been there... Firstly, he'd been sacked three months ago, and secondly, he was meant to be "accidentally" dying in a fire at his house several miles away.'

Nicholas was silent, listening to Mervyn with polite interest.

'You were the only one who could have got Sheldon on that set. Only the producer could have done that. Why was he there, Nicholas? Did you lure him on set and kill him? Why kill him at all?'

At last Nicholas became animated. 'I didn't want to kill the little sweetie! What do you take me for? I'm not a murderer! Why would I want to do that?'

'I don't know. I was hoping you could tell me.'

'I'm afraid the answer is much more mundane, and sadly tragic, dear heart. I didn't lure him. I *begged* him. You remember what it was like on that final day, Mervy. Everyone was pulling a sickie. No one was turning up for work – including Smurf. The Styrax were only built to be operated by dwarves. I was desperate to find someone to work the damn things.' Nicholas pulled out a handkerchief and mopped his brow. 'I rang him up and paid him out of my own pocket. If he kept quiet, just did the work, stayed inside the Styrax, then no one would be any the wiser.' He sighed, wearily. He looked almost glad at the chance to unburden himself. 'I came back at the end of the day, and he'd just... died. Inside the Styrax. So I did kill him. You're right. It was all my fault.'

Mervyn was shocked. 'So it was an accident.'

'No, you were right the first time. I killed him, old love.'

Nicholas looked distraught. Mervyn was in the odd position of persuading the murderer that he shouldn't feel bad about it. 'Nicholas, don't get upset. You weren't to know he'd die in there.'

'But I *did*. The reason why Sheldon was let go was because he had a bad heart. You ever hear of achondroplasia?'

'Yes, I think I read it somewhere.'

'It's the condition that dwarves suffer from. Not that they'd say 'suffer', of course. Positivity and proud to be wee and all that, but the inescapable fact is, achondroplasia doesn't just make you small; it brings all sorts of health problems too. Heart problems in particular.'

'So that's why Sheldon got Smurf to take his medical for him.'

'Exactly, old love. Sheldon wanted to carry on working, but he knew the results would send him into early retirement. Unfortunately for Sheldon, he and Smurf started squabbling again; two little boys with two little toys and all that. Smurf told me he'd taken the medical on Sheldon's behalf, and landed Sheldon right in the poo, so I had no choice. I had to let Sheldon go.'

'So, you smuggled him on set, hid him in the Styrax, and he just...?'

'Indeed. Maybe it was a heart attack, perhaps it was heat exhaustion. But the fact remained, I had an uninsured unauthorised dead midget on my set, whom I had smuggled in and used illegally on the show, knowing full well about his dodgy little ticker...' Nicholas actually started to weep. 'I was looking at the end of my career, old love; not to mention the end of the show. We were only two years in and we were a success. *The Late, Late Breakfast Show* incident was only six months old; do you think we would have been allowed to continue, no matter what the ratings were? I couldn't let the plug get pulled on *Vixens* all for my own silly mistake. So I bundled him into the boot of my car, propped him up inside his house and set fire to it. Then I returned to the BBC and checked for any evidence of Sheldon's presence on the set. I was most meticulous, and I didn't find anything incriminating.'

Mervyn supplied the information. 'Mainly because on that final day, Bernard decided to steal the Styrax... Luckily for you Bernard had a problem with reading. All the time he had it, he didn't examine the writing on the inside as closely as he might have done.'

Nicholas composed himself, dabbing at his eyes with his hankie 'Absolutely, my old fruit. The words on the inside might as well have been Egyptian hieroglyphs for all Bernard knew.' He sighed. 'But then it came into Simon's possession, and then came you, my sweet, and your deliciously destructive backside. My luck ran out, as your bum smashed it into pieces and revealed the evidence for Simon to discover.'

Nicholas got up out of his chair. Mervyn wondered whether he was going to make a run for it, but he just wandered over to Mervyn's bedside table and picked up Vanity's autobiography. He thumbed through it.

Mervyn knew the bit that he was looking for.

'These fans know everything, dear boy. They collate material like MI5 and have it all inside their heads, ready to use at a moment's notice. The moment Simon saw Sheldon's signature scribbled in the inside he knew something was up...' He pointed at the fragment of Styrax. 'That bit you've got there was just a tip of the iceberg, Mervy. Sheldon covered the inside of the bloody thing with gloatings about another term for Mistress Thatcher, "Four more years", "Maggie! Maggie! Maggie!"' He thumbed the pages of Vanity's book. 'Simon knew that Sheldon wasn't supposed to be there at that time. How could he be? It was in the script, the production notes and every tiresome little fact-check thing they write on the internet. And of course, he'd already just read this piece of lurid kiss-and-tell from Ms Mycroft.' He read aloud.

> Early morning, and everyone was setting up cameras and stuff. I saw his little Styrax in the corner of the props area. It waggled one of its claw thingies, so I knew he was inside. So I hurried towards it. But damn and blast my luck! I had to hide behind a pillar. Ace producer Nicholas Everett was leaning on it, going through the shooting script with Smurf. I could see the top of Smurf's adorable little head poking out the back, and occasionally an arm came out, and pointed at bits in the script. Mervyn Stone our cuddly script editor came over and had a quick discussion with Nicholas, and they put Smurf's hatch on for him. My goodness! If the props boys had seen them handle the Styrax, they would have been up in arms! It would have been an instant strike; lights out, all out and they'd be standing outside round their braziers, waving their placards. Anyway, they left Smurf alone, and finally I could make my move.

Nicholas closed the book. 'You see?'

'Oh, definitely. It's proof that you knew Sheldon was on set. You talked to the dwarf in the Styrax, went through the script with him – Vanity saw you. You had to know it was Sheldon.'

'Precisely.'

Mervyn smiled, despite himself. 'Do you know, that bit of the book earned me a blackmail note from Simon too.'

Nicholas was surprised. 'You, old ducks?'

'Of course. The chapter reads like I knew Sheldon was there too. Simon must have hedged his bets, and assumed we were both behind some kind of sinister midget murder. Look.' Mervyn produced his blackmail note. So did Nicholas.

They were both holding photocopies of the lump of Styrax interior with the writing: 376 – 229 – 22. HANDS OFF – GINGER! SAFE. They turned the notes over. Each had suitably ambiguous messages from Simon on the other side.

'Snap,' said Mervyn.

Despite themselves, they both laughed.

'I assume you got a copy of Vanity's book too, with Chapter 13 highlighted.'

'Snap,' said Nicholas. This time there was no laughter.

Mervyn looked at his blackmail note thoughtfully. 'The thing is, even after all these years, I *remember* coming over to help you put the hatch on. Smurf didn't speak, and I couldn't see his face. I just *assumed* it was Smurf. I'm ashamed to say it, but in the dark of a Styrax interior one dwarf looks very much like another to me.'

Nicholas smiled. 'Which brings us nicely to Vanity.'

CHAPTER FIFTY-FOUR

Minnie's words had given Mervyn the key: *How rampant and self-obsessed do you have to be to sleep with the wrong person and not even notice?*

'So on that day, Sheldon didn't stay in his Styrax all the time, did he?'

'Alas no. I asked him to, but when my back was turned he was enticed out by the siren call of the Mycroft in heat.'

'They did the dirty in the big Styrax. And she didn't realise in the dark she'd had sex with the wrong midget.'

Nicholas gave a tired smile. 'Typical Vanity, eh Mervyn? Who knows? It might have been the sexual exertions that finished him off.'

'So that was another secret that stayed hidden until Vanity wrote her autobiography. No wonder Smurf went ballistic. He was telling the truth. He didn't have sex with Vanity; he hadn't even turned up for work that day. He was nowhere near her naughty bits at the time... And he wasn't the father of Vanity's daughter.'

'Smurf wanted to clear his name, dear heart. He wanted to prove to his girlfriend that he didn't do the dirty with La Mycroft. *He wanted to take a DNA test...'* Nicholas looked imploringly at him. 'Can you imagine what would have happened if he had?'

'Of course I can imagine. Even if Simon was silenced and all the evidence of Sheldon's presence in the Styrax was destroyed... If Smurf had taken the test and proved that he wasn't the father, the question would still remain, "Who was the father of Minnie Metro Mycroft?" Attention would turn to the only other dwarf at the BBC who had ever operated a Styrax. Vanity would realise she'd been with Sheldon. She would have been an eyewitness – well, not an "eye" witness exactly, but...'

'Quite so.' Nicholas spread his hands helplessly. 'I had it coming to me from both directions, if you pardon the expression. Material evidence... DNA tests... I was planning to return to producing, my first love, but all this nonsense was going to scupper all that. Worst, it was probably going to put me in prison.'

'And becoming a multiple murderer was going to stop you going to prison?'

'I'm not a murderer! I didn't kill anyone!'

'Not a murderer?' Mervyn exploded. 'Are you serious?'

'I know it sounds incredible, Mervyn, but yes, I am serious old petal. I'm not a murderer.'

Mervyn feared the worst. Nicholas had gone completely mad.

CHAPTER FIFTY-FIVE

Roddy continued, to the obvious pleasure of everyone present. 'It's bally lucky you conscripted me to head this little campaign, which I have dubbed "Operation: Styrax Genocide"...'

Much laughter from the crowd. Roddy was on form this year.

'... But I must say I was less than pleased to be conscripted by Josh, for all my previous campaigns; having a chap over a barrel because he has a few measly unlicensed firearms on his premises...' He gave a petulant frown. 'I mean, if a chap can't have a couple of Webleys, a few Tommy guns, a Bren, a Howitzer and the odd rocket launcher for his own personal use, then what's the world coming to?'

'Erm... Major...?

'It's political correctness.'

'Are you okay?'

Roddy looked at Morris, as if noticing him for the first time. 'Gone mad.'

'What?'

'Political correctness. Gone mad.'

'Oh.'

'How can you deny it?'

'Because it's not true, dear heart!'

'Do you deny meeting with Simon Josh? Do you deny him blackmailing you? Do you deny getting him drunk that night? Sticking him in the Styrax, turning the engine on and running a hose from the exhaust and sticking it in Simon's face? Do you deny scrabbling around in his room and faking a suicide note?'

Nicholas frowned. 'Well, if you put it like that, Mervyn, no I don't deny any of that.'

'And do you deny tampering with Smurf's Styrax with the intention of killing him?'

'Ah... No. I don't deny that either.'

'And do you deny visiting that fan's room to get this lump of Styrax off him? And attacking him when he wouldn't sell it?'

Nicholas's mouth opened and closed.

'Do you?'

'No I don't. I don't deny it.'

'But you're not a murderer.'

'I know this sounds incredible Mervyn. I did do all those things you so vividly described, but I didn't kill anyone. You know me, I hate unpleasantness in all its forms.'

'You're insane.'

Stuart was still in the wardrobe, recording everything. Then he stopped. The red light winked off the camera.

Nicholas stood up. Mervyn moved back a step, instinctively. He hoped Stuart could see all right and would be able to escape the wardrobe if Nicholas tried anything.

'Here's the thing Mervyn, old love,' said Nicholas. 'I did those things to Simon – he was demanding I hand over my whole business for flip's sake – but I couldn't bring myself to *kill* him. The night before last was so horrid. It was cold and wet, the rain just chucking it down, the annoying little man had drunk all my whisky, and he kept dribbling on my shirt as I carried him outside. The hose kept dropping out of the hole, I just couldn't get it to stay in – to coin a phrase.' He gave a tired wink. 'I just gave up, old son. I took it as a sign I was never meant to be a murderer, so I removed the hose and went back to my room to get a grip on myself. I knew I wasn't a murderer. I told myself to sort myself out; be a man, dear heart! I just had to refuse to get blackmailed, let Simon do his worst, and face the consequences. When I emerged to tidy up the car park, I found him, just as you all did, with the engine running, the hose fixed neatly back in place and Simon dead.'

'Are you serious?'

'Never more so. I know how this looks, old stick. When I rushed out into the car park that night I was as surprised as anybody. But *after* that night, what was a girl to do? I knew if Simon's blackmail came out, everyone would assume I did it, so I just kept trying to cover things up, trying to get Smurf to calm down and not take his DNA test. Yes, I briefly flirted with Dame Homicide once more; I inspected his Styrax with half a mind to tampering with it. I had a little look at the gas cylinders, and even opened the nozzle on one, but it was all smelly and made me feel sick, and there was no way he wouldn't notice the odour when he got inside, so I resealed it and left...'

'And the next thing you know, Smurf and his Styrax have been scattered over half the hotel.'

'Precisely.'

'Do you have any idea how fantastically mad that sounds?'

'My darling boy, I wouldn't even be telling you if you weren't confronting me here and now. They'd lock me away in the rest home for deranged and homicidal producers – if they still had room for one more.'

'So you seriously deny everything? What about John the Stalker?'

Nicholas shrugged. 'You mean the chap with the bit of remaining

Styrax? The one with the T-shirt with the improbable lady on it?'

Mervyn nodded. 'That's him.'

'Well I did go to his room and asked to buy the piece back, and of course he wouldn't sell, and I did get a bit cross and pushed him a little – to my own horror, I might add... I touched him! He was so smelly! Anyway, he wasn't impressed with my macho stance, and I retired defeated. Why, has he made a complaint?'

Mervyn was stunned. 'He's dead.'

'He's what?'

'You killed him.'

'Who says? I only pushed him dear heart, a girly slap.'

'You caved his head in!'

'Look at me old love! I couldn't knock the head off a daffodil! I'll repeat myself, once more, for a take: I didn't kill anybody! I quickly decided I was not cut out to be a mass murderer! I have no technical ability, I swoon at the sight of blood oranges, let alone blood; I can't even forge a decent suicide note...'

Mervyn suddenly realised something. His blood went cold. Suddenly he remembered he'd forgotten something important. He realised he'd been wrong all the time. He realised who the murderer *really* was.

He edged towards the door of the hotel room.

'Where are you going?'

'Shhh!'

He quietly fished out the suicide note from his jacket. He'd completely forgotten about it.

'The suicide note you put in the Styrax?' he hissed. 'Was it this one?'

Nicholas took it. He looked at it with astonishment. 'Yes... I found it in Simon's room on a pile of photos and thought it would do. I thought they'd make quite good last words. Why have you got it?'

'It was on the floor of the Styrax.'

'What? Then what did you give to the police?'

Nicholas was speaking far too loud. Mervyn held a finger to his lips. He slowly turned the handle of the door.

'The *other* suicide note. The one on the dashboard.'

'What other one?'

'I didn't tell anyone that there were two... The one I gave to the police was the one on the dashboard. It was perfectly written, brilliantly forged and looked great. Yours, on the other hand...'

'Was crap.' Nicholas sighed. 'I know, dear heart. My murder attempts were just, how can I put it delicately? They were rubbish, lame...'

The wardrobe door creaked open.

'They were ropey,' said Stuart.

Nicholas looked, astonished, at the young man who emerged.

'Ropey. Just pathetic,' said Stuart. 'Your murders were rushed. There was no planning, no thought put into any of them. Is it any wonder I had to improve them?'

CHAPTER FIFTY-SIX

'Nevertheless,' continued Roddy. 'This is a time of war. And me having a couple of shooting irons under my bed is very fortuitous. And I am sure the local constabulary will forgive my firearm licences being AWOL, in the circumstances...'

Morris gave a mystified look to Roddy, to the audience, and back to Roddy again. 'We have no idea what you're talking about, Major. Shall we just give you the Last Salute and let you dismiss the troops?'

'How can we dismiss the troops when we're at war, Corporal?' thundered Roddy, his sudden bark distorting the microphone.

'Um... We can't?'

'No we bally well can't! Not until I lead the charge against the robots!'

'You,' said Mervyn. His voice had imploded and it was now a dry squcak.

Stuart didn't respond to the accusation. 'The murders were rubbish! The business with the hose? All it took was an old rag and it completely stayed in place! Just a bit of thought, that's all!' He sighed wearily, like a parent explaining for the millionth time what a potty was for. 'It's just like "Assassins of Destiny – Part two" all over again. You can't be fussed to do a proper job, and it's up to fans like me to come along and do it properly!'

'You killed them? Why?'

Stuart looked at Mervyn with deep exasperation. He pointed at Nicholas. 'Watching him wrestle with the gas cylinder was just painful. All it took was a well-aimed bullet and he was sitting on a home-made bomb! Much more effective than gassing him!'

'But... why? Why do it?'

At last Stuart answered Mervyn's question. 'I wanted to do it properly, Mr St– Mervyn,' he said simply. 'And I wanted to give you something to do that you were good at; give you a bit of self-respect back. Just like when I paid you to write for me in Peterborough. I knew you were disappointed we weren't Hollywood big-time boys, but when you wrote our little fan play... I could see it in your eyes... I mean, I knew. I knew you felt more... Alive.'

Mervyn didn't feel very alive at the moment. He felt like he'd died and gone to heaven, only to discover it was just like a science fiction convention, with endless queues of shuffling people waiting for God's autograph. Would the madness never stop?

Nicholas spluttered. 'You knew... All the time, about me?'

'Oh yes, Mr Everett. Nicholas. The moment the Styrax got broken. I knew exactly what Simon knew. I mean, gosh, it was obvious wasn't it? It was there, lying in the bits for all to see. Any fan could have worked it out.' He gave a cheery grin. 'I followed Simon, and I watched him photocopy his lump of Styrax in the office and I watched him leave his little blackmail notes, and I watched your meeting with him, and I watched you get him drunk, and I watched you put him in the Styrax Superior, and I watched you and your sloppy murder attempt, and then you went away... and then I did it properly for you.'

Mervyn looked hollow-eyed. 'And then you contacted me.'

'Of course! What a chance! Mervyn Stone with a proper murder mystery with proper bodies! What an opportunity to see you investigate in reality! Wow! Mervyn Stone deducing a real murderer!' His bottom lip popped out. 'But disappointing, too. My goodness it was hard prodding you in the right direction! Reading out the book to you, pulling out the blackmail note you'd missed in the envelope...' He slapped his forehead in exasperation at the foolishness of it all. '... Pointing out the Styrax were padded with papier-mâché, actually *giving* you a piece of Styrax... You didn't want to try and fit it all together. Even when I dragged you to a computer and showed you what the numbers meant, you got all excited, and the next thing I know you'd given up and were checking out of the hotel! I didn't expect to have to do the last murder all by myself, but you didn't seem interested in doing a proper job either! It was just like the script for "Day of The Styrax" all over again, just so sloppy, so half-hearted! You just kept missing the connections, I had to do blummin' everything! Kill the fan, put the evidence in an easy-to-spot place and then escort you to the murder victim!' He rubbed his forehead theatrically. 'Talk about hard work!'

He stopped talking. Finally.

The looked at each other uncertainly; the detective, the almost-murderer and the detective-turned-proper-murderer.

'So, my darlings...' said Nicholas, with an arch of an eyebrow. 'What now?'

'Yes,' said Mervyn, fearing the worst. 'What happens now?'

'Well,' grinned Stuart, 'I've got brilliant footage of you accusing Nicholas of being the murderer, and Nicholas admitting it. I haven't recorded this last bit, that would spoil it. But the first bit is going to look so good on my website, after I've cleaned it up and sorted out the sound issues...' He tapped his finger on his chin. '... I'm kind of thinking that, and this is just off the top of my head here, you two have a fight, and kill each other, and everybody leaves the convention thinking that Nicholas murdered everybody, including the man who discovered his guilty secret. That's you Mr St– Mervyn.'

'I gathered,' said Mervyn drily.

'Sorry...' burbled Nicholas, confused. 'Let me just clarify. You want us to... kill each other?'

'Oh no. You don't have to do that!' laughed Stuart. He pulled out an automatic pistol. 'I'll shoot both of you, and leave the gun in Mr Everett's hand, sort of a suicide thing, how's that sound?'

Mervyn tried to keep his voice steady. 'I don't know. Is there a plan B?'

'Not really,' said Stuart cheerfully. 'It's the best I could come up with in the circumstances, sorry.'

'I don't know,' sighed Mervyn. 'It just seems rushed and sloppy. It's kind of like what we'd do in the old days, eh Nicholas?'

Stuart frowned. He was hurt.

'I mean, who's going to believe a man who murdered three people to keep his secret buried is just going to commit suicide after killing a fourth? It's just not logical, is it?'

Stuart blushed furiously. 'Well it's the best I can come up with given the time.'

'Oh they all say that,' snapped Mervyn. 'We've heard it all before. All the excuses. "We had no money, the budget had been cut again, the lights were too bright, the studio was too small, we couldn't afford this, we didn't have time to do that, the unions were pulling the plugs out at ten, and we had to get it in the can..." All the usual tired old excuses...' Mervyn pointed at the gun with disdain. 'And the fact I contrived to confront Nicholas in my own hotel room, just at the point when Nicholas *happened* to have a gun in his pocket? And I didn't see it? Bit of a huge bloody coincidence isn't it?'

Nicholas was staring at Mervyn, his eyes threatening to fall out of their sockets. 'Mervyn, this is serious, old fruit. I thought I'd told you to stop thinking like a fan...'

Stuart waved Nicholas quiet with a flap of the hand. 'No, no. Shut up. No. He's right. He's right. He's got a point. It's sloppy. I'm sorry. So, Mr– Mervyn, Mr script editor, what do you suggest?'

'Well...' Mervyn frowned and 'hmmm'd. He walked to the desk. 'Perhaps Nicholas could have come into my hotel room very quietly to shoot me? I could be sitting at this desk here, working away, my back to the door. Perhaps he suspected that I was near to the truth and had come to shut me up.' Mervyn aimed his finger at the desk. 'He shoots me – but not fatally. I struggle with him, and with my dying breath I wrestle the gun from him and shoot him too.'

'That's great!' fawned Stuart. He clapped his hands like he believed in fairies.

'No, it's crap,' muttered Mervyn, brutally. 'It doesn't explain your camera footage. I had to have known he was coming. If you're going to use the footage on your website, then the story has to be as is, with me confronting Nicholas by the wardrobe.'

Nicholas piped up. 'I've got an idea, sweethearts. Perhaps I *don't* get killed, I run off and you can all blame me? Just call the police and make them comb the country to search for me? I've got some holidays coming up.'

'That might work,' frowned Mervyn, ignoring the sarcasm. 'What do you think Stuart?'

'I don't know Mr – Mervyn. If he gets caught, he's bound to tell the police that I did the murders for him.'

'Yes, but who's going to believe him, with all the evidence you've got about Sheldon? And will your mates in the police seriously believe you'd murder three people just to give me something to investigate? And then murder me too? It's just completely unbelievable. You can just say Nicholas killed me when I found out about his crimes, and it's your word against his – the word of an overweight, over-the-hill producer with an unfashionable beard, a dead midget in his past and a chronic drink problem.'

'I'll have you know this beard is my trademark, Mervy...'

'Hmm... All right. Okay,' said Stuart. He twitched the pistol toward the door. 'Off you go then Mr Everett.'

Scarcely able to believe what was happening, Nicholas walked to the door. He stopped and turned. 'I can't leave you, old love...'

'It's fine.'

'I just feel rotten about what's happened. I feel it's all my fault.'

'It is, in a way, Nicholas, but that's fine too.' Mervyn grinned. 'Better get running. You'll be a wanted mass murderer in just a few minutes. Better get a disguise. Shave that damn beard off.'

'Never get rid of the trademark, old petal.'

And he was gone. Stuart and Mervyn were left alone.

'So,' said Mervyn.

'So...' said Stuart. 'What do you suggest we do to iron out this bit of plot?'

'I suggest I should be shot on this side of the room, in the back. I could have allowed Nicholas to go into the bathroom to compose himself before I ring for the police to arrest him. He's been my friend for years, and I would allow him that. I'm a pretty decent sort of chap. He would have gone into the bathroom, got his gun out...'

'Oh! I thought you said the gun was too much of a coincidence.'

Mervyn sighed wearily, a long sigh. It sounded like the sigh of a man tired of having to point out the obvious, but it was cover for a man whose brain was thinking furiously.

'Well! It *would* have been, if he'd had it in his pocket when he was confronting me by the wardrobe. Who walks around with a gun in their pocket? Contrived or what?'

'Contrived,' echoed Stuart.

'Talk about a plot device.'

'Plot device,' echoed Stuart, again. He knew the words. The words were comforting to him.

'But the gun would have been in his *bag*. That makes far more sense to me. Perhaps he was going to use it to kill John the Stalker but he never got a chance to use it, so he stowed it in his bag, remembered it was there, asked to go to the toilet, got it out in the bathroom and shot me in the back.'

'Okay, good,' said Stuart. 'A great solution. This is brilliant Mervyn. You are a great detective, and the best script editor ever.'

'Thank you, Stuart. Now you need to stand near the bathroom door, so you can pretend to be Nicholas, and I'll stand here with my back to you, unawares...'

Mervyn turned, closed his eyes, whimpered and prayed.

'Okay, Mr Stone. I'm ready...' He said it in the manner of someone playing hide and seek.

'Don't worry, I'll try and kill you outright.'

'Thanks Stuart.'

It was then Minnie made her move.

She had been in the bathroom for some time now. Of course, she had lied to Mervyn about leaving him alone – she was that kind of girl. She wanted to spook him one more time so she'd used the room key she'd taken from him, sneaked into his bedroom and waited in the bathroom, ready to rush out with a kitchen knife upraised like Glenn Close in *Fatal Attraction*. She'd waited for Mervyn to be alone. And waited. And waited. And listened. And watched.

And heard everything.

It was just as Nicholas said 'So, my darlings... What now?' that she'd managed to catch Mervyn's eye through the crack in the door. Mervyn struggled to conceal his surprise. She winked at him, and waved the knife.

Ever since then, unknown to Nicholas, Mervyn was contriving a way for Stuart to stand by the bathroom door.

The door crashed open, colliding with Stuart. He howled in pain and surprise. Minnie flew through the door, embedding the knife in his arm. Stuart fell backwards, tumbling over the bed, staring in stupefied horror at the knife sticking out of him like an alien appendage from a particularly cheap fan-made costume.

Minnie dived over the bed and ran for the door. Mervyn was well ahead of her, and they both pelted off down the corridor, overtaking Nicholas, who was huffing along as fast as he would do. He goggled in surprise.

'Aren't you dead yet?'

Gunshots from the other end of the corridor interrupted any retort Mervyn planned to make. 'Come on!'

CHAPTER FIFTY-SEVEN

'These robots have killed, sir!' Roddy stood up, swaying slightly as he did so. Stewards clustered around him at the edge of the stage, preparing to catch him if he fell.

'They killed Josh, their spy, their faithful puppet, and we did nothing! They killed the little chap who tried to control them and we fell back! We have taken casualties and done nothing! We have had their filthy claws around our throats for far too long! We have been crushed under the jackboots of their tyres and retreated like Frenchmen! Well, no more!' He pulled a Tommy gun from behind the chair and pointed it in the air.

'Um, Roddy, I'm not sure you ought to do that...'

Roddy pulled the trigger.

A bang. Bits of plaster fell from the roof. The gun wasn't firing blanks. There were screams. People started rushing for the exits.

Roddy aimed at the last remaining Styrax, sitting at the side of the stage. 'You've had this coming. you robot scum!' he yelled. He squeezed the trigger. 'The Day of the Styrax is over!'

He pumped a dozen bullets into it. This Styrax must also have been 'souped up' with propane gas cylinders (most likely Bernard's handiwork) because something exploded inside. A column of flame leapt upwards, scorching the ceiling and melting the plastic chandeliers.

There was pandemonium.

Mervyn, Nicholas and Minnie were running, pounding down the corridor, the vomit-coloured splat shapes a blur under their feet. More shots were heard; louder, nearby. One of the tiny lights on the corridor walls shattered and Nicholas screamed and threw his hands up.

'Go to the stairs,' gasped Minnie. 'We can't risk the lift.'

'Good point,' said Mervyn.

Nicholas didn't say anything. He was throwing all his concentration into moving his stout form along the corridors at an acceptable rate.

What an interesting thing it is, the life of an amateur detective, thought Mervyn. *Just an hour ago I was in fear of my life hiding from Minnie, and just a half-hour later I was terrified for my safety as I readied to confront Nicholas. Now here I am, running for my life alongside my two chief suspects.*

They reached the stairwell, and started clattering down it.

'I can see you.'

They froze. Stuart was at the top of the stairs. They hugged the side of the wall, trying to stay out of his line of sight.

'I can see Mr Everett's shoe.'

Nicholas pulled an embarrassed face and moved his loafer back to the wall.

'All right, you can see us, so what?' shouted Mervyn. 'It's over, Stuart. You might be able to shoot one of us, but another one of us will get out and tell someone.'

'But what's the point? It's over.'

What?

'What?'

'Come on Mr S– Mervyn. Don't say you didn't enjoy the adventure, the detecting, the thrill of the chase...'

'I don't deny it. But this is real life. You've killed people, and I would rather have had them alive if it's all the same to you.'

'But it's over now. We've explained everything. We've solved the murders.'

'You don't solve the murders by creating the dead bodies in the first place. Kind of defeats the object.'

Stuart continued as though Mervyn hadn't said anything. 'The adventure's over now. You're just prolonging it by running away. Making it messy. No one likes long, drawn-out endings...'

'That's life, Stuart. It's just one long, drawn-out ending.'

'Remember what you said to me: "Anything's better than just fading away, dining out on past glories..."'

'I've changed my mind. I'll take fading away, thanks.' Mervyn lowered his voice. 'The fire doors,' he hissed at them, pointing at a green sign. 'When I say "Go" we split up. You run into the hotel and raise the alarm. I'll run out the back through those. I think he'll go after me.'

'I'm not leaving you,' said Minnie fiercely.

'You're going that way to get help,' said Mervyn, even more fiercely. 'If you get shot there'll be hell to pay. Even if Stuart doesn't kill me, your mother will. And prison uniforms are very unfashionable. Do you want your mother wearing luminous orange?'

She look annoyed and shook her head. 'I'm *not* leaving you!'

'Don't make me fire more than I have to,' Stuart's voice floated down to them. He was coming closer. 'I've already damaged the hotel's fixtures and fittings. The convention will get the blame. They might not let us back next year.'

'I'm sure they'll understand,' shouted Mervyn.

Minnie scowled. 'Look, I was a member of the TA!'

'Then look after the civilian who needs looking after! That's what they train you to do, isn't it?'

While they were arguing in whispers, Nicholas had been silent. He was pale and his hands were shaking. He looked at Minnie imploringly.

'All right,' she said grimly. 'Follow me, Mr Everett.' She grabbed his hand in readiness.

'Good. Go!'

Minnie and Nicholas made a dash for the doors leading into the foyer. Mervyn also broke cover, ran into the middle of the stairwell and towards the fire doors.

They wouldn't budge. They were locked.

Mervyn allowed a whimper to escape. He turned.

Stuart had reached the bottom of the stairwell and was facing him.

'This is getting really boring,' said Stuart. 'If I was making a film of this with my friends, I'd cut this bit.'

Mervyn pressed his back into the door. The door moved.

No, they weren't locked. They were just a bit stiff. He hadn't pressed the bar down hard enough.

He spilled through the door and ran outside, just as Stuart fired, shattering the door panel and creating a hailstorm of glass shards.

Stuart ran after him. 'Someone'll have to pay for that!' he shouted.

CHAPTER FIFTY-EIGHT

Nicholas and Minnie ran into a curiously deserted foyer. Bits of alien were scattered on the carpet. Schedules that had been fastened to pin boards had been allowed to fall drunkenly to the floor. It was like the hotel had been victim of a sudden tsunami.

They went to the desk to find the receptionists cowering behind it, eyes wide with shock.

'There's a madman with a gun inside the hotel!' barked Minnie.

'We know!' they chorused.

They looked behind them. Roddy was there, holding his gun

Stuart ran out of the fire door and around the hotel, head twitching in all directions. *Where?*

Mervyn couldn't have got out of sight in so short a time. There weren't that many places to hide, a few scrappy bushes, some cars...

The Styrax. The Styrax Superior.

The door on the Styrax.

Slightly open.

Stuart's characteristically sunny grin reappeared on his face and he dashed over. As he got nearer he saw that the front lights were on – the ones that represented the 'eyes' of the Styrax. They were not immediately noticeable in daylight, but they were definitely glowing. Someone had turned the ignition.

He reached the car, slowed, walking gently so as to not crunch the gravel underfoot. His fingers curled gently around the concealed handle. Bracing his feet on the tarmac, he wrenched the door open.

No one there.

He climbed inside, checking under the seats, behind the seats, looking in the back. That was when Mervyn saw his chance and dashed from behind the withered palm tree by the hotel, pelting along the slip road and up to the motorway.

Behind him, he heard an engine splutter and a monstrous revving sound. He whipped his head back and saw the Styrax Superior judder into life. It edged towards him, slowly at first, but then picking up speed.

Brilliant, thought Mervyn. *I've successfully manoeuvred myself into running from a homicidal maniac in a car.*

The Styrax growled towards him. The lights were activated, and the now familiar call of 'DEATH TO ALL PEDESTRIANS!' boomed out of the speakers. Stuart was completely mad and no one had even noticed. *Let's face it,* thought Mervyn wildly, *If you're mad and you hang around sci-fi conventions all your life, who would ever notice?*

The Styrax reached the edge of the car park and was about to turn into the open road. Mervyn was standing on the lip of the hard shoulder, surveying a sea of concrete and tarmac. There was nowhere to go where the Styrax couldn't follow.

Mervyn had no choice.

He deliberately feigned exhaustion (not that that was a hard act – his legs felt as if they were ready to drop off), wilting and slowing, staggering like a runner 15 miles into a marathon. He waited until the Styrax was almost upon him and dodged to one side, haring back to the relative safety of the hotel. The Styrax pirouetted like an angry bull and roared back the way it had come.

If he could just get back into the hotel...

Mervyn could see the Styrax very clearly now, its huge wedge-shaped bonnet distorted a hundred times over, reflected in the windows of the hotel. Running back here had seemed like a good idea at the time, but now Mervyn wasn't so sure. Stuart didn't care about concealing his crimes any more; in his present state of mind he could see him crashing the Styrax right through the fascia of the hotel and ploughing into the reception desk.

He staggered about (not acting now) half running, half crawling to the glass doors that revolved invitingly. He was half hoping there would be steps up to the doorway, Styrax didn't do steps. But no, it was just a flat plain of flagstones; there was nothing to stop Stuart pursuing Mervyn up to the doorway and beyond. His addled, panicked brain cursed all disabled and wheelchair users for their insistence on removing all impediments to the menace of the Styrax.

Disaster. His shoe caught the edge of a paving stone and he went sprawling, flat on his belly, the tips of his fingers brushing the edge of the revolving door as it swept past his head. His mind immediately switched from wheelchair-hater to that of injured victim, concocting a plan to sue the hotel for their dangerously uneven flagstones. He cursed his brain for dwelling on such nonsense in the last seconds of his life.

Someone was standing over him. He craned his head up...

It was Roddy Burgess, gun in hand, staring at the Styrax. It was bearing down on them both, lights flashing and guns unfolding from its carapace. From the look on Roddy's face, it seemed that all his worst nightmares had come true.

'I knew sooner or later you'd come for me, you robot fiend.'

He levelled the gun, and pumped every bullet it held into the Styrax Superior. It veered, hit a potted palm and hurtled into the air, colliding and landing on a BMW and a Mondeo. Mervyn hoped they were owned by the bastards who had been revving their engines the other day. Finally, the Styrax came to rest, teetering upside down on the BMW.

Mervyn didn't know what Bernard had done to the Styrax Superior to 'augment' it, but it must have been something flammable.

Because it burst into flames.

Roddy and Mervyn were engulfed by a tidal wave of *Vixens* fans, running and screaming past them. Some of them saw the gun in Roddy's hand, but ignored him as they rushed to save the most priceless piece of *Vixens from the Void* memorabilia ever.

But it was too late. The last of the Styrax was no more.

CHAPTER FIFTY-NINE

It is said by many experts that in the event of nuclear armageddon, the only thing left would be cockroaches.

But if those experts also survived the impending holocaust, crawled out of their bunkers and examined the eight-foot tall cockroaches lumbering around the remnants of civilisation, really looked at them closely, really, *really* closely, and looked through the little hole in the mouth...

... They would find a science fiction fan sweating away inside the costume. Because fans survive.

Stuart survived. He was thrown clear. His face and body were horribly burnt, and it took several months in hospital, but he was finally given a new face by the doctors. He called the doctors his ‘restoration team’. Stuart was delighted with the results, and proclaimed his new face ‘much improved’.

Mervyn attended the trial, of course. He was a key witness.

It was one of the more interesting murder trials. Nicholas’s lawyer was very creative, and soon got all of the murder charges against the ex-Producer dismissed. Moreover, he argued that the lesser charge of ‘attempted murder’ did not apply because simply thinking about murdering someone, having a half-hearted go and just giving up was hardly a criminal matter – otherwise every hen-pecked husband who bought rat poison, briefly considered sprinkling it on his wife’s food before dismissing the notion and using it to kill rats should also be in the dock. It wasn’t Nicholas’s fault that someone came along after and ‘finished the job’. All charges against Nicholas for the deaths of Simon, Smurf and John the Stalker were eventually dismissed.

There was the matter of Sheldon’s death back in 1987 – and even Nicholas’s wily lawyer could not get around that. But he could helpfully point out Sheldon’s willingness to work on the show, knowing full well the risks to his health. Sheldon was hardly an unwitting participant in his own demise.

Nicholas was charged with criminal negligence and sentenced to six months in prison – which he’d already spent inside, waiting for the trial to start. He emerged blinking in the sunlight to waiting *Vixens* fans, baffled at finding himself released but incredibly glad to be free to start writing his memoirs.

To tell the truth, Nicholas’s wily lawyer was considerably helped by Stuart.

Stuart insisted on attending the trial in costume. He also insisted on taking the credit for all the murders, much to his lawyer’s despair. He claimed that, even though the initial ideas had been down to Nicholas, the success of the murders was down to him. He was sentenced to 30 years.

He had already been asked by Morris if he could attend a future convention and share some anecdotes about his murder spree. He had been pencilled in for ConVix 45.

The book about the serial killer at the science fiction convention – called *Geek Tragedy* – had sold extremely well. It eclipsed the sales of Vanity Mycroft's autobiography, outselling it three to one. It hovered on the outer fringes of the WHSmith bestsellers chart for a good year and a half, made the author a lot of money and gave him a stepping stone to a successful writing career, creating dramatic accounts of real-life murders.

The only trouble was the author happened to be Andrew Jamieson.

After the dust had settled and the murderer convicted, he'd seen an opportunity, and in a rare burst of energy actually produced a book in six weeks, handing it into the publishers well before the deadline.

Mervyn had a feeling he should have done that. Better hurry up and finish his novel.

Nevertheless, Andrew's book had made Mervyn a minor celebrity. He'd enjoyed being the centre of attention for a change. He'd done some talks, got interviewed by Radio 4 arts shows and even went on Alan Titchmarsh. This time it was *his* photo staring out of *The Telegraph* media supplement, leaning on a (fake) Styrax with ray gun in hand.

Inevitably, however, the media's attention started to turn elsewhere; to other murders, other scandals, other books. The interviews and speaking engagements slowly dried up. All except *Vixens from the Void* of course. *Vixens* was eternal.

Surprisingly, he didn't mind one bit. Perhaps it was the fact that fate had granted him a rare spurt of good fortune, but what seemed claustrophobia-inducing a year ago was now a reassuring corner of continuity. The eternal devotion of the fans.

VIXENS FROM THE VOID

CULTFEST 09

TIME SEGMENT TWO (VFTV)

4.00PM

EVENT	LOCATION
MERVYN STONE Geek Tragedy - Remembering Convix 15	Excelsior's Shrine (Main Hall)
AUTOGRAPH PANEL - • VANITY MYCROFT • ROGER BARKER • PETRA DE VILLIERS	Medula's Throne Room (Room 4B)
DIRECTING VIXENS • Ken Roche • Guy Hollis	Daxatar's Workshop (Room 4F)
'FUGITIVES FROM SPACE' - Episode Screening	The Arena of Magaroth (Room 12J)
WHY 'VIXENS FROM THE VOID' IS BETTER THAN 'DOCTOR WHO' (PANEL) with • Graham Goldingay • Fay Lawless • Craig Jones • Darren Cardew	Hyperion Engine Room (Lounge Bar)

CHAPTER SIXTY

Another place, another time...

Another convention.

Cultfest '09 to be exact. In Birmingham. Or was it Stoke?

Mervyn was on stage, being interviewed by a bespectacled man. He'd just been asked a question from the audience. He was enjoying himself. He was also trying not to glance towards the female steward, who was looking murderously at him from one of the exits. Oh dear.

'Well, I think I first suspected something was afoot when I found the second suicide note on the floor of the Styrax. I think it's somewhere in the first third of Andrew's book...'

'Chapter 14,' someone in the front row blurted out. There was a spasm of laughter from the crowd.

'Yes... Thank you for that. Of course, that was Stuart's first mistake. He thought that Nicholas was so shoddy he hadn't even bothered leaving a faked suicide note, so he obligingly wrote one for him, not noticing Nicholas's own terrible effort lying under the seat.'

'Unfortunately you forgot about it.'

'Oh yes!'

There was more laughter.

'But that was lucky in a way. If I had chosen to mention my discovery to Stuart, he might have realised his elementary mistake, decided thc game was up and that he couldn't play detective with me any more. He would have cut his losses and my throat in the process.'

The interviewer scanned the darkened hall. 'Any more questions?'

A hand shot up. 'Who's got the suicide notes now?'

Mervyn shrugged and looked helplessly at the interviewer. The interviewer leaned in to his own microphone. 'I believe they were sold at auction to Graham Goldingay. Any other questions?'

'Following on from that suicide note... Is there anything that you look back on now and think, "Oh, I should have picked up on that..."?'

'Oh, loads of things,' said Mervyn cheerfully. 'The whole fancy dress competition for example. It was themed the "Sheldon Ellis Memorial Fancy Dress Contest". The whole thing was designed so Simon could communicate to Nicholas and me that he knew Sheldon had died in mysterious circumstances, and he was ready to meet with us both. Unfortunately, I had no idea I was about to be blackmailed for something I knew nothing about!'

Laughter.

'There's just time for one last question... Anybody?'

A final hand glided up.

'About William Smurfett...'

'Yes?'

'I think we can all agree it's a sad loss...'

There was a low rumble of agreement from the audience.

'Yes?'

'Um... I wondered whether, did he mention if he'd recorded any more DVD commentaries?'

'Um, what? I don't know. You'll have to ask the people who organise the DVD commentaries that.'

'Because there are several stories that haven't been released yet, and he did have a lot of anecdotes that were pertinent to those stories, and I was thinking – there were rumours. Did he give any hint before he got exploded that...'

'No. No he didn't mention that.'

The air seemed to escape out of the room. Mervyn knew murder and carnage was all very well, but it would always take a dimly lit backseat to what was really important; which was that the conveyor belt of merchandise thundered on.

The interviewer chipped in. 'The DVD production team have a panel tomorrow morning. You can ask Robert Mulberry then.'

Slightly reassured, the audience filed out of the hall.

He was back in his room, folding his black corduroy jacket and putting it in his suitcase beside his other black corduroy jacket, when he heard a click – which seemed to come from his door.

He barely looked up when the door opened and Minnie slid through it. She was wearing a bright orange sweatshirt with Cultfest '09 stamped across it. Keeping her back to the door, she pushed it closed with her bottom, all the while keeping her eyes fixed on him. She tapped her nose knowingly with a piece of square plastic.

'I wondered where my spare pass key had gone,' said Mervyn.

'You are so careless, Mr Stone Ranger; you have to keep an eye on your jacket at all times. There's no telling what dangerously unbalanced fans are about...'

'You don't have to tell me that.'

She sashayed towards him, pulling her jumper over her head.

'I think you owe me, Mr Stone, for saving your life.'

'So I do.'

Her head disappeared inside her T-shirt and her breasts and belly button popped out the other end.

'I see you got your bra back.'

'Yes, Mum did give it back. Of course, she wouldn't speak to me for a week after...'

Mervyn smiled. 'You save me from being shot, I organise it that your mum doesn't speak to you for a week. I think that's quits, isn't it?'

She laughed, and unfastened her bra, unleashing her breasts like attack dogs. 'Sorry I blanked you in the hall earlier today, but I had to pretend I was cross at you, for Mum's sake.'

'I see.'

'I knew she wouldn't approve of me seeing you after all that's happened, so I had to convince her I never wanted to see you again.'

'Very convincing.'

'That's not the least of my talents.'

'I am packing to go.'

'You've still got half an hour left on your room. I checked.'

'My taxi is due any moment.'

'I cancelled it.'

'Oh. Well there's no reason why I can't hang out for a bit...'

'Yes, you "hang out". They have paid for the room, after all.' She walked towards him. 'Did you know that this convention was set up using the money they got selling Simon Josh's memorabilia?'

'I didn't know that.'

'Then I'm definitely sure he'd want you to get his money's worth. Here.' She pulled his shirt out of his trousers and started to unbuckle his belt. 'Let me help you unpack.'

His trousers were settling around his knees when his hotel phone rang. He skipped out of his trousers and answered it while Minnie slipped into bed and removed her jeans.

'Hello, Merv darling. What did you think of my performance?'

'Vanity?'

'Sorry I had to attack you so hard at ConVix, and sorry I've not spoken to you since, but I had to make it look good in front of darling daughter. She'd go crazy ga-ga if I even contemplated crawling back under you after all that's happened. Had to allay her suspicions before I went behind her back, darling.'

'Vanity...'

'We've still got a half hour left on our rooms, darling, and my meter's running...'

'Vanity –'

'I'll be up in five minutes.'

Mervyn looked helplessly at the receiver, and then at Minnie, who gave him a saucy wink.

He could only imagine what was going to happen any minute now.

But that's another story.

The Mervyn Stone Mysteries Book Two

❖

DVD EXTRAS INCLUDE: MURDER
by Nev Fountain

Mervyn Stone is invited to take part in a DVD commentary discussing one of the more controversial (and, let's face it, blasphemous) episodes of *Vixens from the Void*. And he's about to turn amateur detective. Again.

The whispers begin as the bodies pile up: 'Act of God?' Mervyn's pursued by crazed fans, mad actresses, suspicious policemen and mental fundamentalists. And he's starting to feel like God's got it in for him, too...

❖

The Mervyn Stone Mysteries Book Three

❖

CURSED AMONG SEQUELS
by Nev Fountain

It's the announcement all the fans have been waiting for! After 17 long years, they're bringing back *Vixens from the Void*. But Mervyn Stone is not sure it's a good idea. And to make matters worse, someone is trying to kill him.

Is it the incompetent director who hates Mervyn from way back? The mad fan who wants the relaunch stopped? The producer with a guilty secret? Mervyn is learning something important. Perhaps the past should stay in the past...